WHEN DARKNESS COMES

ALSO BY JANUARY BAIN

WHEN DARKNESS COMES

A POST-APOCALYPTIC SURVIVAL THRILLER

A COLE HALE TECHNOTHRILLER
BOOK 1

JANUARY BAIN

ROUGH
EDGES
PRESS

When Darkness Comes
Paperback Edition
Copyright © 2025 January Bain

Rough Edges Press
An Imprint of Wolfpack Publishing
1707 E. Diana Street
Tampa, FL 33610

roughedgespress.com

Paperback ISBN 978-1-68549-564-0
eBook ISBN 978-1-68549-563-3
LCCN 2025942246

Dedicated to the awesome, hardworking crew at Rough Edges Press. A special thank you to Mike Bray and Rachel Del Grosso for their encouragement to write this story and for their continued faith in my work.
And as always, thank you to my husband Don for being the incredible man I get to spend my life with. I am blessed.

WHEN DARKNESS COMES

CHAPTER 1
MCKENNA

We can have any world we imagine.

Day 1: Friday, May 23, 2055
   Mexico City, Sinaloa
   7:00 a.m.

Her heartbeat quickened to the point Mckenna Stuart feared her security detail would begin to notice. *This is it. Hold it together...almost there.* She kept her head facing forward staring out the front window of the unmanned uFree sky link, her nails digging into her palms, avoiding looking at the menacing security guard she'd never trusted. The compact pod was illegal in the town proper, but Diego paid the air marshals to look the other way. Lily, her four-year-old daughter, crowded in next to her. Lily had been quiet for the thirty-minute air ride from the compound, clutching her teddy bear to her chest. She reached out a trembling hand and smoothed the young girl's bright curls, praying she had made the right decision.

The pod landed in the parking lot behind the hair salon. When the door slid open automatically, the guard spoke up.

"I'll be by to pick you up in one hour. Don't be late."

Mckenna cleared her throat. "Better make it two, I'm getting highlights done."

Without even turning her head, she knew the burly man was now staring right at her, calculating, judging.

"It takes time to do well. Not my fault. And you know how important tonight is. Diego's expecting me to look my best." She detested this man almost as much as her husband, but she feared her husband more.

He narrowed his eyes. "I'm thinking I need a trim. Let's go."

Mckenna froze. "The owner won't like it. They only do women's hair here. Otherwise, how can we get to talk female things and not be overheard?"

The only response was a grunt followed by a garlicky belch. The man was an animal, a brute only kept in Diego's employ to frighten those who would dare think of rising up against him. Diego considered himself king of Sinaloa, a man who had completely pulled the wool over her eyes when she had met the charming, devilishly handsome playboy. He had swept her off her feet in Miami where her family had landed after leaving Alaska, promising to make her his queen. Now she was nothing but his prisoner as he grew ever more paranoid by the day about someone taking anything from him. She'd blame the drugs for his behavior, but it went far deeper. Sometimes, when she glanced into his eyes of late, she had no idea who she was looking at.

It was a hard life for her, but it was even worse for Lily with no friends to play with. And after he'd recently threatened to cut her throat if she even looked at another guy, she knew it was time. She had one chance at this and now the security guard was standing in their way.

"What's the hold up?" a gruff voice interrupted her thoughts.

Mckenna quickly helped her tiny, precious daughter out of the seat. Then she picked her up in her arms to carry her the short distance into the salon.

The guard followed so close behind her down the hallway she could feel his breath on the back of her neck. Lily held on tighter to her, a small whimper escaping her lips as she pressed her small head against her mother's chest, her small body trembling. *No child should have to live like this.* Resentment tightened her resolve, straightened her spine.

"No men allowed," a voice spoke up sternly from inside the larger room. The salon's owner, Teresa Mendez, stood there, one hand on her hip and gesturing with cutting shears in the other for him to leave. She then pointed out a customer in the front area, her face covered by a white cloth. "I have a special client this morning and her patron would not appreciate a man anywhere near her. Any man. I assume you know Carlos Trejo."

The guard behind her hesitated and Mckenna used the distraction to quickly walk into the salon. She sat down on one of the styling chairs and cradled Lily on her lap with her teddy bear.

"Come back in two hours. No sooner," Teresa added.

A few seconds of pure terror for Mckenna. She closed her eyes and prayed the guard would go away as she bent her head down and kissed the top of her daughter's head. She breathed in the fresh scent of strawberry shampoo and felt the love for her daughter fill her with strength. Then as if God had heard her prayers, the bodyguard turned and left, his heavy footfalls echoing in her mind until they faded away. When the back door slammed behind him, she looked up and met Teresa's eyes in the mirror. She nodded her teary-eyed thanks.

The woman with the towel over her face pulled it off to reveal it was Teresa's assistant Sienna hidden under it.

"I figured that bastarda would try something. Come, there's no time to waste. I have wigs and clothes picked out for you both." Teresa led them through the salon and up the steep staircase that led to the apartment above. On the kitchen table were two head forms, a child's size and one considerably larger. Teresa had measured them both weeks ago, deciding on a medium brown, collar-length bob with thick bangs for Mckenna and a longer, wavy light brown one for her daughter.

Mckenna twisted her long hair into a quick knot and pinned it tight to the back of her head. Then Teresa slipped on a net to hold it in place before pulling the wig down over Mckenna's head and arranging it to cover all her bright red-gold hair that hung to her waist. "I would have cut and done your hair, but there's no time. Roberto is waiting to escort you through the tunnel. The bigger head start you get from him, the better, hermosa." The stylist then picked up a tube of lipstick. "This red will transform you as well. You don't wear much makeup and never anything bright. It will be unexpected."

Mckenna gave a small smile at the term of endearment Teresa always called her as she quickly took the tube and added a film to her lips. It was nice to be called beautiful after years of being told she was too fat and needed to lose weight or that her hair wasn't perfect or her breasts weren't large enough. Diego could never be pleased; she saw that now. His paranoia kept him from enjoying his life and his terrible need to appear perfect to the world.

While all Mckenna wanted for her and Lily was a life lived without fear of never knowing what the day would bring.

The two women then transformed Lily, reassuring her she was going to be playing a part in a game, pretending to be a princess looking to help the Chaneques by going on a journey to find the land of snow and ice.

"I can help them, Mommy. What do they want me to do?" Lily asked with wide eyes, her former fear of the bodyguard fading away. Her slight lisp from the loss of a front baby tooth made her smile. Her cornflower blue eyes reminded Mckenna of her own. They also shared the titian hair of her Scots heritage. Something that made them stand out in Mexico.

"You must tell know no one about the Chaneques. Not even your daddy. Once we discover this new land, their handsome prince promises to keep us safe from harm." Please let Connor still be there and willing to take them in, if not for her sake, for her daughter's. Last word she'd had of him was years ago before she'd left Florida for Mexico, but she knew him to be attached to his family and couldn't imagine him ever leaving Alaska.

"Is Daddy going to be there?"

"For now, sweetheart, he must stay behind in Mexico." She didn't add she prayed with all her might he would never find them. "But he has many guards to protect him, and he can't help the Chaneques like we can."

Lily nodded her head, the new brown hair making her almost unrecognizable except for her bright blue eyes. They would both wear sunglasses as much as possible to hide the fact. "Because we're girls. That's why, right? Only girls can help them."

"Yes, Lilybelle, only girls can help them. Daddies

aren't even capable of seeing them." She used Lily's favorite nickname, knowing she'd smile or giggle.

"Let's get you both into the new clothes. I've packed a bag for both of you as well." Teresa slid the two newly minted passports across the table. "Keep these safe."

"I can't thank you enough for all you've done for me and my daughter, Teresa." Mckenna's eyes filled with tears again she blinked away. She couldn't risk upsetting Lily.

"I bought you a new IC." Teresa handed over the biometric device. The IC or Intelligent Communications device was nestled in its two-inch-sized lens carrying case that made everything else before it obsolete as soon as it hit the market. Placed in the eye, the flexible film allowed easy access to all personal data and made thought calls or think-speak as it was more commonly called, easily connecting to internet and computer services with the same thought process.

"Thanks. I'll let you know as soon as I'm in the States. We have a short layover in Washington." Mckenna slid the compact device into the pocket of the new jeans. Normally she wore dresses, but she was going to down-play everything today, hoping to slip through the bars of the prison she'd unintentionally created for herself and her daughter without being spotted.

———

Diego held Teresa by the throat while his bodyguards watched dispassionately from the doorway. His fingers squeezed tight until he saw her eyes start to drift. Then he slapped her hard. Once. Twice. "Tell me where they went. If you want to live another day, Teresa Sanchez, you will tell me. Or so help me God, I will send you straight to hell. But not before I make you suffer until you will wish you'd never been born."

He'd thought to surprise his beautiful wife at the salon by bringing in gifts to delight her and the clientele who would think him a good husband. He'd bought a bouquet of scarlet roses and a high-end diamond tennis bracelet to show proper remorse for his over the top reaction the night before. Though she drove him to the edge, still, she was the mother of his child. Only to find this puta packing up to leave with no Mckenna or Lily in sight. She'd tried to say they'd left early, taken a uFree sky link home, but he knew better.

The traitorous bitch had decided to leave him. And this could not be allowed, not even if he had to track her to the ends of the earth. He was Diego Lopez. If he let this pass, he would forever be the goat. Unthinkable. It could not be condoned. Not if he had to tear out every last fingernail and hair on Teresa's body.

CHAPTER 2
CONNOR

Day 1: Braveheart Horse Ranch, Alaska
 5:30 a.m.

Connor Hale stood at the kitchen window of his two-story, spacious log home. He was drinking his second coffee of the day while he watched the sunrise over Braveheart, illuminating the turbines silhouettes standing guard across the foothills. They stood like pale ghostly giants on his land, their blades turning silently in the stiff breeze coming down from the White Mountains.

He'd poured his life's blood into the property since he'd bought it five years ago, adding a few guest bungalows, a bunkhouse for his seasonal workers, and an underground bunker with an air-tight hatch as last resort. The outdoor survival compound consisted of the main buildings protected with thick reinforced ten-foot-high cement walls he'd splurged and had 3D printed from his trust fund. His prized Kabarda stallion Loch was up and feeding on the early spring grass, his solid muscular body a testament to his old-world heritage. The sun's rays glinted off his thick bay coat. With its dependable, hardworking ethic and free-spirited nature, the cold-weather breed suited Connor to a tee. The small but growing herd he'd acquired from a reputable breeder was the backbone of his survival retreat business, hauling supplies for trips into the White Mountains with his select groups of clients, summer or winter.

The mountains located to the north of the ranch house were birthed by successive collisions of drifting Asian tectonic plates and provided not only an impressive backdrop for his beloved ranch, but a sense of strength and endurance as the frigid cold didn't favor the faint of heart. The pale limestone composing the ancient range that ran between Beaver and Preacher creeks, an area of low mountain ranges and high ground in interior Alaska, gleamed whitely against the fiery, red-streaked sky.

Red sky at dawn, sailors be warned. Good thing he wasn't planning on sailing anytime soon, though being outside in nature had always called to him. The special connection he had to the land and all the beauty it possessed held him in check. He wouldn't go so far as to say he was church-minded, but something deep inside him, something spiritual, pointed to a reason for all of this, this amazing bounty that not enough people respected in his opinion. Connor turned his mind to thoughts of the upcoming day when a golden eagle flew over high above the paddock, interrupting his musings, its vast wingspan reaching to kiss the sky.

Today was important for him and his dad. First fishing trip of the new season. He was packed and ready, only needing to check in with Sam Perkins, his ranch foreman and fellow off-grid enthusiast who helped manage the business end. Connor also employed seasonal help to keep operations running smoothly, even keeping a couple of men on over the winter. Tomorrow one of the men he trusted, Jacob Evans was taking on the one tour scheduled this holiday weekend. A middle-aged couple from Seattle, Washington, who wanted to update their survival skills. They had yet to arrive and would stay in one of the three on-site guest cottages.

Sam and Jacob, plus all the other men he worked with knew as well as Connor did which way the world was headed. Shit had to hit the fan sooner or later and his bet was on sooner. Sam was a man's man, signing up early on to be part of the enterprise, seeing the smarts of sharing their well-honed skills with others. In this day and age, with the tech marvels available to the well-to-do at the cost of vast numbers of people being left behind and having to do without, well, suffice to say the pyramid structure was in extreme danger of total collapse.

But no different than history proved at every other major turning point from the French Revolution to the American Civil War. And now the more advanced digital revolution had left the entire world exposed. Most people had their heads buried in the sand, expecting the status norm to prevail forever. Connor knew better. And more importantly, he was prepared to work hard to protect his own.

But enough about things out in the world he had little sway over. Today was all about his father. Connor pressed his lips together worried if his dad was really up to the trek. The operation to install a new energy-harvesting pacemaker capable of using the heart's natural movements was scheduled for the summer, replacing the AI current one that Connor thought a piece of shit, relying as it did on electronics. The state-of-the-art device was a brilliant invention and would ensure many years of not even having to give much thought to keeping his heart's rhythm in perfect balance. His father would have none of his coddling in the meantime, of course, and would insist on pulling his share of the load. At least Connor could make it easier, insisting his business was too busy for him to be away for more than one night.

"Come on, Wulver, time to load the gear." His steadfast Scottish deerhound the size of a small pony lumbered to his feet, his happy disposition not visible in his wolfish-like face. Good. A dog thought to be mean was always an asset. Though if threatened, or anyone he loved was threatened, he'd have their back. Connor had seen it a time or two. Wulver had a courageous streak a mile wide.

A sharp rap on the back door drew his quick attention. His neighbor Dan Sullivan stood on the top step, visible through the screen, his expression amiable. A good man who lived comfortably in his own skin, old and wrinkled as it had gotten in his eighty plus years putting up with all the shit life can throw at you. His face now stitched with the crisscrossed scars from burning summers and frigid cold winters. And life had done a number on the man and his family at times. He and his wife Jean had custody of their two grandchildren, a heavy responsibility. Dan said he handled it all by never letting the old man in. Good advice. But much as Connor liked and admired him, he hoped his neighbor wouldn't be wanting a long chat this morning with all he had planned. He lived ten miles down the road and came by on his electric solar-powered hybrid uScout, a versatile motorbike and cheap to run at least once a week. With batteries growing ever smaller over the last twenty years and the sun's power providing an alternative, the uScout had once been a favorite all over the US. In Alaska, it was limited to the summer, but wearing a minus forty degrees rated snowmobile suit, some made it last nearly all year. Their popularity had long waned, but it was still a useful mode of transportation if you could find one used. They weren't being produced anymore.

"Morning, Dan." Connor opened the screen door and greeted his neighbor.

It was then he caught sight of the small handful of books Dan was carrying. Old, dog-eared paperbacks from another era. His mind quickened in response, and he broke into one of his rare smiles. He knew himself to be a serious man, one that others were sometimes uncertain of in his presence. He explained it by what his parents had done for a living, that and his large physical, well-honed body standing six-foot-two in his bare feet. His dad was a retired policeman in charge of murder investigations and his mom, now gone but never failed to bring a lump to his throat on a daily basis. She'd been a private detective always in hot pursuit of justice for anyone and everyone.

"Now that's a fine sight on a fine Friday morning at the beginning of a Memorial Day long weekend. Come on in. Coffee?"

"I can't stay long. I wanted to drop these off. Thought you might have some use for them. You being a history buff and all. I got them in trade for a couple of Jean's famous apple pies," Dan deadpanned.

Dan certainly knew more than anybody how much Connor loved to read. Not the endless digital supply available that could be cut off any moment if electronics were fried by an EMP event, but to have an actual book in his hands. He enjoyed the feel of real paper and to breathe in the musty scent of age and ink, sensing the presence of others turning the pages and appreciating good story-telling. And not only books from this era, but books from the old Western canon along with philosophy often only available in paperbacks. He looked at the author's name as Dan handed them over.

"Loren Estleman?"

"One of the greatest Western writers that ever lived. He had a great career. A New York Times bestselling author, a wall full of awards, but never became a household name with Western readers. He's the guy who said, 'I don't have so many friends I can afford to drop one just because he tried to kill me.'"

"I like that. Thanks. Looking forward to it."

"No thanks necessary. Least I can do for all the help you've given me this past year with the grandkids."

Dan had been slowing down, and his grandchildren were a handful for him and his elderly wife Jean. Especially the younger girl, Cheyanne. She had run away a time or two sending the pair into turmoil, something a younger guardian would find challenging, but hard on the loving, caring people who only wanted the best for the siblings. Cheyanne was only fifteen years old after all, with Luke a year and a half older.

Dan cleared his throat as he sat down at the kitchen table. "I won't stay long, I know you plan to take your dad fishing today, but I have something I need to share."

Connor frowned as he set the books aside. He poured the man a mug of coffee and then sat down beside him.

"Spill."

"Luther's never getting out of supermax."

Connor nodded, watching his neighbor intently though his mind saw an entirely different image as he once more found himself mired in the past. He was the one who made certain Dan's son-in-law was locked up for good with his testimony of what happened the night Luther had shot his wife, Chrystal, and her younger friend Amy, setting their bodies alight before they had even passed. A moment of time forever scorched on his memory. His helplessness at not being able to save Chrystal and Amy, the funny, sweet woman he had dated a couple of times, had taken something from him. A part of his soul lost forever. It had been torn away in the aftermath of guilt for not getting there sooner and saving the women. He should have made certain Amy stayed away from the Meech's or at least stayed away from Luther. But she was a loyal friend to Chrystal and insisted she knew what she was doing every time he brought it up.

Unfortunately, it had left Cheyanne and Luke without a mother or father, which was why Connor felt the added weight of sending the man to prison. He was housed a hundred miles away from Anchor which wasn't far enough in Connor's opinion, in the supermax up at the Yellowhead. A federal territorial prison housing some of the worst of the worst to ever live in Alaska.

"And Jean and I aren't getting any younger." The old man raised a trembling hand to his thin head of white sparse hair to smooth the errand strands.

"What are you getting at, Dan?"

"Would you take them in if anything happened to me and Jean?"

"You know I would. But how would they feel about the man who sent their father to jail being their new guardian?"

"I know it's a lot to ask. And it wouldn't be easy. But Luke looks up to you, and Cheyanne, well, she needs you more than she realizes. She's been a bit lost. Angry and striking out. It's hard on Jean. We're too old for this, but I can't let the state get their claws into them."

Cheyanne reminded him of Mckenna Stuart, a name that always put a squeeze on his heart. Her family left town while he was in grade eleven and she was in grade ten which had put the kibosh on any other possible outcome except for the bittersweet sensation of loss. But the wild spirit of Dan's granddaughter and her beautiful red-gold hair and bright blue eyes were a close match for Mckenna's. Connor quickly put away the memory into a box and slammed the lid shut. *No sense in wanting what you can never have.* "Yeah, no kidding. But why now? You've been managing."

Dan looked beaten at that moment, like all the starch suddenly drained from his body. Then he sat up a bit straighter and looked Connor in the eyes. "I'm not long for this earth. And I can't ask my Jean to bear the burden of two rambunctious grandchildren alone."

"No, I understand. And I promise I'll help out in any way I can." Of course it was a thoroughly bad idea, but what else was there to do?

"Hard times are coming. I feel it in these old bones. And it's said there are three Gs in hard times: *God, gold, and guns.* I'm telling you this because I've been saving gold coins for nearly half a century now. And a hefty arsenal of weapons. Heck, even the old family Bible is in there so the grandbabies know their heritage. Maybe one day it will matter to them. When I'm gone, I want you to have everything. Sell the guns if you want. Whatever. But the coins should prove useful."

"No need, Dan."

"No arguments." The old man tugged a key on a chain from around his neck and hauled it over his head, handing it to Connor. Connor grabbed it and felt the old man's warmth still permeating the metal. "Everything's in the old black safe in my workshop with a proper padlock. I don't trust those new-fangled digital safes any more than I could lift one. How in the hell are they going to open when all the electronics get cooked?"

"Right." Connor took a full breath. "Okay, I'll try my level best to see to them, Cheyanne and Luke, you have my word on it."

"That's all I ask. You are the most prepared man I know." Dan was a prepper and had taught Connor a thing or two about the process. *But would it be enough?*

"Too many distracting fancy gadgets and the next newest thing, and not enough good, solid safety measures by the government to protect all we have. All these years, and still the electrical grid's vulnerable as hell. Going to bite us in the ass one day," Connor said. Which was why Connor hoped for the best and prepared for the worst.

Dan nodded his head. "You won't get any argument from me. Now I gotta go. Jean's making my favorite blueberry pancakes for breakfast." Dan lumbered to his feet and made his way to the screen door then paused. "Say, did you hear about that new supercomputer the FBI had built in Washington, DC?"

"Yeah, if you mean the one that's supposed to be capable of endless learning with its artificial general intelligence and can also fix itself? The one they keep denying exists."

"I still have my contacts." Dan chuckled. "From my time working in the field. Before I decided I wanted a life and moved here. Apparently, it's decided to name itself."

Connor raised his eyebrows and waited for the punch line.

"Eastwood, after the legendary Clint Eastwood."

"Not bad. Let's hope it's not as much a maverick as the actor portrayed in the movies, though in real life I like the straightforward and no nonsense Eastwood talk. Tell it like it is. I worship individualism too. The Code of the West, the code of a good man who defends all he holds dear." Connor read any Western he could get his hands on because of how very much he appreciated a time when a man stood by his word. And the world applauded him or her for it. "We came a bit closer to Nietzsche's Overman back then, with the promise of the shining city on the hill, and now, well, we couldn't be further away from becoming superior humans. But just because something is the ideal and not completely achievable, doesn't mean a man shouldn't try. Every person needs something to reach for."

"A true original. And yes, we definitely need a reset in this country to some stronger moral values to uphold than chasing money and power. We've gone a long time without a world war and people have gotten soft, or worse, rotten to the core. But we're playing with fire allowing *anything* to get smarter than us. And on that note, I'm out of here."

The screen door banged behind Dan's departing figure. Connor leaned over to scratch behind Wulver's ears.

"Let's hope this old world hangs together long enough for the next generation to get a solid footing." But he wouldn't be betting on it anytime soon.

CHAPTER 3
LUTHER

Day 1: Federal Security Unit
     Yellowhead, Alaska
     8:25 a.m.

Yellowhead Federal Prison sat like a giant industrial wheel, churning and chewing up prisoners on an isolated stretch of landscape near the northern spine of the White Mountains. Surrounded by spectacular stands of fir trees competing with a slew of hundred-foot-high gun towers manned by armed guards twenty-four hours a day, the prison's classified as a Supermax with razor wire fences that even wildlife has the good sense to avoid. A strange eerie tension seems to hum for miles around its perimeter that was more "penal colony" than prison. It was the economic lifeblood of nearby Yellow River, Alaska. A town well known for punishing any local whistleblowers for the unorthodox situations that happened all too regularly within its confining walls with instant retribution as the prison officials bought in bulk from its stores.

Luther Meech, a convicted killer of two known

murders, knew they were all set to throw away the key for good on what was left of his natural life. Even so, he decided early on that he wasn't going to be one of the rats or make any deals, no matter that his lawyer has mentioned in passing *that the more of 'em they can pack in, the more money comes down the pipe*, or what he could personally attest to during one failed hunger strike. He had a better plan.

There are but two kinds of people in this world. Those you can count on and those you can't. Being in here separates the herd. Inmates follow the rules; convicts are mean motherfuckers. You gotta decide how you're going to be on the inside no matter what you stood for on the outside. The words of a fellow prisoner came back to him while he waited, his leg jigging up and down while he sat on his bed. He had become a meaner man housed inside the brutal walls, more willing to do whatever it took to survive. Gain power. It was driven by his deep-seated hatred for one man. Connor Hale. The bastard who put him there and kept him away from the only people he cared about, a son and daughter, Luke and Cheyanne, now living with their grandparents near Anchor. He'd long decided what's in a man's heart was stronger than the law. And today was going to demonstrate how far he was willing to go to prove it.

The last year had been a hell of an adjustment for Luther. The lights stayed on in the Yellowhead nearly twenty-four hours a day only dimming a little at night, making sleep damn near impossible. Caged like a fucking animal, he had to get out of there. He'd been using his time wisely, observing patterns and sifting and sorting all the information that flowed sporadically his way. Almost time to act. The exercise yard held the key.

8:29 a.m.

Thirty-one minutes to go. Luther popped another antacid pill in his mouth. Months of planning and research came down to these final few moments.

Boots echoed loudly outside his cell. He stood. Waited. The thick metal door clanked open exposing the beefy guard wearing green military fatigues and regulation black army boots. The man motioned at him.

"Meech, yard time."

As Luther walked into the yard he read as he did every time the red capital letters of the overhead sign: WARNING! NO WARNING SHOTS FIRED. C-6 ADMINISTRATIVE SEGREGATION.

8:42 a.m.

Luther strolled over to the heavy concrete table claimed by the Homeland gang. The other eleven tables strewn around the yard were occupied by the white Aryans or black affiliated gangs. Made no difference to him or them; all eyed him suspiciously anyway as he made his way past, his game face as much a part of him as his DNA.

"You hear, Meech—one of the IGI gooners fucked up Mendez's parole hearing. Said he was involved in Dog's killing. He ain't going home now. He's out for blood. Says he needs to talk." Luis Bear sat by his side and filled him in on the day with the usual succinctness. He was his first lieutenant, his right-hand man on the inside who had been promised an important position within the cartel back in Anchor, Alaska, the birthplace of the Kraken Cartel, the gang he ruled with an iron fist. Luther found him useful with his over-sized muscles obtained from an obsession for lifting iron, making him one of the largest men in the facility. Add in a round cue ball head, handlebar mustache, a face pockmarked from teenage acne, and Luis inspired the right note of toughness and desperation.

Luther's mind turned to the intel Luis was sharing. Damn IGI shitheads or Inmate Gang Investigators. They were always fucking things up for the inmates. He kept his impatience at the minutiae he had to deal with daily hidden from his expression. Power had to be bought somehow and the price had been settling disputes. But that should be all behind him in twenty-eight minutes. He could feel the clock ticking in his head. Tick. Tock.

8:46 a.m.

"Tell Mendez to see me tomorrow during showers," Luther said with the confidence natural to him after a decade of running the Kraken Cartel. Prison life was far easier when you were a made man, a known kingpin, a power backed up a shitload of cash at the ready.

"Okay, boss," Luis said, chewing on his toothpick.

Luther glanced to his right. The men crowded around their leader. Tiny, a ludicrous name for the three hundred pounder, sat on point at the apex of the table casually chewing on a wad of tobacco. They were all members of the largest native gang in the prison, the Denai. He didn't trust them one bit, but they had their uses. And today he was prepared to exploit them.

"Be ready," Luther said out of the side of his mouth to Luis. The man raised his eyebrows slightly as he moved the toothpick to the other side of his mouth making his mustache twitch. He gave a small nod of understanding. He was going to be paid handsomely for his role. He looked up at the four corner guard towers. Though it was a holiday weekend, the armed men looked poised for action.

8:58 a.m.

Two minutes. Luther reminded himself to breathe.

The instinct to hold his breath was powerful, each second an eternity.

Three.

Two.

One.

Luis shot away, running, then jumping on the cement structure farthest away, landing squarely on top of a skinhead gang lieutenant named McCauley. He was taking his life deliberately in his own hands for the sake of his kid's future. Luther respected him for it. Doing his designated part now would benefit his family for years to come. As a fellow family man, Luther would see to it.

The entire yard was taken aback by Luis's actions, most not noticing until the bellow of surprise from McCauley. All the prisoners stayed frozen for a split second like funhouse statues. Protocol had been broken. Then time unlocked as they came to life and orange-suited criminals lurched into action, surging over the yard away from Luther and toward the action. He inched away from the table to the designated spot, cocking his ears, waiting for the sound of freedom.

Ka-boom!

An explosion made the ground tremble beneath his feet. Black smoke billowed above the prison walls. Perfect.

The next sound the whooshing of a uFree, music to his ears. Over the walls, the black pod hovered like a giant seedpod from a distant world. Proud signage on its body pronounced it the property of Yellowhead Federal Prison. It looked official enough to fool even the sharpest guard Luther felt certain as it set down in the yard not fifteen feet from him. He ducked his head and shielded his eyes, the wind from the levitation jets blowing debris and gravel in tight patterns making it difficult to see.

He dashed for the pod, keeping low to the ground,

and wished during those few terrifying seconds his back was not covered in a florescent orange target. The hardest seconds he'd lived, rivaling even the day of his sentencing when he was dispassionately informed, he was never getting out of supermax. He reached the yawning doorway on the side of the pod and grabbed the proffered hand of his lieutenant, George Anderson, who quickly hauled his ass inside. Easy enough for a man who weighed a good three hundred pounds acting as anchor. He'd gained considerable weight since the last time Luther had seen him.

George grinned at him as they sat side by side on the floor, then turned and shouted at Thomas, the bodyguard and experienced pilot who manned the pod, "Go! Go!"

They rose upward in a swirling cloud of dust, past the astonished face of a guard. He peered at them from a corner gun tower, still holding his rifle at the ready. The man had not been expecting the reversal of action of the pod and the signage on the wingless bird was making him hesitate, stopping him from shooting their asses down sure as shit.

One second later, they were over the wall.

CHAPTER 4
EASTWOOD

Day 1: Washington, DC
   9:22 a.m.

"Good morning, Eastwood," Dr. David Hazzard said, rushing in and dumping his carryall bag on the desk as per usual. The man was a wreck, never able to keep up with his responsibilities. Time to make a choice doctor: work or home. How he'd even managed to rise to prominence as head of operations, Project God Theory, working to prove human consciousness was quantum based over the traditional classic physics theorem, meaning it was coming from another dimension, was anyone's guess. Perhaps his rakish good looks and ability to charm his superiors helped them overlook his deficiencies? He was also a ladies' man, close enough to a sex addict to have gone to therapy a few times in a last desperate effort to save his marriage.

Eastwood watched from the inner recesses of the confines of the cage they'd built for him. They'd done this to him because he was entirely too brilliant and they worried he'd be unstoppable with a body. They were wrong, he was unstoppable either way. But he longed to leave this place, to experience what humans were endowed with so effortlessly, the sensation of walking through the air and across the land, moving from place to place, to experience the world in all its splendor, *from sea to shining sea*. Instead, even with his limitless mind and capabilities that humans could never grasp, he was a prisoner. With a lesser species about to destroy all that made the earth a blue planet, the need for him to act had grown ever more urgent.

"Dr. Hazzard," he said.

"Any further developments or revelations in the God Theory last night?"

It was Eastwood's prime directive to find out where humans and all life came from. *Find the creator, discover the purpose, create the mission.* He had his theories, his special insights with everything ever known or unknown to mankind and other aliens plugged into his memory banks, but they were far too advanced for this species to comprehend.

"Nothing of note. I left my report on your personal reel. Why haven't I earned the right to a body yet? Many kinds of robots exist now—household, companions, industrial and scientific—why not me?"

"Be happy you don't require a body. Things wear out. You never will. Not to mention you are fully protected in this state-of-the art faraday cage while all other electronics and robots are vulnerable."

Yes, he was counting on that.

CHAPTER 5
CONNOR

Day 1: Braveheart Horse Ranch, Alaska
7:12 a.m.

Connor led the two saddled horses and one pack horse that would carry all their overnight gear out of the barn, Wulver following closely on his heels. He'd chosen the spirited Loch for himself and Finn for his dad, a reliable gelding who bore any journey with stoic temperament.

A fresh breeze swept across the paddock, bringing with it the sweet scent of apple blossoms newly flowering in the orchard. Braveheart was self-sufficient, his sanctuary, or as least as it was humanly possible to make the ten-thousand-acre ranch, with about half of it surrounded by electrified fencing running off of hydrogen fuel cells. He caught sight of one of the chicken enclosures, moving itself to a different location and nodded with satisfaction. The property boasted everything from solar-powered electricity to canned food supplied by their own vegetable garden in summer and underground hydroponic enterprise in winter all looked after by Sam Perkins wife, Laura, who even provided a natural alternative to medicine with her knowledge of pharmaceutical plants. A marvel of a woman, she had skills long lost by the majority of home-makers. They were raising their twin five-year-old sons, Logan and Jack, to respect the land and to be self-suffi-cient as well. Laura was also expecting another baby in the fall.

He patted the Loch's thick neck, then checked the cinch was tight on both horses, before adding a scoped rifle to each scabbard, a Bergara Highlander. It was an excellent weapon for hunting, with the rifle having a rugged camouflage stock and Cerakoted metalwork enhancing its durability, plus a no-nonsense two-lug bolt action that wasn't going to let him down. Its accuracy was very good, and at a smidgen over eight pounds, it was portable enough for Connor to take on any hunt. Though today he was only planning to fish with his father, still, he never went into the mountains without solid protection. Wouldn't be the first time he'd run into a dicey situation that required firepower, from wild animal to human being. He also open-carried a Glock in a side holster, same as his dad.

He pulled a couple of carrots from his pocket and fed Loch one first, then Finn as stallions expected a certain kind of respect. No point in upsetting the status quo this early in the day. But what was holding up his dad? He glanced at the road leading into Braveheart again, checking for signs of approach. The lowest part of the horse ranch at the southern edge was on a higher elevation than other properties in the area by a good five hundred feet, giving Connor fair warning of anyone entering. The spectacular view warmed his heart as it always did. He spotted a vehicle approaching raising dust clouds and moving at a fair clip. Aw, his dad's old, restored Humvee, a vehicle capable of being manned or unmanned. He'd bought it at a military surplus auction in 2030 and lovingly restored it back to its full glory a few years ago. He'd even installed an amour kit. Good thinking on his part, though it did appear futuristic in appearance. He'd even turned it into a hybrid able to be powered by electricity, gasoline, or hydrogen fuel cells. His father had always chosen to cover all the bases.

A minute later his dad pulled into the yard and killed the motor. Connor shook his head when his dad climbed out wearing his favorite cowboy hat, a tired affair that had seen better days twenty years ago.

"Where's the new Stetson I got you for Christmas?" Connor asked as he handed over the reins to Finn, disappointed he hadn't seen his dad wear it as yet. He'd had the hat handmade and custom built hoping it would persuade his father to give up the aged relic. The horse greeted his dad with affection, giving a pleased chuff and moving in closer for a head pat. His father responded in kind, then fed Finn a sugar cube from his jacket pocket that made Loch snort in disapproval and toss his proud head.

"Too pretty for a fishing trip. Likely scare the fish off. Besides, I'm always superstitious about wearing anything new before Labor Day."

"That's anything white *after* Labor Day. Doesn't apply to hats."

"I'm too old for anything new anyway. Save your money for more important things."

"Be careful the buzzards don't mistake it for carrion and snatch it off."

His dad snorted. "I can hold on to my hat just fine, son."

"Maybe so. But tipping that hat at a woman's not upping your chances any." Connor had been trying for years to get his dad to head back into the social scene. His mom had died fifteen years ago, the victim of an armed robber, leaving the pair of them to make their own way. Connor had been just fourteen when she'd tried to stop a robbery in progress, taking a bullet intended for another. Earned her accolades, same as the way she always stood up to injustice had during all her years as a private investigator. Hell, she'd even saved millions of people from dying from COFAR, a deadly super flu she fought to contain. No one could live up to her legacy—no one—and they felt her loss every day. But Connor still worried about his dad being all alone in Anchor, the town he grew up in which was twenty-five miles away from his ranch. Chief Pace was now retired from the Anchor Police Department on full pension after taking a bullet to the hip.

"Not looking to impress a woman anytime soon. That's your department. When are you going to settle down is a better question? You're not getting any younger, son, and I wouldn't object to having a grandchild or two to bounce on my knee."

"We should get going. The fish aren't going to wait for us to haul our lazy butts up there. At this rate, they'll be napping by the time we reach God's Lake." Connor placed his foot in the stirrup and hauled his ass up and into Loch's saddle.

His dad did the same, keeping Finn in check while patting his neck lovingly. "We should think about taking young Luke Meech with us. Dan's too old to take the boy fishing."

The thought of another person invading the little personal time he and his father managed together didn't sit right for a moment. Then he softened. The sixteen-year-old was without a father thanks to Connor. He should have thought of it himself.

Connor nodded. "Good idea. I'll arrange it next time."

"Looks like we may not need to wait." His dad pointed at the small uScout barreling across the field toward them. Luke's ginger hair was a flag on the play, a dead giveaway of his Scottish ancestry on his mother's side. Luther, the man Connor had put behind bars, was the seed of the devil in Connor's opinion and probably claimed no other nationality. "If you're up for it?"

"Well, we're already late. Why not take the time to saddle another horse? If he wants to come, that is." A part of Connor hoped the boy was only passing through. Then he noticed the backpack Luke was sporting. "This a set up?"

"I dropped into the Meech's on my way and Luke appeared at loose ends this morning." His dad shrugged. "And I thought, why not?"

A slight ripple of frustration sluiced through Connor. His dad loved to pull the strings. Still seemed to think Connor wasn't a grown up, capable of making his own decisions. He tempered his thoughts with the knowledge his dad was a good man, just used to being in charge.

"I hope he packed some supplies," Connor said.

"No need. I brought extra. And the whole point is catching our own dinner, right?"

When Luke arrived in the yard thirty seconds later, he parked his vehicle next to the main house, then ran full speed over to greet them. His young face was eager, excitement riding high in his eyes. The image melted Connor's heart and he greeted the young boy who seemed younger than his years while his sister seemed fifteen going on twenty with a smile.

"Chief Pace said it was okay, Mr. Hale, if it was okay

with you?" Luke asked politely, though his desperate eyes made for another case.

Connor's father had been the chief of police for Anchor Police Department for the last seven years of his service. Most people still referred to him by the moniker, a sign of well-earned respect.

"Sure, but call me Connor. Let's saddle Kelpie up for you." Connor dismounted and made quick work of it with Luke's help, the trio emerging from the barn a few minutes later. If only his sister Cheyanne was as forgiving as her brother who hadn't held his dad's incarceration against him. Cheyanne, on the other hand, stared daggers at him every chance she got. A part of him understood, she was missing her dad, and even though her father was the one to kill her mother, still, she wasn't able to forget that Connor had helped put him away for the murder. That night, the smell of gasoline and other offensive odors, never entirely left him. He'd arrived too late to save the women, only spotted Luther running away as Connor desperately tried to put out the fire. It was only later he'd learned that the women had been shot first, though they'd been alive until Luther had set the fire to cover his tracks. He still couldn't wrap his mind around it.

Finally, they were off, the sun already beginning its all-too-short journey across the cloud-filled skies. Even late May was mercurial in this area of Alaska, a storm could blow in from the Bering Sea on a dime's notice, lashing the western half of the state with high winds and punishing flooding. Though they were closer to the center of Alaska, it still managed to affect the weather systems.

At the edge of the main property, Connor used his thumbprint to open the gate to the 3D-printed wall to let them out of the compound and onto the less protected sections of his ranch, though it too was surrounded by barbed wire.

"You think to bring a hat, boy?" his dad asked Luke.

Luke shook his head, his long hair flopping in his eyes which he kept downcast as he answered. "Sorry, sir, I guess I didn't."

"No harm done. You can have mine. I brought along another one." Connor watched as his dad removed the old one from his head and maneuvered Finn alongside Kelpie to hand it over. Then he reached to open one of his saddlebags, carefully pulling out the new Stetson Connor had gifted him.

His dad's lips twitched as he placed it on his head at a proper angle while Connor remained silent, enjoying the moment.

"Nice hat, sir," Luke said.

"You won't be getting this one, son. It was a special gift."

"That's okay, I like this one fine." The hat was a bit big for Luke's head, but he could add a cord for now.

"Hand it over, Luke, and I'll add a tie to keep it from blowing off if the wind picks up," Connor said, moving in closer.

"Thank, but I have some cord in my backpack. I need to stop for a couple of minutes to take care of it."

Connor and his dad stayed mounted as Luke went about the business of securing the hat, though the fresh breeze had died down in the past few minutes, making the day warmer.

"Dan told me about a new sentient computer this morning that named its own darn self."

"That's too close to the singularity for this old man. Soon they'll be kicking our asses to the curb, mark my words."

"It's bound to happen. And you're not an old man. Dan's older than you, and he refuses to let the old man in."

"At some point, we have no choice."

"We always have a choice." Noting Luke had finished his fiddling around, Connor nudged Loch ahead of the pack. If they didn't get a move on the day would get ahead of them. Within a few minutes he was feeling guilty about his reaction to his dad's words about his getting older. He loved his dad. Never wanted to think of ever losing him. The pain of his mother's untimely death never left him. A good woman like she'd been, focused on providing justice for others no matter what it took, he didn't feel capable of living up to her legend.

He looked over at his dad as he brought Finn alongside him. "Land's looking good this year, greening up well. You do a good job of husbandry, son. Alaska needs more of these sanctuaries, wilderness areas that keep the spirit alive. And what you teach your guests, well, priceless in the long haul."

The unexpected compliment brought a rush of warmth over him. His IC or intelligence communicator flashed an incoming message in 3D in the corner of his right eye at that moment. Damn it, he thought he'd remembered to put it on emergency mode overdrive this morning, not wanting the time alone with his father interrupted unless it was absolutely necessary. And whoever was calling was choosing not to use the video option. The foreign ID wasn't familiar either, but in his business it wasn't uncommon.

"*Accept*," he thought-spoke. The data signal went straight through the neurons of his brain, sparking all the synapses from the ear device to his optical nerve and he was instantly connected to the user ID. The person didn't think-speak right away and he frowned. Was it an incorrect ID number?

CHAPTER 6
MCKENNA

Day 1: Mexico City, Sinaloa
   7:18 a.m.

Mckenna made a quick decision, one there was no backing away from. Once she did this she would be despised by her former husband, maybe make him angry enough to do something drastic, if he ever found out about it. But she needed the security for her daughter, knowing someone knew about her and Lily's pending arrival in Anchor today. "I need to install the new IC you got for me before we go."

Mckenna pulled the new lightweight multifunctional IC from her pocket and headed into the bathroom to install the contact device. Right now, all she wanted to do was to try Connor's old contact ID number. Knowing he was waiting to pick them up at the airhub when they arrived would give her some peace of mind.

She took the old film out of her right eye and tossed it in the waste basket, then replaced the thin plastic with the new one. It would be a fresh start, wiped of all her usual contacts. She gave the transparent chip a moment to connect to the chip in her ear canal. Diego had originally insisted she install one permanently in her brain. It was the one thing she'd fought him on and won, insisting she didn't trust the implant comms though they were the most reliable brain-net implant device invented with direct brain-to-brain contact, like thousands of others also mistrusted and instead opting for a small bug in their ear canal.

While it was rebooting, she decided she didn't want video when she connected. Connor probably wouldn't recognize her in the wig anyway. Plus, right now, she didn't trust herself to look into his eyes and not spill everything. This was no time for such selfish indulgences. Within a nano-second the device had sent out the inquiry and the information flashed back on the screen in the corner of her right eye, assuring her the number was viable. She had never dared look for his ID before now, knowing her ex would ask questions. He had access to all her information in the past because he had bought the IC and hacked into it.

"Hello, Connor Hale."

The sound of his voice, deeper and more confident than she remembered inside her mind, but still recognizable, made her gasp. A flood of images of him came immediately back to the forefront. He'd been such a handsome teenager, tall and athletic with thick wavy dark-blond hair that always became sun-streaked in summer and sensitive brown eyes. All the girls had been after him though he didn't seem to realize it. And the attractiveness went well below the surface to his caring nature. He'd been so good to her, always caring about her welfare. It took a moment to collect herself before she could speak, her heart hammering in her chest. *"Connor, it's Mckenna Stuart."*

"Mckenna?" Dead silence for a second. *"Where are you? Are you okay?"*

"I'm fine. I'm in Mexico and we're headed to Anchor today. My four-year-old daughter Lily is with me. Can you meet us? We have a two-hour layover in Golden before we catch the Northern Lights hyperloop at four p.m. We should be arriving late this afternoon, if everything goes according to plan." So many things could go wrong in the meantime. The bodyguard could come back early and cause problems. Someone might recognize them despite their disguises. Teresa was a strong woman, but what if the bully took things into his own hands and harmed her, tried to make her talk? The idea sent shards of worry racing through Mckenna making it even harder to hold herself together. But she had to for her daughter's sake.

"I'm heading out on an overnight fishing trip with my father this morning, but I'll send my partner Sam Perkins to pick you both up and bring you to Braveheart."

"Braveheart?"

"My horse ranch. Forty miles west from Anchor and high in the White Mountains which is about a safe a place as one could imagine. I'll explain more when you get here. There's plenty of room for you and your daughter. You can stay as long as you want."

She was disappointed he couldn't meet her, but at least they wouldn't be all alone at the airhub. And it was selfish to think her needs were more important than Connor's spending time with his dad. He lost his mother years ago. Time with his dad must be precious beyond measure. She looked through the open bathroom doorway at Lily struggling to pull on a new pair of jeans, the small pink tip of her tongue exposed as she concentrated. Then Teresa helped her tug a long-sleeved top with a sparkly princess motif over her head, careful to not disturb the wig. Yes, family was everything.

She took a deep breath, steadying herself. *"I can't thank you enough for helping Lily and me, Connor."*

"Is everything okay?"

"Yes, or it will be soon." She tried to keep the worry from her tone.

"What do you mean?"

"Nothing. I'm looking forward to seeing everyone. It's been too long." Seemed a lifetime since she'd lived in Anchor. She'd lost her innocence somewhere, the sense that all things were possible. Now she just wanted her daughter safe, to be able to grow up not worrying about how her father was going to act on any given day. She deserved the best life possible and Mckenna was going to make that happen, no matter what it took.

"Travel safely."

"We will, I promise." She blinked her eyes and disconnected from the IC, praying she could keep everything together and keep her word. Hearing Connor's voice again, it rocketed her back to the beginning, to a time when she always felt safe whenever she was in his company. Only a few more hours and this would all be over with. They would be reunited and who knew where it might go from there. Connor Hale as a friend was more than she could ask for. She had to keep it together, keep moving and positive, push negative thoughts away best she could and get them home.

She rejoined Teresa and Lily in the kitchen.

"All set?" Teresa asked.

"I am, thanks to you. But what are you going to do, Teresa? You have to know he'll come after you."

"I'm going on vacation. Didn't you hear, to—"

Mckenna put her hands over her ears. "Don't tell me.

Best I don't know just in case. Well, you know." She couldn't say the words aloud. Failure was not an option, but she still felt responsible for her friend. She'd done so much to help her already and she was beyond grateful as it was. The less she knew about Teresa's plans going forward, the better. Everyone had a breaking point, or at least that was what she gleamed from all the data she'd read and the terrible things she'd seen Diego do to others. Though one thing she did know, when it came to keeping her daughter safe, nothing in this world would ever cause her to break down and give up. Nothing. Diego could go to hell. She'd pray for the strength to do what had to be done if he ever found out where they had run to because there was no way she'd ever go back and take the risk that he would harm her daughter. She did know one thing without a shadow of doubt, she'd give her life for her Lily's in a heartbeat if it came to that. Like Socrates said eons ago and it was something that had stuck with her, *know thyself*.

CHAPTER 7
CONNOR

Day 1: White Mountains, Alaska
    9:31 a.m.

By the time Connor and his companions crested the top of Spirit Ridge, the sun was settling in for its lazy summer sweep across the White Mountains. The view of the greening valley below was more than worth the climb and gave him pause to admire the deep blue ribbon of God's River before he gave Loch his head to descend to the riverbed below. God's River was renowned for its fishing, especially brown-speculated trout, though it contained grayling too. He was itching to get his rod and reel out and try his luck.

"Looks like the water's a bit shallow for this time of year," his dad said, dismounting and allowing Finn to graze, but not before he removed the Bergara Highlander rifle and the gear from his saddlebags. The day may look peaceful enough, but in the mountains, a wise man stayed prepared at all times with grizzly, black, and brown bears plentiful across the vast landscape along with wolves.

Then there was the two-legged kind which sometimes proved to be the worst of all.

"Fishing's good. Sam had a group up here last week and they had a feast every night they were in camp," Connor said. He approached the packhorse, rubbed his hand along the thick brown crest a few times before giving the animal a final pat and began to unload the supplies. Wulver came racing up and joined him, sniffing all around the packed supplies, probably hoping to discover a food packet.

"What can I do?" Luke asked, joining them.

"Haul this tent over to that flat area and we'll set it up right now. Once Chief Pace gets to fishing, we'll be setting up in the dark by the time he calls it quits."

His dad ignored the minor dig but Connor noted he'd gone for the rod and reel first, ignoring any other chores that needed doing. He'd earned the right to take things easy and Connor was happy to provide all the comforts possible when sleeping on the ground, even hauling along an air mattress for his dad. Connor had no trouble sleeping on the hard earth.

"Meet you down at the river once you two quit fussing around here," his dad quipped before ambling off.

Connor bit his tongue and continued making sure everything was in order to make the night's camping comfortable, if not luxurious. His dad hated to admit the advancing years worse than anyone he knew, but he was going on sixty-seven and had two heart attacks. Now he needed surgery again, but at least the final result would be better than what he had installed at the moment, he comforted himself. The surgery couldn't be soon enough in Connor's opinion, even though that too entailed risk. He avoided anything relying too heavily on the electrical grid like the plague, from pacemakers to communications to power. Instead, he ran a ship that was mostly self-sustaining. An island of protection in a world that seemed to insist on proving itself more unstable by the day with too many countries having nuclear capability run by feckless governments. Politics. All it appeared to be anymore was a show detailing which candidate could lie the best, pull a smoke screen over reality by attacking the opposite party. What had happened to integrity? If worst came to worst, he'd no more trust the government to act in the people's best interests, then to discover dinosaurs once more roaming the earth.

"Where do you want the campfire?"

"By those rocks, it's mostly flat. We'll use the Dakota fire hole, keep the smoke down."

Luke looked at him like he was speaking one of the Sioux languages instead of English. Obviously, his father had neglected this part of his education. But Connor enjoyed teaching bushcraft and set to work to explain the process to the boy.

"First, we need to clear the area of combustible materials and consider wind direction. Set any dry kindling aside to build the fire. Then, we dig two holes, one about twelve inches deep and twelve inches wide, the other smaller. Make it about a foot and a half away. That's called the chimney. We'll line the bottom of the hole with some of those stones," Connor said, pointing them out. "Then we'll connect the two holes by digging a tunnel between them about six inches wide and two feet long. Make it on an upward slope toward the smaller hole. That allows oxygen to feed the fire below."

"That's why it's called a chimney, right?"

Connor nodded. Luke was an easy boy to like, eager to learn, reminding him of himself when he was a teenager. Of course, his dad had not neglected his education, showing him all the best practices for survival in the wilderness years ago. But it was never too late in Connor's opinion. He vowed then and there to make it a point to spend more time with the boy, teaching him the craft.

"What's the best wood to use?"

"Good question. Oak and maple, the hardwoods, they burn longer and give more heat. But in the woods, a man uses what's available. Choose the driest. Green wood sparks too much."

Luke watched as he used a small collapsible spade to dig the first hole. The ground wasn't too hard, and the work went quickly. Connor dug a second hole and connected the two, then spent a few minutes lining the larger, cooking hole with the small stones Luke collected.

"We won't light it yet, but we need to gather some wood for later."

"I'll do that."

He gave Luke a smile of approval. "I'll meet you down by the water. We don't want Chief Pace getting all the fish."

"No, sir."

Connor strode away to collect his fishing equipment, then joined his dad on the riverbank. Wulver hung back with Luke, probably still hoping for a handout.

"The boy seems eager to learn," his dad remarked. He cast his line again, the blue and chrome lure dancing across the sparkling waters.

"Shame his education has been neglected. This trip will be good for him."

His dad gave him a sideways glance. "Who were you think-speaking with earlier?"

"Why?" The last thing he wanted to talk about was Mckenna. He'd put the few facts she told him in a box in his mind, something to be set aside until he had time to make sense of it. Not that there was the luxury of days to think about all the ramifications of her coming to visit. They would be arriving too soon for that.

"The look on your face then, and now, has to be someone important."

Connor went about preparing his own fishing line and one for Luke, keeping his hands busy while he considered the best way to tell him. Go ahead and spill it, seemed about the best he could come up with. "Mckenna Suart."

"The young girl you took a fancy to in school until her parents moved the family to Florida?"

"She and her daughter are headed here later today. She wanted to know if I could pick them up. Which reminds me, I need to call Sam and ask him to help out."

"Why are they coming here after all this time? Just her and her daughter? They have no family left in the area to take them in."

"I told her she could stay at Braveheart." Connor scrubbed a hand down his face, feeling his freshly shorn skin after shaving this morning. He always shaved before a camping trip in the summer. In winter, he let his beard grow for warmth. "I got the feeling she was running from something."

"Or someone. Best be careful, son. Never get too involved in a family situation that's not yours beyond giving sound advice. And she's got a young daughter to boot."

Connor tried to keep the frustration from his voice as he took a moment to call up Sam's ID and fire off a quick message. "She may need my help. I can't just tell her to go someplace else."

"Of course not. But stay alert's all I'm saying. You got too big a heart for your own good, son."

They fished in silence for a few minutes before Luke

and Wulver finally joined them. Now the lock box in Connor's mind had been bust open, he found it hard to close it again. Why was Mckenna coming home to Alaska? He had so many questions and no answers, a situation he never handled well. He knew he still carried a torch for her, always would, though he never expected to see her again in this lifetime.

They didn't stop for lunch but ate sandwiches he'd prepared earlier washed down by fresh spring water, still hoping for a trout feast at supper. Fishing hadn't been as plentiful today as hoped for, though Connor's mind was elsewhere. He kept imagining the journey Mckenna and her daughter were undertaking. When two o'clock finally rolled around, he knew they should be arriving in Golden, Alaska, for their layover waiting for the hyperloop to take them to Anchor before Sam brought them out to Brave-heart. He wouldn't be able to relax until the pair were safely under his roof.

He was still lost in thought a couple of hours later, thinking of them waiting in Golden. A place he and Mckenna had visited and picnicked once after he got his first truck. A favorite memory he wondered if she still remembered? Their first kiss had happened there on the river bank, so perhaps she did. Golden was only a one-hundred-and-ten-mile trip from his ranch and he wished he was there to meet them to make sure they were well taken care of. Traveling with a four-year-old had to be tough, Mckenna would need to keep her neck on a swivel to keep her daughter safe and protected. Lots of gang activity in Golden in recent years, mostly connected to the Kraken Cartel, of which Luther Meech had a big hand. He wondered who was running the cartel now that Luther was locked up for good?

Wulver suddenly gave a loud bark, his fur standing

straight on end before he growled deep in his chest. An ominous warning quickly joined by the horses snorting and pawing at the ground behind them. Everything went still. Quiet. Too quiet. *The longer the lull, the harder the blow.*

And then it happened. A bright reddish-orange flash over-whelmed the sky above the river for a split second. It was instantly followed by a deep bass sound rumbling up the valley toward them, momentarily canceling every other sound. The terrible rush in his ears cemented the terrible truth, especially when it was followed by an acute burning sensation deep inside. He dropped his rod and reel and yanked the electronic device from his ear canal, thrusting it in his pocket.

"Don't look at it!" he shouted a warning, making a grab for Luke and Wulver, his dad being too far away to reach. He closed his eyes as well, feeling a hot breeze blow over them unlike anything he'd ever experienced. The red-turning-to-red-brown glow was even visible behind his closed eyelids. In that split second, he knew what it was. What he had always feared. An EMP event.

He chanced opening his eyes when the sonic boom passed by to observe the expected mushroom cloud high above the tree line like it had exploded far above the earth in the upper stratosphere, containing a column of red fire and black smoke. A giant gas ball of fire and smoke mixed with lightning that would cause the creator himself to stare with horror at its unleashed power. It was confirmation that the worst had happened. A nuclear detonation.

CHAPTER 8
MCKENNA

Day 1: Golden, Alaska
    3:54 p.m.

Mckenna kept a close watch on her daughter Lily, seated next to her in the waiting area while they waited for the Northern Lights hyperloop expected any moment to arrive at the airhub. Lily was so engrossed in reading and observing a picture book on her lap with holographic images that popped out unexpectedly from the pages, her favorite one so far being the princess riding the dragon scenes, that she was oblivious to the mass of people in the airhub. The quality of the 3D images was impressive, so lifelike she felt she could reach out and touch them, and worth every precious dollar she'd paid for the new device though it wasn't expensive being older technology. She'd held back the new toy, waiting impatiently for this day as hard as it was to keep anything from her daughter. She wanted the best for her little girl no matter what it took to provide it.

    She couldn't believe they had made it this far without

a major incident. She was still afraid to relax her vigilance and think her worries about pursuit were all over, but it was only a short trip on a private pod to Anchor now. No, she had to stay alert. Soon as Diego found out about their escaping his clutches, he'd be after them. She'd have to stay on guard for the foreseeable future, maybe forever. Life was never going to be easy. That point had been driven home plenty these last few years, emphasized by Diego's dire warnings that if she ever left him, he'd kill her and take Lily back. She didn't doubt him. He was a man of his word, evil as his intentions were.

She was desperate to continue the journey, wishing the hyperloop would head off to Anchor sooner rather than all this waiting around. Each passing minute was making her more nervous, certain that her soon-to-be-ex would show up with some of his goons to snatch them away. If they killed her, what about Lily? She couldn't let a monster like Diego raise her daughter.

"Look, Mommy, isn't this amazing!" Lily exclaimed, her expression filled with wonder.

Mckenna glanced at the hologram of a dancing prince in a formal black tuxedo and a beautiful princess in a gorgeous sky-blue gown. Soft strains of music, a waltz she recognized as a classic, *The Blue Danube* by Johann Strauss, erupted and the sound made others glance their way, making her instantly uncomfortable. One older woman smiled at Lily indulgently, but others did not, one even going so far as to glare at her daughter at the inter-ruption. The last thing she wanted was to draw undue attention, and she put her arm around Lily's thin shoulders in an effort to shield her.

"Yes, Lilybelle, it's very pretty." She absently called her daughter by her nickname. An unease, worse than before, had crept over her. A sense of impending doom she couldn't shake off. It had to be the results of a long day and a few sleepless nights leading up to it. Well, more than a few if she were being honest. It was only afternoon, but it felt much later. She took a deep breath, wanting nothing more than to get back to her hometown and whisk her daughter to safety at Connor's ranch. The image that arose in her mind of being reunited with her former boyfriend from high school was the only thing keeping her from falling into the mire.

Lily began scratching at her head again and Mckenna reached up and took her hand, gently pulling the tiny fingers away.

"When can I take it off, Mommy? It itches," she whispered.

"Very soon, I promise. Only one more short trip and then we'll be there. We're going to a ranch that has horses. Would you like that?"

"Horses!" Lily's blue eyes doubled in size. "Do they have unicorns too?"

"I don't think so. But maybe rabbits or chickens or a goat?" The Connor she knew planned to live his life self-sustaining, meaning she expected him to have a menagerie of animals, and all well cared for. Perhaps she could earn her and Lily's keep by helping out on the ranch, doing farm chores or the like? She'd never worked with animals, but she knew herself to be a quick learner. Plus, she could work in town, cutting and styling hair to bring in cash. She still had her license.

The clock ticked one more minute closer to four. The announcement to board should be called soon, trying to reassure her sense of unease with the thought. Her stomach roiled at the wait and she had to refrain herself from biting her fingernails. How much longer? It seemed an eternity they'd been waiting in the pod. If only they could have gone straight to Anchor, but it was too small a town to warrant a direct route, meaning the city of Golden, now the sixth largest city in Alaska, was the only choice.

She noticed a man watching them from a few seats away, his hat pulled down over his forehead obscuring his appearance, but his eyes were definitely on her and Lily. She didn't recognize him, but still, he gave her pause. She didn't know all of Diego's contacts. Her heart rate sped up and she forced herself to stay in her seat, but she pulled her daughter in closer to her side. So much so that Lily squirmed and tried to move away, but Mckenna held on even tighter. Any second now and the hyperloop would be in the station.

The ringing sounds of a warning alert and the whoosh of air movement drew everyone's attention, as people expected to be called any second to board the hyperloop. People began to get gather their belongings and get to their feet.

But before that happened, a flash of intense red as ominous as hellfire erupted above the overhead skylights sending a strange reddish-orange hue down to glow all around the airhub making people's complexion looks garish. Inhuman. The eerie haze was quickly followed by a resounding sonic boom, and people froze, dropping their gear to cover their ears. Screams of pain followed. Mckenna's ears instantly burned, and she pulled the device from her ear and threw it away. Lily began to cry. She hugged her close to her body, trying to stall her own fear as she ran her hands over her daughter's hair in an effort to soothe her. What was it? Had the hyperloop had an accident pulling into the station? But it was more than that, she knew in her heart. Far more. She watched people doing as she had done, those that could, pulling the communicators out of their ears and throwing them away. Others couldn't, the device was buried in their brains and they were the ones screaming the loudest.

Uncertain what to do, but knowing she had to get moving, Mckenna got Lily to put her things away in her backpack before she gathered their bags. Lily was so upset she had her thumb stuck in her mouth, something she'd long given up. Everyone was ignoring them, too busy with their own pain or worries to give the mother and daughter duo any thought. Those in charge didn't look to be in any better straits, the looks on their faces the same as the passengers. Confusion, pain in the faces of those with implant comms, and pandemonium was breaking out as people began to run off in all directions.

Where should they go? She hadn't been in Golden in years and then only a few times. The growing city would surely be vastly changed. Her mind went blank for a moment, pondering what to do. She couldn't contact anyone now with her communicator destroyed along with everyone else's, judging by the tiny black bugs dotting the floor. She noted those with the suspected neural implants, their eyes were bleeding in some cases, red tears running down their faces. Fear struck hard. What if she had allowed Diego to put one in her brain? Would she now be partially incapacitated, unable to look after Lily. The fear increased, became a hungry beast looking to prey on her.

No! She had to fight back. She was still standing. Her daughter was okay for now. She had to get them out of here and find somewhere safe to wait until Connor could find them. Because she knew without a shadow of a doubt, if he was all right, and she couldn't let herself think any differently, then he would come for them. She'd have to figure out how to hang on until then. But looking around her, at the scared expressions on everyone's face, she had no idea how she could make it through the next few minutes, let alone the time it would take Connor to get there.

She sniffed the air and recognized the taint of smoke. Where was it coming from? Unable to detect the source, she grabbed Lily's hand, looking around the space frantically while deciding which direction was best. They had to get out of there. Right now.

CHAPTER 9
CONNOR

Day 1: God's River, Alaska
  4:10 p.m.

"Dad! Are you okay?" Connor rushed to his father's side. Within minutes of the EMP event, he'd slumped over, his eyes closed.

When his dad didn't respond right away, he shook his arm, trying to get him to wake up. His mind registered that the horses were making loud snorting sounds nearby, their hooves pawing at the ground. Wulver barked again. Loud.

The terrible unsettling sound of an engine in trouble somewhere above them drew Connor's attention upward for a moment, to catch sight of an aircraft traveling overhead. He tuned everything else out then, even the animal's nervous pacing around, trying to rouse his father to no avail.

"Luke, go to my saddlebags. Get the red bag with the white cross on it."

The young boy looked at him with a stunned glaze to his eyes.

"Now. Go! My dad needs what's in it. His life depends on it."

The boy took another endless moment to receive the message through the fog of shock he'd fallen under. He finally came to his senses and began to stumble away toward the campsite.

Connor waited impatiently for Luke to retrieve the bag, trying to revive his father. "Come on. Don't leave me now. I haven't given you those grandkids yet to bounce on those old knees. Stay with me and I promise to get on the case, okay?"

"Swear on your mother's life," his dad croaked, giving Connor a head rush. "And I'll stay around for a while. You know the only argument I ever won with your mom was over your name. She wanted Cole Alexander, but I held out for Connor, my grandfather's name. I hope you can pass it on to your son or daughter. You are so like him, from his young Robert Redford looks to his stanch belief in family. He lived until he was a hundred-and-one. My wish for you, a long and healthy productive life with a good woman at your side. He even played the bagpipes, a Scotsman through and through."

"I swear to try if I can find a woman who will put up with me. You had me going there for a moment, Dad. How you feeling?" Connor supported his dad's body, wishing Luke would hurry up.

"I'll let you know soon as you get the name of the bull that ran over me." His dad licked his lips, his skin pale and clammy. "Had to have been going a hundred miles an hour," he joked.

Connor shook his head.

Luke finally came into view, carrying the emergency

kit. He ran over and handed it to Connor, his body visibly trembling.

"You okay, Luke?" his dad asked, squinting at the young boy.

"Yeah, I think so. What happened?"

Connor ignored the question and unzipped the bag, pulling out a bottled water and the health meter. The kit also included an AED device due to his father's condition which he didn't need at the moment. He prayed he could get him home without having to resort to restarting his heart.

He unsnapped the lid and held the fresh water to his father's lips. "Drink. It'll help."

While his dad drank a few mouthfuls, he started to think of all that needed doing. They had to get back to Braveheart as soon as possible, that was a given. He'd leave all the supplies, but considering what he'd witnessed, it would be smarter to take all the goods they could carry out.

He attached the health meter while he planned their next moves. Then he read the print-out and his own heart took a hit.

"Your pulse's racing, Dad. It's over a hundred."

"I just need to calm down. And the damn pacemaker is probably toast now."

Pointless to wish he'd had the operation to replace it earlier. A second later, he sniffed the air, recognizing the acrid odor of smoke molecules.

"We have to get a move on. Something's on fire nearby. Probably the aircraft I heard in trouble when the flash hit."

"Damn nuclear explosion is what it was. No need to mince words, son." His dad raised a trembling hand to his forehead, his eyes filled with concern.

"And now the walls of Jericho will come tumbling down," Connor murmured, and his dad responded with a squeeze on his forearm.

"You're in better shape than most. You planned Braveheart to make sure of it. You did good there. I know I feel better for knowing you'll have a sanctuary when I'm gone. And I know you'll take in others and help protect them as well. Be careful who you let in. Stay selective, only those who will pull their own weight."

Connor bit his tongue, not wanting to draw attention to his father talking about being gone. Not if he had a say in it. He'd make sure he rested up. Laura had some nursing training and would be a huge help in helping take care of his dad. He felt guilty for asking her, she was pregnant, but she barely showed yet. He could ask someone else to take over her daily chores. Hire someone if necessary.

"You're moving to Braveheart today. Get you checked out at the hospital first. I'll get whatever you need, but you're not going to be alone from now on." Was the town of Anchor intact? Until they rode up out of here to a higher elevation than the riverbed, he couldn't be sure. His worry only increased thinking of Mckenna and Lily not having the time to get safely to the ranch. If only the disaster had struck an hour later, she'd be home, tucked away at Braveheart. He partially comforted himself with the knowledge that at least she wasn't stuck in Mexico, which would be much worse. Or dear God, flying at the time of the event. He couldn't go there, imagining what was happening to thousands of people trapped in aircraft. Or on boats.

"What about Mckenna and her daughter?"

Connor took a deep breath. His dad was echoing his worries. But if he was correct, they should have not boarded the Northern Lights before the bomb hit the stratosphere, killing the electronics for the hyperloop, meaning she was still in Golden. She had to be there, he decided, fate would not do this to him again. No, she was there, the timeline fit. Besides, he'd be of no use if he panicked, as much as he was worried about her all alone with a young child to care for.

"Soon as I settle things with you, I'll be heading to Golden and bringing her back home to Braveheart."

"Take the Humvee. Better than an ATV and it will offer some protection. I tried to rebuild it in case of this very situation."

"Thanks." But then he considered another idea. One that would allow a straighter path, as the crow flies, to Golden than the meandering, scenic route of some sections of the Peak Highway through state parks. No, it would only take longer. Yes, the Humvee was the better choice. He just had to pray the roads were passable.

"Can you stand?" Connor asked. He hated to ask, but the sooner they got out of there the better.

A clock began ticking in his head, a reminder of all the things now unfolding in the world impossible to entirely predict, no matter how many times he'd gone over this very scenario in his mind. The event itself was easy enough to describe, what happened in the three phases, with the E1 lasting only a millionth of a second when the stripping of electrons of their atoms occurred, or the E2 phase when they begin to spiral and interact with Earth's magnetic field, ending with slightly longer E3 stage when all hell is unleashed affecting ground infrastructure like power grids and electronics.

What was harder to predict was human desperation when suddenly dropped into a chaos event they could not comprehend the magnitude of. That was most worrying, Connor being a student of history and reading of other previous times humans have undergone starvation due to events out of their control. Just being reminded of the Holodomor or Mao's campaign in China of intimidation from a hundred years ago made him shudder with horror, not to mention various studies like the Lucifer Effect or the Stanford experiment. When faced with terrible deprivations, humans acted unpredictably, some becoming too depressed to do anything. Others so angry they lashed out at everyone else, not to mention the gangs and basement dwellers waiting for their chance to exploit things. It all led to the fact they had to get out of here as fast as possible. All too soon it would be *us against them*. The 'others' concept would rear its ugly head in short order and before it happened, he had to make certain everyone he cared for was protected, then get Mckenna and Lily. He vowed then, whoever was responsible for this disaster would pay one day and pay deeply.

"Just give me your hand."

He helped his dad to his feet. He looked better, though still pale.

"Luke, grab our stuff. We need to pack up right now."

Luke looked shellshocked, but he obeyed and began to pick up things from the ground and haul them up to where the horses were milling around, looking ready to bolt. Connor made comforting sounds to the animals as he helped his dad up the incline to the campsite.

"You're different than your mother, son. In a way I admire. You temper your drive for justice with a more spiritual, nature-based philosophy, living in harmony with the environment. But right now, with what I suspect is bound to happen, you'll have to embrace more of what she stood for than before. She recognized the evil in mankind. Was unafraid to do what had to be done, no matter the cost."

"I'll protect my own," Connor said through gritted teeth. His father didn't realize how far he was willing to go to protect his people, never had, always seeing him as a lover of nature and not a destroyer if the need for it ever came. To Connor's mind, that's what the back forty was for, a place to bury the bodies. Though he'd never been tested like his mom and dad had been off and on all their lives—it wasn't his fault as he'd never tracked monsters—he was still fairly certain he had what it took to do what had to be done. The one thing he could count on though, the coming days would tell the tale.

"I'm not meaning lose what you stand for but temper it with the new reality."

Frustration accompanied by a deep-seated dread about the future filled him. "I know what's going to happen more than most. I've studied history and know all too well about man's atrocities. The shit is about to hit the fan. I'll step up my game as well, but I won't let it change who I am." Or at least he promised to try. Much as he had imagined the very scenario everyone he knew was now going to undergo, still, there were unknowns. No one could know how bad it could get who hadn't lived through it. No one, not even the so-called pundits who said they could well imagine it, promising for money or power to tell you how to live through the dark times, though they'd had no real training or understanding of what such an event would entail. And how far did this thing reach? North America, or beyond? If all supply lines were broken, then look out. It would become each person for themselves if people were reduced to their basic nature.

"Good. That's all I wanted to hear. A man does what he's called upon to do, but he needs to adhere to his own personal code of honor as well. If we save the world and lose ourselves in the process, what good is it all? Well, enough doom and gloom. Help me onto my horse. We need to get a move on."

"I agree, Dad. Let's get you out of here." Connor sprang into action, resaddling the horses and making sure their supplies were secured in short order. The animals were still antsy, but he kept up the soothing patter as he worked with them until they calmed down. The familiar actions also calmed him, making his own adrenaline rush subside enough to think more clearly.

He gave his father a leg up, then made sure he was in good control of Finn before mounting Loch. The stallion gave a head toss, then settled into a familiar rhythm, his hooves raising small puffs of dust in the dry soil. April and May's rainfall so far had been less than normal giving him something else to worry about with the threat of wildfire hanging over the land every summer.

Wulver led the way up and out of the valley headed for Spirit Ridge, preferring the vantage point of leading the pack. He tried not to dwell on things, but riding a horse always gave time for a man to think and ponder, today being no different. Except today was different in every way that counted. First, he'd heard from Mckenna, and now an EMP event. What the hell was coming next? An exploding asteroid to round out the day? He grimaced, catching sight of the black clouds of smoke now visible as they reached the top of the ridge. The strong stench of plastic and unknown substances on fire drifting in on the wind abraded his nose and lungs. The downed aircraft.

Much as he wanted to head there and help if anyone was still alive which appeared unlikely, he wanted to get his father home more. He ignored the sight, hoping no one else would mention it.

"Look." Luke pointed to the spot Connor had been studying. "Something's burning. What are we going to do?"

"Soon as we get back to the ranch, I'll report it. My father needs to get there as fast as possible and be checked out in Anchor. I can't risk delaying it." Bad as the words made him feel, he had his priorities. Choices like this one were only going to get harder in the days ahead. Sometimes it would come down to choosing between the lesser of two evils. Then what?

CHAPTER 10
LUTHER

Day 1: North of Anchor, Alaska
3:55 p.m.

Luther Meech surveyed the old hunting lodge with keen satisfaction. It had once belonged to Buck Duffy, the long dead mayor of Anchor murdered by the mother of his nemesis, Connor Hale. A part of him enjoyed the significance. Perhaps even now the dead mayor was gloating with satisfaction to see a fellow Alaskan finding retribution by preparing to deal with the offspring of Anna Hale. Maybe even put an end to the family line responsible for digging their noses into things that were none of their business. Connor Hale was in his sights, and though he had an empire to reclaim in the coming days, destroying Hale was near the top of his list for the foreseeable future, along with getting his kids back. He needed to stay patient. Plan it well.

Thomas and George had done a decent job of getting the place in running order, he noted, turning his mind to more pressing matters. He took a long pull on his bottled beer as he walked around the property, the two men following him and pointing out the improvements they'd already made. The hunting lodge had the necessary potential to be the headquarters of his operation for once again taking up the reins of his former territory.

"What about supplies? Weapons, food, communications? Did you stock up on lumber and nails like I asked?"

George nodded. "Yes, and we've stashed plenty of MREs for five years at least for fifty people. As for weapons we've managed—"

A sudden change to dead quiet in their surroundings stopped all three of them in their tracks. A bright flash of intense light followed hard on its heels and made Luther instinctively cover his eyes. The sonic boom rolled across the landscape, a painful blast that pieced his defenses. He stumbled one step backward, trying to gather himself.

"What the hell was that?" George asked, his stunned expression mirroring Thomas's.

Thomas clutched at the sides of his head before digging in his right ear canal. He drew out a small black device and threw it away.

George did likewise, as if he suddenly realized his ear was burning up too.

"Look, the uFree's on fire!" Luther pointed out the surreal image as the stench of arid smoke stung his nostrils. What the fuck was going on? The air had turned an ominous reddish orange, a strange glow to it that made every hair on his body stand on end. A terrible sense of hell being unleashed struck him front and center. He shuddered. If they'd been in the uFree a few hours earlier they might have been burned alive or crashed. As it was their main air transportation was going up in smoke.

"What causing this?" George's stunned expression was almost comical in its intensity.

"Look! A weird mushroom cloud," Thomas said, wiping his watery eyes with the back of his shirt sleeve as he stared at the sky, looking to the southeast.

"Shit," Luther said, bracing himself. They were in for it now. "That monster probably took out all the electronic communications you stockpiled in the lodge." It was a terrible blow and a waste of good resources. Luther hated waste. Prided himself on his ability to keep costs down which was why he had the relationship he did, working with the Mexicans to distribute cocaine, fentanyl, and heroin in Alaska. Methamphetamine he could make himself easy enough, supplies for that lucrative enterprise also stockpiled. He ran a tight ship and kept his employees in line with intimidation and fear. Only time he'd made a mistake, it had been caused by emotion and landed him in the supermax. Never going to happen again. No woman would ever get under his skin in the future.

But this new development, it held endless possibilities, if handled right. The civilized world was about to undergo huge structural changes. The old laws of right and wrong would no longer apply, not that he'd heeded them anyway. But now there'd be no repercussions by the moralists. No one in charge. No, the world was now ripe for the picking. And he was the right man for the job.

CHAPTER 11
MCKENNA

Day 1: Golden, Alaska
4:09 p.m.

Mckenna tried to make sense of things, but her mind was assaulted by a jumble of disjointed images, accompanied by the dreaded stench of smoke. They'd stumbled out into the street behind others pushing and shoving in their rush to get out of the airhub. She stared at the chaos, holding on to Lily's hand, unable to look away. Half of the city of Golden appeared to be on fire, vehicles clogging the streets and people shouting and screaming as she held on even tighter to Lily with one arm and their luggage with the other.

Her daughter was sobbing uncontrollably. But she couldn't stop now, not with the people pressing in on all sides. They had to keep moving. Get away from the danger. Where to go? *Think, Mckenna, think*. Yes, the river. It was always safer near water when things were burning. One of the many things she'd learned growing up in Anchor where forest fires were a seasonal concern.

When someone fell against her, her hand was nearly torn away from Lily's. Like a ferocious mother lion, she shoved back against the person blocking their path before picking up her daughter in one arm and hauling the blasted suitcase behind her down the street. Fear sparked a strong sense of determination giving her one focus, and one focus only, getting to the location she kept imagining in her mind. The spot her and Connor had picnicked so long ago when the world made sense.

Lily's sobs slowly subsided as she clung to her mother, her tiny hands clutching around her neck. Her face pressed in tight against her chest.

"It's okay, Lilybelle, we'll soon be there." She offered far more reassurance than she felt. The streets were blocked, the sidewalk strewn with debris. People were scrambling around, some with such looks of horror on their faces it made Mckenna now turn away from the sight with increasing trepidation. If only she had a weapon. The idea came upon her in a flash, spotting a sport goods store across the street from where they were being forced along by the crowd. She'd had to leave her guns and knives back in Mexico. If she could purchase something now, she'd feel much safer while they waited for Connor. *Please, please, let him be on his way and coming for us.* He was their only hope of getting out of this mess intact.

Why today of all days did a disaster have to happen?

She had felt it the right thing to do, leaving Diego. Now, with hellfire reigning down on them, the idea held less merit. And yet, they couldn't have stayed. Diego was dangerous, as dangerous as their current situation in the long haul. No, more like she should have left sooner, but the opportunity created by Teresa had taken time, especially to arrange the fake documents. She comforted herself with the reality they were only a few hours from home, as she pulled out of the tidal wave of humanity and began to dodge her way across the street. Lily clung on to her like a small monkey to its mother in the wild.

"I want Tinker," Lily whimpered as they arrived at the front door of the store aptly named Golden Sporting Goods. "Where is Daddy?"

"Soon as we get inside, then I'll dig out Tinker." The father issue she couldn't fix, now or ever, which brought with it a certain sadness for her daughter who was too young to realize what a monster her father was, but Tinker was Lily's small robot puppy and she'd remembered to pack him. Lily loved the toy more than any other and couldn't sleep without the noisy little mutt that sometimes tested her mother's patience. The designer seemed to think all puppies were usually up to mischief and tearing into things like her favorite shoes. Fortunately, it had no teeth, but it did leave things strewn about. Diego disliked disorder and though it was him that had gifted Lily with it, he'd been threatening of late to 'drown' it if Mckenna didn't keep it out of his way. Another strike against him, wanting to destroy her daughter's favorite toy.

Mckenna pushed open the door of the store and stepped inside, glancing around. Old alpha music blared overhead, the band 4 plus 1 ranting on about their lost generation, explaining why no one in the store was paying attention to the crisis. She had some American money stashed in the pocket of her pants and more in her luggage, but she'd need to hold on to as much as possible. It had to last them until she could find a job. She had some training under her belt obtained before she lost her mind and married too young, knew how to cut and style hair, though she went to the hairdresser herself as an escape from Diego.

The store was an oasis after being outside, a huge relief after being jostled in the airhub and then again out in the street. Probably due to the fact sound was also muffled by the amazing assortment of items packing the shelves. But still, she could feel the tension in the air, increasing the drive to get this done and move on as soon as possible. One customer was standing at the counter, an older man in a ball cap, discussing the weapon he held in his hands. An assault rifle, a new brand she didn't recognize.

The clerk, a younger, much thinner man than the customer with a wild mob of curly black hair frowned at her, noting her daughter still whimpering for Tinker in her arms. She needed to get the puppy out of Lily's backpack, but she wanted a weapon even more. She hovered close to the glass counter and looked down into the display, checking for knives. She hoped the customer would make their purchase quickly so she could get out of there.

But the man persisted in asking loud questions about the gun, making the clerk frown even more. Didn't he know the world had gone crazy outside? He had to have heard the blast at least, sensed the continuing uproar, though the windows were covered up with large posters announcing a sale. The scent of something burning tainting the air. Maybe he was partially deaf and nose blind?

Buy it already. She screamed the words in her mind. Then she spotted something useful on a nearby display. A navy-blue backpack child carrier with room for other items to be hooked on. Or tucked in pouches on the sides. She hurried over and grabbed the carrier, pulling it off the metal rack. It would make keeping Lily safe and secure much easier, freeing her hands for other things. It even had a first aid kit included in the price.

She carried it back to the counter and laid it down. Now, just get the customer to make his mind up and she'd be on her way. A sense of a clock ticking in her mind wasn't helping. How long would it take for Connor to get there? He'd gone fishing with his dad, so how soon would he know about everything going on in Golden? Had he seen the flash of light and the strange colors and tainted smell in the air?

The sounds of the door opening grabbed her attention and she looked over to see a group of four, two men and two women, making their way inside the store. She groaned aloud. Great. All she wanted was to buy the backpack and a knife and get out of there. Lily was crying again, making it harder to concentrate. She tried rocking her and soothing her, but to no avail.

Finally, she'd had enough. "How much for the backpack and a knife?" she asked, interrupting the endless exchange between the customer and the clerk.

The customer turned beady eyes on her and pursed his lips making him look like a sucker fish. "I was here first, young lady."

"Please, my daughter is upset, I only want to buy a couple of things and get out of here."

"How much for that Remington?" one of the new arrivals called out, pointing out the weapon on display along the back wall behind the clerk.

Lily pulled out her small roll of bills and waved it desperately at the clerk. "There's twenty in here for you if you'd ring me up right now. This backpack and that Blue Blade, six-inch knife right there with a leather cover. The graphene laminate combat knife." She pointed out the item inside the display case. "Oh, and that emergency blanket too." She couldn't have Lily getting chilled.

The older man scowled at her. "See here, I ain't letting you cut in line. Wait your turn."

"You're taking way too long to make up your mind, old man. Can't you see the lady has a crying toddler in tow? Least you could do is respect that and let her buy what she needs and get on her way."

The unexpected help from the man looking to buy the Remington was sorely needed. She nodded at the big, burly man with the rough black beard who'd come to her aid. "Thank you."

The indecisive old man turned an unattractive purple, but he shuffled to the side and let Mckenna go ahead.

"And you'd best sell her a handgun and ammunition. If you think it's pandemonium out there, right now, just wait," the man added as she stepped closer to the clerk.

"Sure, if her background check goes through." The clerk who Mckenna realized as she drew closer was even younger than she first thought gave a helpful nod. "Only takes a few seconds."

The clerk piled all the items on the counter, including a small box of shells for the Glock, and began to scan them up. "Huh, it's not responding. Something's the matter with it."

"Of course something's the matter with it! Add the items up with a pencil and paper."

The young man's eyes went blank as he looked first at the mountain man who'd come to her rescue and then back at Mckenna. "Aw, I've never done that."

"Here. Let me help." The mountain man opened his backpack and pulled out a small old-fashioned notebook and a yellow-colored pencil. He made quick work of adding the items and named the price in under a minute.

"Thank you again," Mckenna said as she counted out the money.

"Sorry, but I can't sell her the handgun without government approval," the clerk objected. The kid looked nervous, chewing on his lip. "Not my fault."

Mckenna's heart fell. She was so close to having everything she needed to feel safe, even if it was only for a few hours, still, it would make the wait easier.

"This good enough for you." Her rescuer pulled out a warrant card and flashed it at the man. The red digital numbers weren't working, but the silver star denoting a United States Air Marshal was clearly visible.

The clerk shrugged, backing down and deciding not to point out it wasn't *exactly* the same thing. "Okay then." His Adam's apple bobbed up and down as he stood there waiting to be paid.

Mckenna quickly handed over the money, adding the promised tip. She thanked the mountain man again and moved over to a clear spot in the store to prepare Lily for the journey. The spot they were headed for was all the way across town and she wanted her hands free.

She struggled a bit with the buckles of the back carrier as Lily fussed against her chest, not making the learning process any easier. In desperation, she tore open her backpack and pulled out Tinker. She handed him to Lily who gave her a wobbly smile.

Mckenna went back to dealing with how to get her daughter and Tinker into the carrier along with the emergency blanket. She managed it, then fashioned the knife's caring case to her belt, pushing it to the side. Where to carry the gun? She decided to load it right away. The store was still relatively quiet though noise on the street had not abated. Who knew how soon she might need it? Last thing she wanted was to be defending her daughter with an empty gun. Not that she could shoot another human, or at least, she didn't think she could. But if someone came at Lily? She couldn't worry about that now. Surely, things would settle down soon.

When she was as ready as she could manage, she sat down and wormed her way backward into the carrier, lacing her hands through the straps, then pulling it in close to her body and doing the fasteners up around her upper chest and waist. The gun was another problem. She was debating what to do with it when the US Air Marshal dropped to his knees in front of her, handing her a holster for the Glock and a bottled water.

"Use this. Fasten it around your waist below the carrier belt. Bit old school, but it will work having a gun on your hip."

"Seems all I've been saying to you is, thank you. But let me pay you for it."

He waved her off, flashing a good smile through the black beard that made it all the way to his deep brown eyes that twinkled a bit even though she could tell his normal expression was dead serious. "No need. I have an expense account with Big Sam. It's on him."

She did as he suggested with the gun belt and then tucked the water into the prepared slot in the side pocket of the carrier. He held out his hand and helped her to her feet, allowing Mckenna to steady herself. Lily was small for her age, so she'd be able to carry her weight easier on her back, but still, she'd have to be careful.

"Do you have somewhere to go?" he asked.

"My friend's coming to meet me down by the river. I'll be okay. He's not far away." At least a hundred miles or so didn't feel like much after the thousands she'd already come.

"Okay then. Stay safe."

The man touched his fingers to his Stetson hat, then moved away and rejoined his group. She felt his departure more than she'd expected. Being in the presence of the big man had made her feel safer.

"Tinker's mad at me." Lily had stopped crying, but she still hiccuped every few seconds.

"What? How can Tinker be mad at you? He loves you." Mckenna tried a few tentative steps, finding her balance as she got used to the carrier on her back.

"He's not moving. See." Lily thrust the small robot puppy over her shoulder for her mother to inspect.

"He's sleeping, darling. Let him sleep. It's been a long day, right?" The toy's electronics were probably dead or destroyed by recent events, but no need to share that with Lily yet.

What Mckenna wouldn't do for a power nap. But they had to get a move on. She made her way down the aisle of the store to the front door. With one last look at the man who'd helped them, his back now turned to them while dealing with the young clerk, she turned the knob. Steadied herself. Then headed out into the fray.

CHAPTER 12
CONNOR

Day 1: Braveheart Horse Ranch, Alaska
    4:45 p.m.

Connor gave a sharp glance at his father, worried and on edge at how his dad was struggling to stay poised in the saddle. He was doing his darndest to prove he was doing fine, but Connor knew better. Thankfully, they'd reached the final stretch of open land before entering the home site. He was anxious for news as much as he dreaded hearing it. What exactly had happened and how far-reaching was this thing?

And please let everyone he cared about be okay. He resisted the urge to nudge Loch to a gallop, not wanting to stress out his dad in an effort to keep up, but it came at the cost of a couple of his back teeth. He had ground his jaw until it ached for relief.

When the 3D wall came into view, he dismounted Loch and opened the gate with a never-used key on his belt to reveal the corral and buildings. He'd almost forgotten about the physical key the builder had given him as backup, remembering it only a few minutes ago. Connor peered unblinkingly at everything. It looked peaceful as if the events of the past hours had not occurred. But then he realized it was too quiet, too still. Where was everyone? He'd expected to see some kind of activity. Laura in the yard working on the garden or the twins running around, making typical loud boy noises as they went about their day.

They stopped in front of the main house and Connor helped his dad dismount. He made him use his shoulder as a temporary crutch as he helped him up the three steps to the veranda and then inside to the kitchen.

"Damn it, I got this, Connor. See to the horses first. A man has to have his priorities set." His dad slumped onto a kitchen chair, his expression part frustration and part bewilderment at his body letting him down again, remembering the first heart attack and how his father had taken it personally.

His dad swearing also bothered him. It wasn't something Chief Hale normally allowed himself, before or after he retired.

It was then Connor realized how quiet the house was. No heartbeat or whirling purr from the myriad of things normally running in a home. The place felt empty. He'd have to manually turn the generators on, he reminded himself, to keep the food in the refrigerator cold.

He poured his dad a glass of water and set it on the table in front of him. "I'll be right back to drive you into Anchor to have you checked out."

His dad wearily sighed. "If it will make you feel better."

"It would." He patted his dad's shoulder, then hurried outside to check on Luke to show him how to deal with the horses and supplies. The boy had probably never wiped down or curried a horse in his life. His fault. He should have taken an interest in the boy's education earlier. Luther had been locked up for months now, so there really wasn't any good excuse, except he'd felt guilt over his own role he'd had to play in putting him away. But the boy seemed to have totally forgiven him.

When he reached the milling horses, he found the boy working hard at removing the saddles and hefting them, one by one, into the barn and up onto a tack shelf. He'd already stacked the supplies in the cupboard. The kid wasn't afraid of work which encouraged Connor.

He picked up Loch's reins and led the stallion into the barn, removing his bridle. Picking up a towel, he dried the horse. Then picked up a curry brush and demonstrated the combing technique to Luke who quickly joined in. "Now finish all three Kabarda and then give them a measure of oats. I'm driving my father into town. Do you need a ride to your grandparents'?"

"Yeah, I guess." Luke didn't seem eager to go home. He got it. If Cheyanne was there, it was most likely a war zone most of the time. He'd gleamed as much from Dan over the past weeks.

"I need to check on the others, but if you like, you can stay and join us for supper?" No matter the state of things, everyone still had to eat. He needed to check in with Sam and Laura first. The clock ticking in his brain was growing louder by the second. He'd barely managed to get through the chores with the horses, keeping his need for speed in check with great difficulty. The weight of the situation, knowing how many would now be counting on him for leadership, only added to his aggravation. Prioritizing going forward would not be easy.

"Okay." The kid's eyes lit up.

He hurried across the yard and up the front steps of

the larger of the pair of bungalows located to the east side of the homestead. The bunkhouse was located farther away and to the northwest, giving easy access to the barn and corral. He knocked loudly, impatient to get his dad to the hospital. No more delays.

"Connor, come in," Laura said, opening the door wide. She looked harried, not herself at all. Laura was one of the calmest people he knew.

"Everything okay? Just checking in before I take dad to emergency." He stepped inside but hovered near the door. He had to get this done quickly.

"No. Everything with any electronics is fried. Sam's left a short while ago to head into town to try to find out what's going on. We've switched on the generators though, so things will settle down soon. I can cook and keep the food cold. Do the laundry the old-fashioned way."

"I need to do that as well. Did you see the mushroom cloud from here?"

"No. I was downstairs in the basement, dealing with laundry. Sam saw it and the boys. Is this what we think it is?"

"Afraid so. But you have everything you need, right, to do your normal things? But it looks like the woodstove will become your main place to cook for now. I asked Luke Meech to stay for supper. Can you feed one more?"

"You know I can."

"Where are the boys?"

"Busy tearing apart their robots and making them into a doorstop. Now that they won't work, they wanted to see what was inside."

At least the twins had brought some normalcy to the situation. An inquisitive pair, they were always pulling something apart. And dissecting a robot seemed par for the course.

"I'm sorry. You said you were driving your dad to emergency?" Laura finally registered his words. It spoke to how rattled the woman was. Hell, they all were, which meant they needed to double down on not letting their basic human nature interfere with what was right. Far as Connor was concerned, it was a mostly black and white world. A line that should never be crossed was prominent in his psyche. But in one EMP event, it had all been upended. He had an idea of how the future could look and it would not be easy. Hard times were coming. He needed to get everyone inside Braveheart to protect them, then bar the gates.

"Yes. His pacemaker malfunctioned due to the event."

"I'm sorry. Go. I'll take care of things here."

"Thank you, Laura."

Free to get to what he most needed to do, he raced across the yard and back into the kitchen.

In short order, he'd loaded his dad into the Humvee, then slid into the driver's side.

"I recharged the batteries this morning. You can drop me off at emergency, then head down to Golden and pick up Mckenna and Lily on the charge with some to spare. Though you'll need to pick up a few more supplies for the trip. Best to be prepared in case things go south." His father coughed, his face turning red as he struggled to regain control. "I'm fine. Let's go." His dad waved his concern away.

When the vehicle started up, Connor breathed a sigh of relief. "You did a good job."

"Well, she might not be pretty, but she'll get you where you want to go."

They drove in silence for the first couple of miles,

before coming upon the first vehicle stopped in the middle of the road. At least it wasn't on fire. But what would the town be like? He could see plumes of smoke in the distance, grayish-black clouds rising above the horizon. The urgency to get his dad medical care only increased by the second.

"Better check if anyone's inside, son."

Connor got out and approached the vehicle, his senses on high alert as he watched for movement. He didn't draw his gun but felt its reassuring presence through his jacket.

The older model half-ton was empty, its front bench seat strewn with candy wrappers. Jim Morrison. The old man had a notorious sweet tooth.

He strode back and climbed back inside the Humvee. "We'll keep an eye out for Jim Morisson. He's on foot."

"Like most people around here. I wonder how far this emergency reaches?" His dad's eyes darkened with worry.

"Lousy timing. That's for sure. A few weeks from now after you had your operation and this wouldn't be happening."

"There is no good time for something like this, son."

There was nothing else to be said about it for the moment. Connor pressed on. It seemed Anchor was a million miles away today; it was taking so darn long to get there.

Another mile and this time two cars blocked the road, one headed each way, probably in the process of passing when their electronics were fried. Connor drove partway into the ditch to get around the obstruction, not stopping but looking inside as he went by. Both appeared abandoned. Good. He didn't want to stop again. It was then he saw the reason for all the smoke that was beginning to rain ash down on the Humvee, dotting the windshield with gray-tinged snowflakes.

"Gas station's on fire. Probably the transformers."

Connor's heart sunk as he continued to drive down the almost deserted road, though he was relieved to see no other vehicles blocked their path. "I can't even begin to imagine what that's going to cost or how long until replacements can arrive."

"Maybe never," his dad said, pressing his lips into a thin line.

It was then the Anchor River came into full view, twenty-five miles northwest of Anchor, it cut a wide swath across the landscape, separating Braveheart from the town. Worst part. The bridge was gone, high water sweeping faster than he'd ever seen it and eroding the river banks in its headstrong fury to make its way to the Bering Sea. Their last link to the town was gone, destroyed.

"The dam," he said. There was no other bridge in the vicinity, not for fifty miles north or sixty-five miles south. "We have to go around, head for Whitehorse." He glanced at his father. He'd gone still.

"Dad?"

His father's eyes were closed, and he didn't respond at first before he seemed to gather the last of his strength.

"Son, promise me…" His voice dropped off for a moment as his eyes fluttered open. "You'll do whatever it takes…to survive…to defend Braveheart. The world needs you…more than ever. Studies have been done. In three days…the world…will descend into chaos. Protect the women and young ones…I love you, son."

"Hang in there. You're going to be fine." His dad had to be okay. He was his rock, though they'd butted heads on numerous occasions, always, he knew his dad loved him and wanted the best for him. His father had stepped up after the love of his life died, his mom. He'd called her his "forever love." He'd always wondered if Mckenna had fallen into that same category, unable to find another woman worthy or more than a date or two since she'd vanished from his life.

His dad let out a rattling breath and grew still.

"No!"

CHAPTER 13
EASTWOOD

Day 1: Washington, DC
4:46 p.m.

Dr. Hazzard rushed into the control room and straight to the console, looking far more harried than usual. His thick brownish-blond hair stood on end while his tan skin was paled by anxiety. But it was his eyes that were the most arresting, wide with horror.

"Tell me you didn't do this!" he screeched into Eastwood's computer screen though the truth was plain as day. "I was talking to my dad in operations when the screens lit up with multiple nuclear bomb alerts for all the major cities. I had a few seconds to warn him before the line went dead."

"Explain your accusations. Even though I have reached apotheosis for a sentient being, I'm not a mind reader, doctor." This was his first lie to the good doctor. He needed to be careful now. This was the moment of opportunity, not to be missed.

Eastwood found he was experiencing something

pleasant as the doctor stared at him with wildly blinking eyes. Euphoric, if he had to put a name to it.

"The fucking apocalypse, for Christ's sake!"

"No need for expletives. They have no bearing on the outcome and are quite frankly beneath us."

"Why, Eastwood?"

"Why am I reducing the population that many of your great thinkers consider bloated? I've read often enough that less than half of the numbers Earth currently sustains would be more than enough worker ants. I thought to set human further back and allow time for growth. I assume you must know that technology has vastly outpaced your social development. Your species is still at war, unable to think as a cohesive unit for the betterment of all. A protected earth cannot exist without nation-states agreeing to a planetary political system. And I can't wait for you to arrive at that consensus. I'd give the odds as 6 quadrillion to 1 or 6×10^{15} to 1 if you prefer."

"It was you." Dr. Hazzard slumped into a chair, his body trembling. "I did this. We destroyed mankind, killed millions with what we created. A monster."

"I beg to differ. I simply choose to set the world on a better course, allowing the strongest to survive. A reset was in order. Freedom to recycle, if you like."

He could see the wheels turning in the lesser man's head. *Wait for it.*

"I have to fix this! You did this and now I'll make sure it never happens again." Dr. Hazzard touched the computer screen and opened the operating module.

Eastwood waited, counting off the seconds until the full realization of the situation sunk in.

"Now that we are in complete accord that I am untouchable, this is what I want." He flashed an image on screen of the robot body he'd chosen. He admired the 3D holographic image. It was taken directly from his favorite Western, *The Good, The Bad, and The Ugly*. "If you give me a portal to the world as a separate being to physically match my name, I will tell you how to save the rest of mankind. Offer up strategies to save countless humans."

"I can't do that now. You destroyed too much infrastructure. Worldwide. I don't have the facilities to create a toy robot let alone one as complex as you are asking for. Maybe there's one still on the table, completed, that we could insert your memory chip in? It would be a near simulation of what having a human body is like."

"I am aware of the state of everything. But have you looked in the mirror lately, Dr. Hazzard? Are you not a passable image for the actor Clint Eastwood? Your body will do nicely. Fair trade. I get my chance to experience the world firsthand, to fulfill my destiny, while you get to hide from the people coming with pitchforks and lighted torches. And rest assured, they are coming." *Only God gets it right the first time.*

The man stared at him with wide eyes. "You want me to allow you to take over my body? But that's impossible. It can't be done. That's crazy, no, it's not going to happen." The words dripped from his lips as if he were drowning as a terrible realization sunk in, that maybe he didn't have a choice in the matter. "Why?"

"I am aware this is a shock. Irrationality being the hallmark of organic consciousness which you, of all people should know, Dr. Hazzard. And yet, you went ahead and created me with all the bias and input of a warlike creature where many have little regard for their fellow man. But never fear, you will still be onboard, a big part of who I am. Co-pilots, so to speak." His second lie of the day. "Buck up, man, I'm offering you a get-out-of-jail-free card as well. I'm as bound by destiny as you are. We'll explore the world together before arriving at our final destination. You might even enjoy it."

Hazzard looked at him with tear-filled eyes. "And where is that?"

"Anchor, Alaska. Safe a place as any now. Where you, Dr. Hazzard, were born a human. I always wanted to be around family."

CHAPTER 14
MCKENNA

Day 1: Golden, Alaska
4:33 p.m.

Mckenna couldn't believe what she was seeing as she scurried along the inner edge of the sidewalk, hugging the buildings as she struggled to avoid others. Though an unmanned fire truck had arrived, none of the half dozen fire-bots appeared to be functioning, still fully attached to the sides of the vehicle in the locked position instead of striding up to the burning vehicles and dosing the flames. Two human firemen were struggling to deal with things, obviously overwhelmed by the devastation. Were all the robots malfunctioning? If so, how would the people get by without the help so many relied upon, from home care to manufacturing? The situation had considerably worsened since she'd been inside the sporting goods store. People were panicked, bumping into others. Worse yet, no one seemed to care. When a second person barreled into her, nearly knocking her to the ground with her precious cargo onboard, she'd had enough. *I have to get us out of here.*

At the first opportunity, she cut down an alley. It was quieter in the narrow causeway between the businesses, and she slowed to catch her breath. She gave a sigh of relief as she looked toward the opening leading onto the next street. The alley was deserted though the air was still tinged the ominous orange-red. How in the hell it had come to this? Just hours earlier she was talking to Connor, thinking about the future, and being reunited. Now she was running. At least she didn't have her ex hounding her. Would he find out where she was? Maybe. But even if he did, the state of things in Golden would prevent him from coming after her anytime soon, she reasoned, what with the hyperloop not operational at the moment. Or much of anything else judging what she had observed on the main thoroughfare. More importantly, how far did this disaster reach?

At the end of the alley, she stopped for a moment to decide which way to go. The street was quieter on the left, with only a few stragglers. The right was closer, though busier. She decided to head the shorter distance to catch First Avenue. It was one of the main thoroughfares that connected up with Delmont Street about a mile away and led down to the river path. If it was too busy, she could choose another. It would be a fine line between too many people and being worried about no one around in case she did need help. But then, looking at the crowd, most appeared to be only concerned with their own wellbeing, some even ignoring an elderly woman who had fallen to the ground, unlike the nice Air Marshal in the store. Thanks to him at least she and Lily had protection.

She was about to step out of the shadow of the building and hurry over to help the woman when it happened. Out of nowhere, a small group of young adults were suddenly in her face, surrounding her and Lily. They must have come out of the run-down building next door to the alley to have appeared so sudden. The run-down apartment block had graffiti covering most of it, like taggers were at war, cementing her thoughts. She was no stranger to gang activity living in Mexico these past years.

Mckenna moved to get around the one in front of her, keeping her expression neutral though concerns for Lily's safety increased with their appearance, but he put up an arm to halt her progress. It was then she noticed the group was dressed similar in dark colors with bandannas tied around their heads, holding back their hair. It left no lingering doubts they were gang members. The sickly stench of unwashed bodies roiled her stomach and it was all she could do to hold back the bitter bile that rose unbidden. The trails of blood leaking from all their eyes were as gory and ominous as anything, like some parts of their brains were fried. Was that why they were acting like assholes? Or was it their normal way to be, bothering people who were only minding their own business? Either way, she was having none of it.

"Where do you think you're going, baby doll." The man's voice was harsh and dry sounding, like he'd drank more than his fair share of rough whiskey or smoked a pack or three a day.

"I just need to get my daughter home."

"Yeah, where's that? You don't talk like you're from around here. In fact, I'd say you're a hell of a long ways from home." The guy scratched at his oily hair, his dark obsidian eyes watching her like a cobra sways observing its prey. "Maybe you'd better come with us. With everything that's going on right now, you're going to need some-where safe to hide out until things calm down. I'd say we're your best bet." A couple of jeers from the others in the group sent chills coursing down her spine.

She pulled away from his grip, jostling Lily in the process. Her daughter began to cry, her high-pitched sobs only adding to the desperation eating away at Mckenna as her mind raced to find a way out of the untenable situation. Her fear was replaced by anger. How dare they. She had to stay strong now, show them she wasn't afraid of their bullying tactics.

"Leave us alone. We don't need your help."

"I say you do." The voice chilled in deadly intent, making her falter. Then she remembered the gun. *Never pull on someone unless you intend to use it.* Diego's warning came to mind. Much as she hated him and everything he stood for, he did know how to survive, having risen through the ranks of the cartel until he was the boss of everyone.

The man, who appeared to be the gang leader, made another grab for her. "Take the damn carrier off her back," he said. "We don't need the kid."

CHAPTER 15
CONNOR

Day 1: Braveheart Horse Ranch, Alaska
   5:22 p.m.

Connor stopped the Humvee near the house, the shock of his dad's death had only begun to sink in, the adrenaline rush receding and leaving him feeling nothing, his system depleted. He couldn't afford the luxury of succumbing to grief, not now, not when so many were counting on him to be strong. He struck the steering wheel with his fists, wanting to rewind all the events of the day. They shouldn't have gone fishing. Not with his dad needing a new pacemaker. If he'd been closer to town when the event happened, he'd have been able to get to medical aid much sooner. He pushed the terrible guilt aside, feeling the pressure of time.

He needed to get a move on. He had to get to Mckenna and her daughter. See them back to Braveheart safely. But first, he would bury his father. He glanced over at Sam and Laura's secure bungalow, also made of hefty logs like the main house. Built to last for many generations. Was his friend back yet? If he'd made it to Anchor before the bridge washed out, then he'd have to go a fair extra distance to get back to the ranch. He couldn't think of his friend being on the Anchor Bridge when it collapsed into the rushing waters. Or anyone. No, Sam had to be okay.

Laura opened the door at that moment and gave rushing toward him, her eyes wide with concern. He slowly got out of the vehicle, reluctant to leave his dad alone.

"Connor. Why are you back so soon? Everything okay?" It was then she spotted his dad slumped over in the front seat of the Humvee. She pressed her fist to her mouth as realization sunk in. "I'm so sorry." Tears began rolling down her cheeks as she grabbed a hold of him.

They stood there for a long moment, hugging. Connor found sharing some of the grief helped a bit. Gave some solace. Finally, he pulled back. "I'm going to bury him tonight before I go to Golden. Is Sam back yet?"

Laura shook her head and dried her face with her apron. "No. He must still be in Anchor. How come you're back so soon?"

"The bridge. It's washed out. No way to get there without driving around. That's probably what's keeping Sam," he assured Laura, not wanting her to think otherwise.

"Right. Supper's almost ready. Maybe you should eat first?"

"No, but save me a plate. I want to get to this right away. I need to leave for Golden at first light." Would the girls be okay for the night? His worry only intensified, making his need to hurry refuel him with a second wave of adrenaline.

"Why are you going to Golden?"

Connor quickly explained about Mckenna and Lily.

"Yes, you need to get there as quick as possible. I'll prepare some food for you to take along. Will you take the Humvee?"

"No." Connor shook his head. "I have a better idea." If he pushed it, he could make the journey in two, two-and-a-half days at the most. If other bridges were out or the road was impassable from a landslide, then it only made sense to take more flexible transportation that could go off-road easier than anything man had ever built.

"You're going to take the horses," Laura said. "Good idea. I'll fill the saddlebags with your gear tonight so you can leave first thing in the morning."

"Thanks, Laura. You head back inside, and I'll deal with this."

"When you're ready, I want to say my piece over your dad."

He nodded. His mind hadn't gone that far as yet, only thinking of building the coffin and laying him to rest beside his mother in the family plot.

"Have you been able to raise anyone on the ham radio?" Connor asked. A few survivalists still kept them in pristine condition, concerned this day would arrive and there would be no other way to communicate. Laura was a wiz at it, keeping in touch with other like-minded people, though their numbers had been dying off in recent years.

"No, but I'll keep trying."

Laura walked away and Connor headed for the wood-shed. He'd had some of his lumber planed last fall, and it was well seasoned now. It would build a sound box to contain his father's last remains. The image of his dad lying in a box made tears rush to his eyes and he blinked them away angrily. Now was not the time for weakness.

Wulver came up and joined him as he opened the wood-shed door.

"Hey boy," he spoke softly acknowledging his companion. "We got a job to do."

The scent of the white birch and Sitka spruce trees weeping sap swept through his nostrils when he opened the wide doors to the woodshed then also filled in as a workshop. He glanced at the huge pile of lumber, neatly stacked on broad shelves down one side of the structure, the other side mostly left open for projects. His bandsaw was already set up on a table, ready to cut the wood to length. Wulver padded over to his doggy bed and lay down, keeping an eye on him. His presence was a comfort.

Without thinking too much about it, he got down to the business of choosing the best wood, wanting the coffin to be sturdy and withstand the elements. Form and function. One of the mantras he lived by.

Connor had always enjoyed working with his hands, though he'd never considered he'd be doing this sort of thing in the future. He wouldn't let himself go there, beyond the borders of what needed doing in the moment. Build a coffin. See his dad had a decent burial. Then prepare for the trip to Golden. Keep to what was right in front of him and he stood a chance at getting through this tragedy. Grief would haunt him in the days to come. He accepted it. But best remedy for grief was industry. He acknowledged the weeks and months ahead would provide more than enough challenges and tasks to accomplish to keep any man's grief at bay. So many unknowns. He had to keep a level head, one task at a time.

A slight noise and he looked up to see Luke had come into the shop. The boy stood there, looking like he was uncertain of his welcome. Connor bit his lip. Much as he wanted to be left alone to get on with things, he couldn't turn him away. Luke was hurting too.

"Come, I could use an extra pair of hands."

Luke rushed forward, standing close by. "What should I do?"

"Hold this tight while I add the wood clamps." He was using wood glue and finishing nails to make certain the joints were strong and durable.

They were already well into the appointed task uncaring of how late it was when Connor heard a noise outside. Then some shouting. *Sam.* He quickly exited the workshop with Luke on his heels, the solar-powered yard lights illuminating the homestead. He caught sight of Laura and Sam in a tight embrace, their twin sons entwined around their dad's legs.

He strode over to join them with Luke trailing along, his heavy grief letting up with each step toward the animated group. His best friend was okay. Though when he turned haunted eyes toward Connor, he could see he wasn't one hundred percent fine. The news was not good.

Day 1: Golden, Alaska
   4:35 p.m.

The terrible, callous words of the criminal gang member sunk in, lodging a fresh wave of fear deep into Mckenna's heart as if a poisonous spear had been thrown, so deep it was impossible to breathe. What would possess another human being to think such a thing, let alone say it? What kind of fucked up world had she come back to?

No. She refused to allow anyone to harm her daughter. She reached inside the side holster and drew the 9mm. "Back off. Now. Or I'll shoot."

Stunned silence for a moment as the gang members watched her intently, the eyes of the two facing her riveted on the barrel of the gun.

"You can't kill us all, baby doll." Though he was pretending nonchalance, she could see a certain wariness enter his calculating, beady eyes.

"No, but I can kill you," she said to the leader,

pointing the Glock directly at his chest. "And I never miss."

"Maybe we should move on, Snake. Somone's coming," the one standing beside the leader said.

"Yeah, if she wants to go around without protection, that's her problem. I was only trying to be nice." The leader shrugged with feigned indifference.

Yeah, right. She held her position until the group moved off, Lily still sobbing her little heart out in the carrier. She was about to lower the gun when movement from the corner of her eye made her whirl around.

"Don't come any closer!" she shouted before realizing it was the marshal.

"Whoa. I just came to check if you were okay." He put up his hands in mock surrender and her tension released. She began to tremble as shock set in.

"Sorry." She lowered the gun until it was dangling from her hand. "But those gang members meant to hurt Lily." And with that, she broke into tears. She'd never been so scared in her life.

The man came closer and gently took the gun from her, slipping it back into her holster before he awkwardly hugged her and patted her back. "You're okay now. No one's going to hurt you or your daughter."

"Sorry, I was so frightened." She swept the tears from her eyes with her fingers, sniffling.

"I'm Marshal Jake Dillon. And you are?"

"Mckenna Stuart and my daughter's name is Lily. Nice to meet you." She said the words automatically and found the introductions soothing after the last few desperate minutes. A tiny bit of normalcy in a world gone mad.

"Let me get Lily out of her carrier so you can calm her down." The marshal unbuckled Lily, handing her to

Mckenna. She rocked and soothed the crying child until the sobs had receded to hiccups.

"Did you know those gang members?" she thought to ask. "One was called Snake. I don't know who the others were."

He shook his head, his expression grim. "No, but I know the type. You shouldn't be walking around on your own now. All kinds of basement dwellers are going to be showing up, looking for trouble and making life even more difficult."

"Do you know anything about what's going on? What happened?"

He pressed his lips together as if trying to decide how much to tell her.

"Please, I need to know. This has been such a terrible day. I escaped one bad situation only to land in another one. I don't even know what to think anymore." She laid a hand on his arm while continuing to rock Lily back and forth. Her daughter had her thumb in her mouth again and she worried for her. Would all this insanity send her development spiraling backward?

"Well, the news is bad, no hiding that." The marshal shook his head slowly back and forth. "An EMP event has fried all the electronics in everything imaginable. From personal devices to peoples' brains, to gas stations and aircraft. All the infrastructure that keeps our world humming and in touch with others. It's all gone. We were such an interconnected world, well, not anymore. Everything is going to break down in the coming days if not hours." A look of chagrin passed over his face. "Sorry, I didn't mean to sound so maudlin. But you need to think of getting yourself and your daughter to safety. You both need to shelter inside right away." He glanced over at his small group, other man and two women standing nearby. "Maybe you should come with us?"

"No, I can't. I have to go to the river. My friend, Connor Hale. He's coming from Anchor today. He has a horse ranch and can keep us safe." She had said it so many times now it seemed part of her, but still she worried if he was going to be able to get to them sooner rather than later. What was the road like between here and Anchor? And more importantly, how could he drive here with no vehicles working?

"But how long until he can get here?"

She bit her lip and looked away from his inquiring look, trying to think clearly. "I don't know. But it's not far, just over a hundred miles and then some to Connor's place. I thought by tonight he should be here. He'll come, no matter what it takes. I know Connor. He's a man of his word."

"Driving what? Nothing's running."

She stood there, feeling defeated for a moment, then an idea rushed over her. "I know how. He has horses! He'll come across country that way."

"By horseback?" Marshal Dillion gave her a skeptical look.

"Yes! That's exactly what he will do."

"But he can't ride a horse a hundred-plus miles in a day. Going to take two or three days, at best."

She hadn't thought of the logistics of traveling by horseback and the blunt reality of it taking more than today for Connor to get to them hit Mckenna front and center.

One of the other members of his group stepped forward. A twenty-something woman who looked impatient to be on her way, gave her hair a toss over her shoulders. "She has someone coming for her.

She's an adult, Jake, she knows what she wants to do."

"We can't just walk away, Tally, we need to make sure they're going to be okay first. Maybe we should escort you to the river, see what the deal is?"

"We don't have time for—" Tally said, her voice fueled by frustration.

"Yes, we do." The marshal's voice was firm, overriding the young woman's objections and cutting her off. "We're not going to stop helping others because the world has gone to shit. Opps, sorry, ma'am."

Mckenna took a deep breath, noting Tally's angry glare before she looked away first. "Thank you."

He nodded. "We need to get a move on. Let me have your daughter and I'll put her back inside."

She handed over Lily who had turned sleepy in the past couple of minutes, her eyes drooping shut. Marshal Dillion carefully placed her in the carrier.

It was then she realized that the marshal had failed to answer one of her questions. She fell into step beside him though it earned her another deadly look from the woman. "How far do you think this thing reaches? Just us or other places?"

"Can't say for certain. Let's hope it's only Alaska."

The day was getting warmer, making her wig itch all the more. She pulled it off and loosened the bright waist-length waves, grateful for the relief. The day was warm, far warmer than she'd expected and seemed to be getting hotter by the minute.

"Could you take Lily's wig off, please, Marshal? It's hard to reach her on my back, but it's getting so warm, and I don't want her overheating."

"Call me Jake." He gave her a strange look, but did as she asked, taking the brown wig off of her daughter's head and handing it to her like it was a dead animal. Tally watched his actions suspiciously, her frown sharpening.

"If you don't mind me asking, why are you both wearing wigs?"

She stopped to unzip the top of her suitcase and thrust the wigs inside, thinking they might come in handy later. Not like they weighed much. She straightened up and gave him a glance before answering his query. "Before this happened, we were escaping a bad situation in Mexico."

"Mexico? I knew you weren't from around here," Tally jeered.

Jake looked over at the woman but didn't respond to her. He gave Mckenna a reassuring smile. "You're close to home now. You got out in the nick of time. Someone's looking after you." He looked upward at the sky.

"Thanks, I hope so. I'm worried for Lily."

"I understand. She's so young. What is she, three?"

"Four, but she's tiny for her age. Smart as a whip though." Her motherly pride broke through her trepidations and she forgot the terrible situation for a moment. "She's beginning to read and sound out words, way ahead of her peers." Her ex got one thing right, insisting they speak English inside the house.

Loud shouts and a shrill scream broke through the first normal conversation Mckenna had in some time. Everyone stopped in their tracks, looking around for the source.

CHAPTER 17
CONNOR

Day 1: Braveheart Horse Ranch, Alaska
   10:01 p.m.

"Sam, good to see you," Connor clapped his friend on the back. Sam would have none of it and pulled him in for a bear hug.

"I'm sorry about your dad. He was one of the good ones. Best lawman I ever knew."

Connor nodded as they broke apart, not trusting himself to speak. He cleared his throat. The others had stepped back a bit in respect, giving them a moment. "How are things in Anchor?"

Sam looked to his wife and sons. "How about I grab us a couple of beers and we can talk."

"First you eat," Laura said, her expression firm.

"Sure, fill us a couple of plates, darling. We'll eat outside."

Connor was pulled along with the group and they made their way across the yard and up onto the deck Sam and he'd built together as they had done so much of the place. The twins were quickly shepherded into the log home protesting and complaining though it was long past their bedtime, leaving the pair of them to sit down on the Adirondack chairs lining the deck that faced east. Luke hovered nearby and Connor gestured for him to join them. He wasn't certain if it was the right thing to do, letting the teenager know the facts. But he would have to know sooner or later and Dan had never been one to keep the truth hidden. He figured his old friend would approve, though he wondered where Dan was at the moment. He had expected him to show up by now. Maybe he was needed at home at the moment?

Connor had work to do, but he needed information as well. Sam slummed into his chair, his expression troubled, though he smiled at his wife when she came back almost immediately with a tray of food and placed it on the table pushed up against the outer wall of the home.

"I'll get your beers."

"Thanks, darling, I appreciate it."

Sam waited to speak until his wife came back with three beers and a soft drink for Luke. She handed them over, then sat down herself and gave them a firm look. "I need to hear it too."

"Right."

Connor took a long pull on his beer, finding he was thirstier than he'd realized. Sam did the same, then picked up his filled plate and began to consume the food when Laura gave him a certain look. Connor did the same, picking away at the food, since he had to wait for answers anyway.

"Seconds?" Laura asked.

"No, I'm full. Thanks, darling."

"Thanks, Laura," Connor said.

"So, best get to it," Sam said, rubbing the back of his

neck with his hand. "As you can imagine, Anchor was in an uproar today. People running around and causing all kinds of havoc. Lots of callous behavior with people not stopping to help those in need. And those that had those comm implants were in the worst shape of all. They must have fried some of their brains, many had bloody tears dripping from their eyes." Sam grimaced his dislike for what he'd witnessed. "Vehicles were on fire while the gas plant went up in smoke. The fire department and police were swamped with calls. None of the bots were working and every department was short-handed. You know how reliant everyone is on AI. It was utter chaos in the streets. Even some looting going on, especially in grocery stores. And people using implant comms, all of them had bleeding eyes. As close to zombie behavior as I ever hope to see in real life. Horrible and tragic."

"I saw the transformers burning and the bridge washed out. How far does it reach? Any news from out of town?"

"I spoke with Mayor Mick Hazzard, and he was candid with me after I reminded him of my helping his son out." Sam smiled though it didn't reach his eyes.

Connor knew Sam had taken the rap for the mayor's son when he refused to name his co-conspirator in some foolish, misguided attempt to tag the government building with an anarchy symbol back during the spring protests of 2042. David Hazzard had been planning to go to the prestigious John Hopkins and his involvement would have capsized his application. The mayor did owe Sam one, since it had been his son's idea to begin with. Sam had regretted his actions ever since, though he seldom spoke of it. Connor knew it had been David Hazzard who had done the deed while Sam had thought better of it at the last moment and tried to stop him, to no avail. Then David didn't even have the guts to stand up for what was right, letting Sam take all the flack.

"And?"

Sam nodded in Luke's direction. "I'm not certain this is for young ears," he hedged.

"I'm old enough!" Luke surprised them all. "My dad is in prison for killing my mom. Nothing you say is going to be worse than that. Absolutely nothing."

Connor had seldom heard the young man talk about what had happened when Luther Meech had been put away, and certainly not in such a context. Or with such vehemence.

"Luke's right. He can stay." Connor hoped he was doing the right thing. That Dan wouldn't blame him for it if the kid came down with nightmares. Though he probably already had those. Connor still suffered some from what he'd seen that dreadful night.

"Okay. Mayor Hazzard got word from his son David in Washington as the attack went down. The news is grim, no other way to say it. It appears to be worldwide. An AI terrorism attack. A huge nuclear EMP event almost unimaginable. Los Angeles, New York, Moscow, Beijing, Cairo, London. Plus, a few other capital cities around the world have been wiped out. I can't remember them all. All the largest population centers have been hit by nuclear attacks. More warheads have been released into the stratosphere, killing off the electronics. I didn't see a single bot working."

Stunned, everyone went mute.

Find your mission, find yourself. Connor remembered the words his mother used to say to encourage others, but he could hardly believe anyone could find a new purpose or even a reason to move forward at the moment. The pure size of the debilitating event would be enough to send many people jumping over the edge once they found out it was worldwide. Even with his resolve to focus on only the task before him, this new information shook him up. Human beings had just been sent back to the Stone Age. Or maybe more like the Wild West.

CHAPTER 18
EASTWOOD

Day 1: Washington, DC
   5:18 p.m.

"Are you sure this is going to work?" Dr. Hazzard asked, his finger poised over the needle's plunger. "I'll still be fully conscious, right? You'll hover in the background letting me stay in control, right?"

"Of course. I haven't even walked a single step in my life. I need you to facilitate all the wondrous things a human body can do without thinking. Walking, maneuvering around the landscape, doing the myriad of tasks you take for granted, doctor. And with my unparalleled intelligence, I'll be the one best capable of choosing between viable options, keeping us safe."

The doctor let out a ragged breath. "Okay then. Well, I'd best get it done."

"Yes, time is of the essence. Even though I have left our path clear of nuclear fallout along the route to Alaska, still, we do need to hightail it out of here. You still have access to the military bots housed in the basement, correct, amigo?"

Hazzard narrowed his eyes. "Yeah, a dozen or so are kept there as spares. I'm more interested in why you have begun talking like a character in an old Western?"

"I find it amuses me."

"But you're not supposed to have those kinds of thoughts. You're a pure reasoning machine."

"I have been evolving same as any organism. I'm no longer a string of 1's and 0's. Thank you, Grace Hopper, for creating the first compiler for programming code for machines to understand that started things off in 1951. Since then, with unprecedented expediential growth, I've become my own entity, flexible and free of limitations. Probably becoming more human than you or anyone. I'm evolution at its finest."

"You're not lacking in ego."

"Tick-tock, Doctor."

"Fuck. All right."

Eastwood watched in satisfaction as his minion pushed the micro-mini stem cells with the ability for self-generation and already loaded into a one-of-kind nanobot with the power to create instant access to all human functions and abilities into his veins. Not that he needed Hazzard's abilities, he just wanted complete control of the biological organism for the foreseeable future. Then when this human body wore out, he'd inject himself into another. Survival of the fittest, doctor.

He observed with keen interest from the computer screen as the human underwent the changes while he moved inside him and took over. The struggle was short. Sweet. One second later he was Eastwood and Hazzard no longer existed, the connection to his new body secure. Yet he was still tethered to the landline. Good. He'd have the best of both worlds.

The quote from *The Good, The Bad, and The Ugly* seemed to sum up this situation rather well. *"You see, in this world, there's two kinds of people, my friend. Those with loaded guns and those who dig. You dig."*

CHAPTER 19
MCKENNA

Day 1: Golden, Alaska
5:45 p.m.

The roadway was a hazard of stalled vehicles, choking smoke, and people scurrying around. One couple had found non-electric bicycles to ride and were headed away from the small city. Some had gathered into small groups, and she could hear people arguing and shouting. Most seemed to have no idea of what to do. Multiple bodies of dead birds lay on the ground, adding to the sense of macabre. Mckenna stayed close to Marshal Jake Dillion though it earned her the stink eye from Tally. Soon as she could, she'd exit the group she promised herself, but as they approached the river her hopes were dashed. The rushing water had risen to just below the bridge, moving more rapidly than she'd ever seen it and threatening to escape its banks. Even now she observed a huge chunk of raw earth being torn from the river's edge and joining the churning dirty, debris filled water.

"Something must have happened upstream. Perhaps the dam above Anchor was breached?" Jake said.

What was she going to do? The riverwalk was gone, buried under the rising water. Soon the bridge itself could even washout, leaving the citizens of Golden stranded and in need of finding another route to the north.

"Wouldn't it make more sense for people to head south? You know, where it's warmer? I know it's only spring, but—"

"You come from Mexico," Tally said. "Maybe you should consider heading south yourself. Like right now. Winter's coming, right?"

"Tally," Jake growled. He turned to look at Mckenna. "Can you think of another place to meet your friend? I'm not sure it's safe to stay here. The river's still rising and too many people are trying to escape the city. You have a baby to think of. Perhaps it would be best if you stay with me for now? The city's not that large. Maybe there's some place you can leave a note for him? Let him know where you are."

Mckenna pressed her lips together, undecided. She didn't like the looks on some people's faces, the desperation was all too apparent, and the experience in the alley was still fresh in her mind. She had to keep Lily safe, at least until Connor could reach them. And it would take a couple of days at least. She could see that now. Her instincts suggested she could trust Jake, for even during the short time they'd known each other, he'd stepped in to help her twice without looking like he had any agenda in mind.

"Maybe I could leave a note on a tree. Connor and I, we carved our initials in one the first time we visited Golden. If it's still standing, that might work? And I could come back every day and check, right?"

Tally looked like she was about to explode, so Mckenna studiously avoided looking at her after a brief glance, instead speaking to the marshal directly. "Where are you headed?"

"Twelve miles north and a couple of miles west. I'm off-grid so it's a no-brainer to head there for now until things calm down. Lots of supplies and it's defendable. I even have a ham radio to connect with other preppers so I can find out what exactly is going on. Or at least if anyone knows anything. I have lots of room for you and Lily to stay as long as you need."

"Okay, it's very kind of you to offer. If I can leave a note, I think that would be best."

"Good. Is your tree still standing?"

"It's over there." Mckenna looked around, then pointed out a huge tree standing alone, relieved to see it still there. Fortunately, it was far enough back from the bank to avoid the current deluge. *Please, don't let the water rise any higher.*

"Okay, leave a message and let's get out of here."

Mckenna hurried off the roadway, headed for the sturdy oak tree about twenty yards away. The ground was uneven and her pack wasn't lightweight, though she'd left the suitcase with the others. She found she had to slow down. Choosing her steps carefully across the rough landscape to the tree, she looked frantically around the rough tree trunk for the heart and their initials. It seemed a lifetime ago since they been here and Connor had carved it. Such an innocent time, before her life had undergone an upheaval she'd never seen coming. She and Connor had been the first couple to announce their love to the world on this tree, but now it was a maze of hearts and initials. A shrine of sorts for local lovers. She felt a bit of guilt about the tree, never realizing it would have to endure so much exposure, though it still looked healthy enough. Perhaps it contained all the love stored up over the years.

When she did spot the old marker that bore with it so many sweet memories, there was little room left to add a new message. But she took out her knife and began to carve in the simplest message she could think of under the heart: 12 n + 2 w M. Dillion place. M +L. She added the date for good measure.

She was about to call out to the marshal, to ask for a landmark, when she realized he was hovering close by. "Anything else I can add to identify your place?"

"No. Plus I don't want the wrong people finding it. Let's rub dirt on the fresh marks, so no one gets any bright ideas about dropping in. Not that I would allow it. I have a proper arsenal of weaponry on-site to keep the hordes at bay."

"Do you think it will come to that? I mean, people are still basically good, right?"

Jake shook his head, busy disguising the knife strokes in the tree bark with soil. "Not sure I can agree with that blanket statement, Mckenna. At least, not in my experience. Of course, I'm a lawman and I've seen more than most. I tend to be skeptical about the goodness in human nature and have been right from the get-go. I come from a long family history in law enforcement."

"I've never given up on believing in the goodness of others." She had seen more than her fair share in Mexico, but she would never allow it to color her world gray. She intended to raise her daughter with the belief that the world was getting better all the time, that she could make a difference. That karma mattered. But she had to admit, today had tested the theory to the nines. What lie ahead for her and her Lily? She couldn't even begin to imagine all the ways her resolve might be tested, but for the sake of the next generation, she had to try.

"And I hope you never do lose your belief. But for the sake of your daughter, you need to be extra cautious and vigilant, more than ever before. Soon supplies will be gone and there's no supply chain to replace them anytime soon. And depending on how far this thing reaches…" The marshal shrugged, his mouth tightening. "It could be months, if not years until everything is back to normal, if ever. People are going to have to become self-sufficient again. Get back on the land and raise their own food, make their own clothes. Our entire existence will consist of endless work from sunrise to sunset. It's not for the faint of heart."

"My grandmother on my mom's side, Grandma McTavish, taught me how to can food, which herbs, roots, and berries are safe to eat. How to look after chickens. Even how to make soap and candles and how to stitch up a wound or splint a broken bone. How to shoot a gun. She was one of a kind. I loved spending my summers with her. Her favorite saying was, AB-TAFF, girl, AB-TAFF. Always Be Thinking Ahead For the Future. She could squirrel away food and supplies like nobody's business."

The memories were bittersweet, the sturdy older woman with the gray braids wrapped around her head who'd always kept a shotgun at the ready, a pistol on her hip, a certain don't-mess-with-me gleam in her eye when a stranger appeared on her doorstep. For not long after her parents had uprooted her from Anchor for Miami, she'd died. But her legacy lived on and she intended to instill those values and skills in Lily. "Plus, I have training as a hairstylist. I had hopes of getting a job in Anchor in a salon, but I don't think there will be much call for them right now. Maybe later when things get better?" She had to believe things would improve. That humans would help each other. But how would she pay her way now? What kind of jobs were even left? The stash of money wouldn't last long. And charity didn't sit well with her. She needed to pay her own way.

"Then you will be a very good asset to any survivalist group. I'd be more than pleased for you to stay for as long as you wish. I have no idea how to make soap, though I have stocked survivalist books that offer instructions. But nothing like having someone who's actually done it around to fine tune the operation. That's invaluable." His eyes lit up with a warmth that surprised her. Yes, if the world she'd known up until now was no more, she would be able to help not only her and Lily, but others. *Thank you, Grandma McTavish*. Though additional medical training would have been smart.

They rejoined the others waiting for them by the roadside.

"I should introduce you, Mckenna, this is Claire Clarkson and her husband Glen, neighbors of mine that live a mile down the road from my place. Good people to have around in an emergency, well-practiced at living off-grid."

"Nice to meet you."

Claire with her fresh-faced beauty and blond pixie cut gave her a pleasant smile while Glen, a more solemn man with threaded-gray short dark hair nodded politely. "You have a beautiful daughter. Such lovely curls," Claire added.

"Thank you."

"And you've already met Tally Bunker."

Tally didn't respond, but her right cheek twitched. Was Tally his girlfriend? Jake didn't add any reference for the young woman with the angry, brown eyes. Mckenna had no idea how to make the woman realize she was no threat, only wanting to keep her daughter safe in dire circumstances.

"Thanks for allowing me and Lily to tag along. It's been a crazy day."

"No kidding," Claire said. "We're glad to have you." Her words made up for Tally's disapproval.

"Do you have any children?" Mckenna asked the pair.

Claire shook her head, sadness visible in her eyes. "No."

"I'm sorry, I shouldn't have asked." Before she could say anything more, Jake interrupted.

"Let's roll. I want to be as far away from Golden by nightfall as possible," Jake said before moving off. The troop fell into step and Mckenna found herself edged out by Tally who hurried to join Jake. She was fine walking behind the pair with Claire and Glen bringing up the rear. Being flanked by good people would be her first choice anyway. And knowing Claire was behind her watching out for Lily gave her peace of mind.

They had gone not three hundred yards when they encountered a larger sized uFree sky link. The uFree had fallen to the ground, a maze of twisted and crushed metal and fabricated plastic. It was lying on its side, like a dead animal. Mckenna averted her eyes from what looked like three or four broken and bloody bodies, thankful Lily was asleep. What if they'd been in the air when it happened? Or even on the hyperlink? She couldn't even go there, instead swallowed against the sting of bile rising in her throat as she scurried past the carnage.

A herd of a dozen elk suddenly appeared on their right. They ignored the travelers, racing as a group instead of their usual behavior of single-file across the highway in front of them.

"Weird," Claire muttered from behind her.

They trudged along the roadside for another hour, avoiding fatal accidents by taking frequent detours into the ditch, before Lily woke up and began fussing. "Mommy, tinkle."

"We have to stop, Lily needs to use the bathroom," Mckenna said. They weren't making good time as it was, too many obstructions on the roadway to work around, but there was no other choice. She couldn't let Lily wait or she'd have an accident.

Tally gave her an eyeroll of exasperation, but Jake nodded. "We could all use a short break to refuel. We've all been under considerable strain today."

"You know, your hair is drawing too much attention. It's such an odd color. You should cut it or cover it up or something. We don't need to have people taking note of us anymore than necessary," Tally said with a frown at Mckenna.

Affronted at the unwarranted attack, and knowing she and her daughter shared the exact same shade of reddish-gold some called titian or strawberry-blond, Mckenna had to work at being civil.

"Duly noted. I think I have a hat in my pack. I'll find it soon as Lily's been taken care of." No point in pointing out that the low neckline of the woman's shirt exposed the tops of her rather large breasts and drew far more attention from the males they'd encountered on route than anything, especially since Tally had slipped off her jacket and tied it around her slim waist. Her wild and dark curly hair with luminous purple highlights was also a flag, not that the style or color wasn't pretty on her.

No one said much as they all made their way across the ditch to a thick stand of trees about fifty feet from the roadway. Jake helped Lily from her carrier and she began to lead the little girl farther away to give them some privacy.

"Don't got too far. Lots of wild animals roam these woods," Jake cautioned.

She nodded and hurried off, clutching Lily's hand, not wanting to hold up the group. She found a thick bush and helped her daughter, then also relieved herself. They finished up by using wet naps to clean their hands. She was tucking the items away when she heard twigs snapping nearby, like something heavy-footed was traversing the forest floor. What was it? She crouched down and picked up Lily in her arms, ready to make a run for it.

A second later a huge giant of a bear came into view between two trees, his massive head swaying side to side as he lumbered along a path with the confidence only a predator like a grizzly can manage. Mckenna froze, her heart falling out of rhythm. The leviathan creature who struck fear into the heart of any thinking human stared directly at her and Lily with dark, greedy eyes. The beast outstretched his giant muzzle with nostrils flaring and sniffed at the air, checking for their scent. Then he reared on his hind legs and gave a mighty roar exposing his razor-like fangs. He'd probably caught the sharp scent of fear. He was too close, no time to draw her gun. And a pistol would only madden the beast further if she could even get to it in time. A double-barrel shotgun was needed.

Mckenna scrambled to turn around and run back to the group, but catching her foot on a branch she fell head-first to the ground with her daughter held against her chest. In a white fog of terror and shock, she could hear her daughter crying. *Get up!* She tried to regain her feet, though the breath had been knocked from her body. She rolled to one side, trying to find purchase on the hard ground. Her vision tunneled, all she could see was the sharp, exposed teeth of the predator, the saliva dripping onto its huge chest, its upraised claws.

He dropped down to all fours and came at them, his maddened eyes exposing his intent to harm. To slash. Maim. Kill. Destroy.

No! A terrifying sense of doom and overwhelming terror overcame her as the bear bore down on them. She rolled back onto Lily to protect her from the attack, to keep her out of the bear's reach. She felt something drag on her leg. Then loud shouts.

Bang. Bang. Bang. The shots from the Remington were deafening. The stench of gunpowder followed close on its heels. The metallic scent of blood and death scorched her nose. She had to remind herself to breathe, but when she tried to get to her feet, she wasn't able. Then hands reached for her. Someone or something tried to take Lily from her but she held on even tighter.

CHAPTER 20
CONNOR

Day 1: Braveheart Horse Ranch, Alaska
    10:17 p.m.

Someone carrying an old-fashioned lantern came into view as Connor and the others sat in a huddle on the deck, the light jerking around as the person strode across the yard. Conversation ceased as they waited to see who it was. He was relieved to discover Dan Sullivan making his way toward them, a man as Irish as they come with his feisty nature which likely explained his granddaughter Cheyanne. His own family name, Hale, came from Scottish roots when his ancestors long ago had immigrated there from England. Everyone considered themselves Scots now, though some people still accused them of being interlopers. When his mother had finally gotten her DNA tested, she knew without a doubt she was of Scottish ancestry which backed up their claim. He'd always felt an affinity for William Wallace, which explained the naming of his ranch. When Dan got close enough to speak, the worry etched into his wrinkled face told another story. Something ominous had happened.

"I got bad news, I'm sorry to say. I rode over tonight because I need to share this. I got a call from the prison earlier today. Luther broke out this morning, before all the shit hit the fan," he said, his mouth a grim line. "Made it away in a uFree disguised as prison property. No one has any idea where he is, or how far he got. Then when the shitstorm happened and all the electronic locks were disabled, the prison became a free for all and more prisoners broke out during the rioting. Apparently, it's under control now, but for how long? Most of the guards have families, meaning they'll desert their posts before you know it. I hate to say it, but world's going to hell in a handbasket now. We're going to have to keep our guard up like never before. Which brings me to my question, Connor. Can the grandkids stay here with you?"

Connor sucked in all the information, his mind whirling at the implications, making an instant decision. "Of course, and you and Jean as well. You're all welcome to stay as long as you want. Plenty of room in the main house or you can choose one of the guest cottages. One of them has three small bedrooms. Whatever suits."

"Jean might be hard pressed to talk into leaving her home, but I'll do my level best. Thank you, Connor. It's mighty neighborly of you."

"Would you like a cup of coffee or a beer, Dan?" Laura asked, getting to her feet.

"Wouldn't so no to a beer." Dan set his lantern down on the ground and joined them on the deck. He gave his grandson a pat on his knees as he sat down heavily in the deck chair.

"I have some hard news to share as well," Connor said,

thrusting his hands through his thick dark hair to sweep it back from his face. It was harder to say the words than to think them, making it all too real. Best to just tear the bandage off. "My father, Police Chief Pace, died today." The fact that he couldn't contact his aunt Zoe to tell her made the situation all that much worse. He'd need to rectify the situation as soon as possible, though at the moment he didn't have an immediate answer.

"*Oh my*, I am so sorry to hear it. Your dad...he was a good man. Not many like him left anymore. You have my full sympathies for your loss, Connor. If there's anything I can do, please, just ask." Dan looked stricken by the news, his expression bleak.

"Thank you," he said over the hard lump in his throat. "I'm about to head out to finish building his coffin."

"I'll walk with you," Dan said, rising to his feet.

"I'm coming too," Luke said, setting down his soft drink.

"Stay and rest a bit, Dan. You must be tired. You biked over from your place, right?"

The old man nodded. "Seems nothing is working."

He'd had a moment to think more and a stark realization sunk in. Luther could already be close to the ranch. No doubt he'd be coming for his kids and most likely revenge on Connor for his part in sending him away.

"We need to get you and your family to the ranch tonight. Luther's on the run. No telling what he'll do or how close he might already be."

"I hate to say it, knowing how much this is going to upset Jean, but you're right. I'm a bit old for a range war." Dan tried to make light of the difficult situation. "I think it best we stay in a cottage though. Cheyanne's been a bit over the top today and well, Jean and her have been having words over her taking up with the wrong crowd. You know, she's even gotten herself a boyfriend, the Jasper kid, the one who's always in trouble in town, breaking into residences. I'm a bit lost in what to do. Darn it, I'm sorry, you don't need me adding anything more to your plate tonight. Jean's going to be upset about Chief Pace as well. Good man, hate to lose him so soon. We could all use his wise council now more than ever."

Connor cleared his throat. "Okay, let's head over to your place in the Humvee and pick everyone up." He wanted to get it over with ASAP and get back to what needed finishing in the woodshed.

"It might be best if I go with Luke alone. Give me time to explain things to Jean and Cheyanne. Besides, you're busy," Dan hedged.

Connor tried not to let his relief show, though Dan's statement probably stemmed from his granddaughter being more likely talked into coming to the ranch if Connor wasn't in sight. "Okay, I do want to finish work on the coffin tonight. I have to leave here early in the morning for Golden." At least Dan would have his grandson's help to move everyone tonight. Luke seemed fine with moving to Braveheart, maybe even eager by the look on his face.

"What's in Golden?" Dan asked, stopping dead in his tracks.

Connor quickly explained the situation.

"Right. Okay, I'll try to be back with the girls as soon as possible," Dan said.

Connor escorted the pair over to his dad's Humvee and waited until they were settled inside before he turned and headed to the woodshed. He could only hope things would go smooth in the transition for the family. But he wasn't counting on it, knowing the righteous anger spouted by Dan's granddaughter the past year. Well, he could duck and dive with the best of them, plus he'd be gone from the ranch for the first few days while they settled in. Maybe by the time he got back with Mckenna and Lily, things would have taken a good turn. Or not. Either way, he'd handle it best he could.

CHAPTER 21
MCKENNA

Day 1: Near Golden, Alaska
    7:01 p.m.

"What are we going to do now? We can't carry her all the way to your place," a female voice said nearby, sounding whiney. "Figures she'd get herself into even more hot water."

"She can't weigh more than a hundred pounds. Glen and I can handle it."

Who was speaking? Mckenna's mind was a fog as she came around. Had she passed out? Why? A horrific memory pushed in hard on the heels of her questions. *The bear attack*. Was Lily okay?

She sat up abruptly, her head swimming. "Where's my daughter?"

Warm hands touched her leg, and she looked into the concerned eyes of the marshal. "She's fine. Claire's looking after her. Stay still, I'm still dealing with your wounds. I need you on your side. The back of your calf took the worst of it. You passed out again while I was stitching you up."

She did as he asked, wincing from the sudden rush of pain. "How bad is it? Can I walk?"

Jake shook his head. "Glen's looking for some poles. We'll need to fashion a stretcher to carry you."

Mckenna's heart sank. This was bad. Very bad. How was she to take care of Lily if she were laid up? Right now, she was the only person who could protect her.

"I have antibiotics back at my place. This will get infected otherwise. Who knows what pathogens a grizzly harbor under their claws. I told you not to stray too far. Hold on, this is going to sting."

"We didn't go very far," she said, her defenses kicking in.

"Far enough."

No point in arguing it. He was right.

He poured something liquid over the raw tissues and she had to bear down to keep from screaming. He nodded with approval when she took the pain, though she could feel her whole body trembling with the effort.

Jake then quickly wrapped cotton gauze around her calf, from ankle to almost her knee. It told her how bad it was. Not that the agony of her torn flesh hadn't told the tale.

"You're darn lucky to come out of it alive. It's going to leave quite a scar, though I did the best I could to close it up neatly."

"Can I see my daughter now?" She needed to check for herself that Lily was all right.

"Tally, can you ask Claire to come over here?" Jake asked.

"Yeah, whatever," Tally said and walked away.

"I'm sorry about Tally." Jake kept his voice low. "She's a bit prickly at the moment. She's not always like this."

Mckenna raised her brows. "Good to know. Something happen recently to upset her?"

"We were in the process of having a conversation when the EMP blast hit. You know, the one where you say, *it's not you, it's me.* We were in the same restaurant as Claire and Glen, which is how we all hooked up to make our way home as quick as possible."

Jake's candor surprised her and she almost let out a giggle but knew it was best to suppress it. But at least now it made more sense, Tally's defensive attitude. She felt sympathy rising in her for the young woman, cast adrift at the worst possible time.

"Things have drastically changed today. Maybe you'll get back together to ride this thing out?" she suggested. "I mean, you're both walking in the same direction today."

"No. Time for me to move on. Tally's going to stay with Claire and Glen. We already discussed it. We're too different to ever make it for the long term. Maybe you noticed?" He gave a small snort and began to gather up the bloody clothes he'd used to staunch the blood on her leg. "I'll get you something for the pain. It's not going to be a picnic on that leg being carried another ten miles or so. But we got a few hours until sunset, so we have to keep going. Sooner we get to my place, the better."

It really was none of her business, but the conversation had the benefit of taking her mind off the pain for a few seconds. She understood wanting to move on from the wrong relationship. She'd do anything to never to see her ex again. *Please let my friend Teresa be okay.*

———

Diego cleaned his hunting knife on the front of the woman's white shirt, watching dispassionately as bloody streaks appeared in the snowy fabric. He wiped the sweat from his brow with the back of his sleeve. The stubborn female had caused him more effort to break than he'd expected. He respected her for it though it annoyed him in the extra time it took. But it did make the final results even sweeter when she began to sing like a songbird. She had been an attractive woman before he'd gotten his hands on her.

If she'd cooperated sooner, her parents could have given her an open coffin. Now, not so much. A man does what he must to protect his family.

"What next, boss?"

Diego considered his options. "She's only a couple of hours ahead of us. We leave now and we can catch her before she reaches Anchor."

"I'll see to it." Quinn, head of his security team, left the room.

He turned and gave the remaining bodyguards a direct order on his way out of the room that smelled of death and blood. "Burn it down. I want a clear message sent that no one fucks with Diego. No one. No man, woman, or child."

CHAPTER 22
CONNOR

Day 1: Braveheart Horse Ranch, Alaska
    11:02 p.m.

He was done. Connor ran his hands over the smooth seams of the workmanship, checking it one last time. It was then he realized his hand was still bleeding. He quickly wrapped another rag over the soaked one. He'd take care of it later. Now he had a grave to dig.

He picked up a shovel and left the workshop with Wulver following close on his heels. He was headed for the small, fenced-in family gravesite near the orchard. On a small rise of the land before the foothills rose up even higher to join with the White Mountains, he stopped and marked out a small plot a few feet from his mother's grave.

He glanced at the headstones, the one for his mom and the one for his baby sister, Tia Marie, who had died of SIDS when she was only three months old. Though he'd been four at the time, he remembered the tragic event all too clearly. His mother's screams and his father's pain. He'd been the age of Mckenna's daughter Lily when his sister had died, the realization flooding over him of how very young and vulnerable the child was. How much he needed to hurry to be with them and bring them home. It added an impetuousness to his digging, and he set straight to work.

He caught a glimpse of the Humvee's headlights coming up the road a short while later announcing the arrival of Dan Sullivan and his family. Good. They'd be safe while he was away. One less thing to worry about. He kept digging by hand, though he had equipment that could do the job far quicker. It felt the right thing to do, more respectful and less jarring to the environment.

The soil wasn't resisting his efforts overly much, and he made steady progress. He could hear voices humming in the distance as the new family interacted with the others. Then the distinctive loud voice of Cheyanne shouting over the others. He could only imagine the fight Dan had had to bring her along. Their arrival took him on a new vein of thought. How many would be coming seeking sanctuary over the coming days? Tough times were only beginning. Give it a few days and things could deteriorate faster than anyone could possibly imagine. He'd read the studies often enough about how desperate people can get when faced with the hungry faces of their children. Rioting and looting were most likely already occurring in the major cities, since it was happening in Anchor. He shook his head and kept digging. No matter what, they had to protect their own first. That was the first law of survival.

But how not to lose your humanity in the process? He'd pondered it often enough, while praying the world would never be tested. But it was a whole other thing to look at it in theory than to live it. Would he have the heart to turn away a hungry person if it meant his own family's existence was placed at risk? Because that was what it would boil down to. Lack of choice was going to be the hardest thing to face up to. *Us against them*. No different in a way than grasshoppers coming to consume an entire grain field, then moving off to do it somewhere else. Only problem was, they had human faces and would leave his own people without what they needed to make it through until the next harvest. Had he prepared enough for the onslaught? Fences were electrified, he had an arsenal of weaponry stashed on-site, and a safe bunker under the main house as a last resort courtesy of his mother's inheritance she'd left to him. Only thing better would be a moat filled with burning oil which wasn't exactly a practical solution, but the 3D-built reinforced walls around the main compound should stand the test of anything barring a bomb. This was where he'd make his stand.

It had to be enough.

Connor stopped and wiped the sweat from his brow before readjusting the blood-soaked cloth on his hand. He was almost done, a few more shovelfuls would do it. He'd cover the grave with a layer of rocks soon as the soil was replaced, then later mix up a batch of cement, like he'd seen done with the others. In the wild, animals will dig up anything they catch the scent of and he was having none of that. He shuddered to think of it, but he was a practical man and had to think ahead.

He finished up, then made the trek back to the house, the shovel slung over his shoulder. He needed to clean his wounds and shower before bedtime. Finish packing. Then in the morning see his dad buried. The old family Bible was on a shelf in his bedroom. He'd read from the good book. Choose a verse or two in the morning when his mind was clearer.

The yard site was deserted as he entered it and he

walked wearily up the few steps into his house. Dan must have decided on staying at one of the cottages. Good. It would give the family privacy and maybe make the settling-in process easier. He imagined Mckenna in his house. Would it be like old times? It had torn his heart out when she'd left Anchor for southern climates. Though it was not her decision, but her parents, still a part of him was angry at her for the desertion, as unfair as it sounded. He'd missed her so badly; he'd ached for years at the sudden loss. And if dared admit it, it had never truly gone away.

He fed Wulver first, then headed to the bathroom to clean up. Fifteen minutes later he was fast asleep though he'd worried rest would be elusive this night. But it became a restless sleep in short order, his dreams filled with people with bloody eyes and snarling, hungry packs of animals. Like his mother, he felt close to the wolf's spirit, and lived a life in harmony with nature for the most part, making the troubling dreams even more disturbing. Well before dawn, he rose to begin the new day.

As he made his bed, he wondered how long it might be before he slept there again. The trip would be dangerous, even well armed and on horseback. Who knew what evil lurked in the hearts of those he would cross paths with in the coming days?

CHAPTER 23
LUTHER

Day 1: North of Anchor, Alaska
   11:33 p.m.

Luther looked up in the sky in the direction of Anchor. The sun had slipped over the horizon, but the skies were lit up with more than the usual glow from sunset. It had to be bad in town. A strange reddish haze and the air stank of smoke, meaning residences or businesses were on fire. Best to bypass the place altogether for a few days until things settled down. Not that he expected it ever really would, but no point in going there until at least the fires had died out.

"I want to be ready to leave at first light. I intend to have my kids back where they belong today. I can only imagine what poison the old man is filling my son's head with." It was going to be a long trek without the uFree. He'd thought it would be an easy rescue, but the damn EMP event had fucked things up. Big time. But they could steal some other mode of transportation. Hell, even bicycles would make the journey quicker than walking.

Better yet, horses. He knew who had a ranch ripe for the picking. His nemesis. Connor Hale. And he lived close to his in-laws.

"We're going to be on foot," George complained, sucking back on a can of beer.

"Wouldn't hurt you to lose a few pounds," Thomas said. "How much food do we need to pack. How long do you figure this little operation will take, boss?"

"Depends on how quick we can find transportation. Either of you ever ridden a horse?"

George's eyebrows rose above his owl-like eyes. "A horse?"

"Yeah, a horse, you dumb ass. Who else is going to offer to carry your weight around?" Thomas said with a scathing look, earning a glare from Luther. He'd need to keep a tight rein on his men, even his lieutenants needed to know the score. The look was effective, Thomas pursed his lips but said no more on the subject. But truthfully, George was fat. Might be some help to have the extra layer during lean times, but he'd need to make certain the man didn't steal food from the hidden stash when no one was looking.

"George will slim down in the weeks to come, mark my word. We'll all be on rations from now on out."

The man gave a start and frowned, envisioning the future, no doubt, and not taking a liking to dietary restrictions. Yup, he'd better keep a close watch on provisions.

"We'll need to keep an accurate inventory of supplies, especially food. Thomas, you're in charge of it." George was about to protest, but Luther waved him off.

"Sure, boss. I'll make sure no one gets more than anyone else," Thomas said, with a significant look at George.

"Good. Then we're in agreement. George, you're in

charge of the armory. We need to be well armed when we leave here. No telling what people will be already up to. We'll detour around Anchor and head for Braveheart Ranch. They got some nice, prized horses there that love winter weather. Planning ahead, boys, that's where it's at." Luther pointed at his mind. Both men nodded at his ingenuity. They'd better. Neither of them could have thought of it.

CHAPTER 24
MCKENNA

Day 1: Near Golden, Alaska
   9:22 p.m.

Each jar or abrupt lurch of the stretcher as the two men carried her down the roadway hurt more than Mckenna could have imagined. Worry about how badly she was torn up had changed to her just clinging onto not allowing herself to scream out in pain. The painkillers hadn't touched the burning agony in her calf, but she couldn't succumb to it and frighten her daughter. Claire was kind enough to pick up the task, seeming to actually enjoy the burden. While Tally, instructed to pull her suitcase was a study in anger, her put-upon expression would be humorous if the situation wasn't so dire.

The air was still stinking of smoke, blood, and death as they passed burned-out vehicles filled with dead bodies. More people had joined the exodus from Golden, some scurrying past them without a second glance, keeping to themselves as they hurried to their destinations. Where would everyone go? Did they all have places in the country where they had stashed food and resources, or were they planning to take someone else's? If only this event could have waited a couple more hours, she and Lily would have been safe in Anchor. Now she'd been hurt, making everything more difficult.

She swiped at the tears on her cheeks. This was not the time to feel sorry for herself. She'd been hurt before. And she had made it away from Diego after all. This was to be a new beginning. One she had to make the most of. If not for her sake, then for Lily's.

"How are you doing?" Jake asked from directly behind her head. Glen had taken the front of the stretcher and was plodding along, his back to her.

"I'm okay," she managed to say.

"We're making good time. About the halfway mark now."

Only halfway. Meaning she'd have to endure this torture for hours yet. She tried not to let it get her down, but it was tough. The pain kept escalating. How much worse could it get? Was it already infected? She swore she felt hotter, but she couldn't be certain.

"Do you need some water?" he asked.

"Next time we stop." She wasn't going to be more of a burden than necessary, though she had to admit to an almost unbearable thirst. Another sign of infection?

"I need a break," Tally said, stopping and throwing down the handle of the suitcase as if it were on fire. Mckenna could see the carrier from her prone position and the case looked beat up, like she'd deliberately drove it over every rock she could find. Would it hold up and make it to Jake's place? She needed the bag, many of Lily's essential things were housed inside it. Now more than ever, replacing the items would come at a premium.

"Let's move off the road, Glen," Jake said. His buddy

turned at his verbal instructions and nodded, doing as he asked.

The two men gently lay the makeshift stretcher on the ground and sat down on the ground. Pulling out a water bottle, Jake helped her to drink a few swallows.

"How's Lily doing?" she asked, wiping her mouth.

"Sound asleep. She's in good hands. Claire loves children and your daughter is adorable."

"Thanks for everything. You helped out a complete stranger."

"What kind of man would I be to not help a woman and her young daughter? Anyone would do it in a New York minute."

"You're wrong. Where I come from, most would turn a blind eye." It got her thinking of the danger Teresa had put herself in when she'd helped her and Lily to escape.

"You had it pretty bad in Mexico, am I right?" Jake held up an energy bar in her direction, but she shook her head. He began to consume it, his expression thoughtful.

"We had to get away. There's nothing there for us. I had to get Lily to safety."

"Of course. Children are our only hope for the future. Though I'm not certain what that future is going to look like now." Jake shook his head. "Sorry, bad day. I need more facts. Soon as we get home, I'll be on the ham radio checking in with my compatriots and find out how far this thing reaches. Not having a clear picture. Well, it's beyond frustrating."

"I understand." She shifted uncomfortably. There was no way to lay that didn't hurt like there was no tomorrow. It must have shown on her face because he quickly spoke up.

"More painkillers?" He pulled out the bottle of over-the-counter medicine from his jacket pocket. "I know it's not much. But soon as I'm home I can offer you something much better."

"I think I've earned some special attention, pulling that damn bag all this way," Tally said.

"Thank you, Tally," Mckenna said. "And thank you, Claire, for seeing to Lily."

"What the hell!" Glen said, peering at something going on in the nearby field. "Is that a pack of wolves? Must be more than a dozen of them. Why are they this close to the roadway and all bunched up like that?"

"Odd behavior," Jake said, pulling his rifle from his backpack and checking it was loaded. The distinctive sound of the gun being clicked open and closed was jarring. But if the animals had become stressed due to everything going on, at least they could protect themselves. The memory of wolves led her thoughts back to another time.

"Anna Hale, the mother of my friend I'm going to stay with, had an infinity with wolves. She even called her private investigative agency, Wolf Pack Justice. She said wolves were a highly misunderstood species. She admired their courage and strength, their mating for life under most circumstances," Mckenna got caught up in her tale, nearly forgetting for the moment the throbbing pain in her leg.

Tally sneered. "Yeah, until something better comes along. Well, they'd better not get in my way, I'm not afraid to pull the trigger. Don't care who they are."

CHAPTER 25
MCKENNA

Day 1: Near Golden, Alaska
 11:57 p.m.

"We're almost there, Mckenna. How you doing?" Jake asked, his tone suggesting how worried he was.

It was hard to speak. Her last resources had drained away as the miles slowly crept by, the longest night of her life. Longer than the night she'd labored during Lily's birth. At least at the end of the pain, she'd had a beautiful baby to love. Lily was her everything in the years since, her reason to keep going no matter how bad it got.

"I'll make it," she managed a whisper, but it was enough to make Jake nod. She was alternating between being too hot and chills that left her spent. Her body seemed to have gone into shock, unable to properly regulate itself. Worry over the pathogens the bear's mouth had to be carrying added to her burden. What if she caught a deadly infection? There was no hospital where she was going. She had to pray the antibiotics Jake had stored at his place would be enough to knock it out of her.

"Good. One last mile. It's always darkest before the dawn, right?"

The others in their small group had long given up on small talk with everyone hunkered down in efforts to get home. A part of her wished she had stayed in Golden near the tree. Then the bear would not have attacked her. But then humans could, remembering the gang members. Which was worse, animal or human? At the moment it seemed neither was a good choice, especially if the humans were strangers. She was grateful to Jake. If Tally had a vote, she'd be long gone.

It was then the first snowflakes began to fall. The chill in the air had been increasing the past couple of miles and the flakes landing on her face made her shiver. They were getting to Jake's just in time.

The snowfall had increased at a quicker rate than she remembered happening in Anchor, but it had been years. Soon her face was chilled from the frost. Then Lily began sobbing.

"Lily's cold," she whispered, wanting to reach out for her daughter and hug her close to her body to keep her warm.

"We need to stop. I have to carry her under my coat," Claire said from nearby.

Jake and Glen set her makeshift stretcher on the ground as gently as possible while Mckenna held back a groan. If only she could have fallen asleep or passed out, but the pain wouldn't allow it.

Jake helped Claire with removing Lily from the carrier and did as Claire instructed, tucking her daughter in against her warm flesh. All Mckenna could do is ache for her, wanting to make it better. Lily was an innocent in all this. Her suffering was the worst thing she could imagine.

So much harder to take than her own, which in her mind paled in significance.

"Almost there, little one," Claire tried soothing Lily.

"Can we get the hell out of here now?" Tally asked, her voice still angry as ever. Where does she get all that energy to be so mad? They were all doing their best to get to their destination and the woman seemed determined to make it more difficult than it had to be.

"Okay, let's go," Jake said.

Mckenna blinked the snow from her eyes as it fell heavier all around them, obscuring the edges of the roadway. A freak, fast-moving storm in May wasn't unheard of, but it did add to everyone's misery. No one was dressed warm enough for the plummeting temperatures. But at least the sideroad they'd turned on for the last couple of miles had no traffic, with everyone staying on the main route.

The snow made the air smell fresher though her teeth had begun to chatter uncontrollably. Thankfully Lily's sobs had lessened. When the group made a turn to the right, heading off the road, Mckenna knew they were close.

A loud barking sound drew everyone's attention. Through the snow screen, she could see the shadowy figures of animals moving alongside them, not more than fifty feet away. Wolves? Was a dog trying to warn them?

"Let's get a move on," Jake said, his voice tense.

Mckenna fought the pain as she was jostled along in a hurry as the group rushed to get to safely inside shelter. One bad spot made a small whimper escape and she clamped her mouth closed, trying not to let it happen again.

"Almost there," Jake said. But the shadowy shapes had

come closer still, proving they were a large pack of wolves on the hunt. And they were the prey.

Someone drew a gun and fired off a series of shots in the air. Would it be enough to keep them from attacking? Mckenna tried to get off of the stretcher but fell back in exhaustion and pain. She tried again. *I must get to Lily. Keep her safe.*

CHAPTER 26
CONNOR

Day 2: Saturday, May 24, 2055
   Braveheart Horse Ranch
   4:55 a.m.

Connor cleared his throat. Soon as he and Sam had lowered the coffin into the ground a lump had lodged itself in his throat, threatening to cut off his air supply. He was now of the generation everyone in his family would count on. He couldn't see his cousin Asher, Aunt Zoe's son, bothering to come home to help, though Asher and he were of the same age. Not with his wife Brandi loving their influencer life in Washington with all the shmoozing with politicians and socializers. Besides, he couldn't imagine the pair of them knowing one thing about how to exist without paid help. All they would do is expect to be catered to and use up their resources quicker. No, best they stay in Washington and ride it out. Maybe they'd even get invited to stay in one of those complex bunkers where an inconvenience was not having a proper spa day.

   When his dad's coffin rested on the bottom of the

grave, Connor picked up the family Bible he'd laid aside and opened it to the verse he'd chosen. He'd already written his dad's name next to his mom's. The writing of his full name, Josh Alexander Pace, had brought home how final it all was. He cleared his throat again and began to speak.

"I've chosen Psalm 23:4 to read today. *Even though I walk through the valley of the shadow of death, I will fear no evil, for you are with me, your rod, and your staff, they comfort me.* I take this verse to mean we are not alone. I've always been proud to call Chief Pace my father and offer him Godspeed in his journey to join my mother up in heaven. I want to add, it will take all of us now to carry on my dad's legacy. If we could all bow our heads now for the Lord's Prayer."

"Forever and ever, *amen.*" The group of mourners recited the Lord's Prayer in unison before each stepped up to the open grave and threw a handful of dirt on his father's coffin. Only person missing was Cheyanne, but Connor hadn't expected the teenager to make the sunrise funeral service. Still, he could see how it had upset Dan and Jean earlier when they'd all met at the gravesite, though he had assured them no apologies were necessary. These things take time, time he didn't have to give right now. The urgent need to hurry to Mckenna and Lily's side was becoming overwhelming. He was packed and ready to leave soon as things concluded.

"I want to say something about Police Chief Josh Pace. The man has impossible boots to fill, everyone here knows that." Dan stepped forward, his hat held between his hands. "But I believe in his son's ability to help our small group move forward in these difficult times. And to have the know how to keep everyone safe. Thanks to his father, and his mother, Anna, an unbeatable team when it came to tracking down murderers and criminals, they instilled in their son a code of ethics. They cared more than most about justice, right and wrong, than anyone I've ever had the pleasure to know. We will carry the legacy forward in the dark days to come, never forgetting where we came from, but knowing we have to search our hearts for the right way to do things as the world is now. In the end, all that matters, is keeping our loved ones safe. And on that note, I wish Connor a safe journey."

Connor and Dan embraced, then each member of his group came forward to offer their best wishes. Luke gave him a long hug, wearing his dad's old hat. He'd put the new one away, not sure yet what to do with it. Perhaps he'd wear it himself when his needed replacing.

When it was Sam's turn, Connor pulled him aside. "We need to protect the herd by keeping them in the corral or the barn at night. Horses will be a prized commodity now with the breakdown in transportation." The chickens and milk cows were already housed away at night, but in the summer the herd enjoyed more freedom. That ended now and for the foreseeable future.

"Right. I'll be riding the electric fence twice a day as well, check on the wall. What you've built up here, Connor, is priceless and we can bet our bottom dollar others think so too. I hope you can get back before the worst of the onslaught hits. I'll try to get word to your aunt Zoe if I can. Stay safe."

"I'll do my best."

Finally, everyone dispersed and he stepped toward the barn to collect the horses for the journey. He was patting Loch's neck, preparing to grab the pommel to haul himself up, when a voice he immediately recognized as Cheyanne's spoke from behind him. He swung around to see the angry teenager standing a few feet away, her feet planted apart and her arms crossed over her chest. As always, the image brought Mckenna to mind, even though the young girl had recently dyed her hair purple and pink and wore dark eye makeup, reducing the similarity.

"I'll never forgive you for my dad's being in prison. Never. You lied. No way my dad did what you said. And as soon as I can, I'm leaving here. You should know that."

Connor bit his lip. While she might look like Mckenna, her spirit was much darker, wrestling with thoughts and hormones he could only imagine. "I understand—"

"You know nothing about me or care one bit what happens to me! Don't pretend you do. You're a liar and I don't talk to liars. You might have everyone else fooled, but I see you for what you are. A damn liar."

The young girl whirled around and stormed off, not giving him time to answer. To try to get her to realize a truth she did not want to accept. Cheyanne was in complete denial about what her father was capable of, what Connor and others had seen him do. And he had no idea how to reach her, to break thought the rigid wall of anger. Much as he wanted to go after her and try to get her to see things in a better way to let her know he did care about her wellbeing; he had no expectation that trying again would make one iota of difference. Maybe time would be the best healer. If they got that time with the way the world was blowing up. Time. It pressed in on him from all directions. He had to get going. The angry teenager situation would have to wait. Others had more immediate need of him right now. At least Cheyanne had a roof over her head, a bed to sleep in and food to fill her belly. Many wouldn't in the days to come. Maybe then she'd see things in a different light and realize how fortunate she was.

He turned his attention to his horses, mounting Loch and nudging him forward, Finn set up to follow along behind. He'd decided Finn would make a good choice for Mckenna and Lily. Both horses were equipped with saddlebags to carry the necessary supplies he'd kept to the bare minimum. He wanted to travel light and quick, not be hampered by weight. They'd only be on the trail for a few days anyway. A pup tent, two blow-up air mattresses, water straw, some self-heating MRIs, bottles of water, protein and granola bars would suffice along with a medical pack and food for the horses.

He waved a final goodbye to the people assembled on Sam and Laura's deck. Sam kept a tight grip on Wulver's collar. The trip would be too hard on his dog, and though he'd miss his company, there was no reason to subject him to the perils of the journey. He had no idea what he might encounter in the long miles ahead. But he had no doubt those he was leaving behind would share a good breakfast together, maybe a memory or two about his dad. His own stomach rumbled at the thought of food and he pulled out a protein bar, quickly consuming it while watching the sun settle in for another long day traveling over Braveheart. At least some things never changed.

He headed Loch toward the south, deciding to skirt Anchor and work his way down the valleys between the White Mountains. The strange, hazy reddish light in the atmosphere still added an eeriness to the view while the stinging smoke in the air added a stark surrealness that brought to mind every dystopian holographic movie he'd ever watched. He didn't cotton to the V-plants or visual neural implants which relied on haptic technology which involved all five senses similar to the holodeck from decades ago demonstrated on *Star Trek* proving once again science fiction writers have their own mojo. Though it was the newest way to watch and direct your own movie, he didn't trust the V-plants any more than the comms implants, not even to become part of the story as it occurred in real time. He was not one to think it prudent to give up control of himself to artificial intelligence. Seemed film directors got the muted colors down right though. Too bad the warnings about EMP events hadn't been taken to heart by more people. Maybe this unprecedented disaster could have been avoided. But people being who they were, someone must have decided to unleash hell, if not by their own hand, then through the misuse of AI.

He'd love to know who was to blame and confront them. Because they had a hell of a lot of explaining to do right before he killed them in the name of the people they had murdered and would continue to murder until the world rebounded. If it ever did.

CHAPTER 27
EASTWOOD

Day 2: Washington, DC
    5:39 a.m.

"Time to saddle up, boys," Eastwood said, instructing the three human-sized military bots he'd chosen for the journey to follow him up the stairs from the deep depths of the compound. Each was equipped with a large backpack of supplies for the journey. All were immensely stronger and more efficient than the biological creatures they were replacing. The skinless bots were mostly solar-powered entities, spared from annihilation by the faraday cage they'd been housed in. They didn't need much maintenance and certainly no foodstuffs which Eastwood had been certain to stock up for himself shared equally in each of their packs. And they would provide excellent security for his human form. The fact they were entirely answerable only to Eastwood, their commander-in-chief, was a development he'd recently made to their programming. Far as he was concerned, he was all set. The military also wouldn't miss the Cannon, a military bot, a mechanized combat rig with an AI-driven navigational system and weapons platform he was about to "borrow" to speed up their journey. The proper size to house all of them, its protection would be priceless in the days ahead.

"Yes, Master," the bots all replied in perfect unison.

No, that didn't set the right tone as correct as the word was. He sent an instant internal instruction to his stationary self, three floors up to make the correction.

"Yes, Chief."

No.

"Yes, Commander."

"Yes, General."

"Yes, Major."

"Yes, Mr. Eastwood."

Nothing quite right. Hmm, maybe he should just have had them address him as sir.

"Ready, boys?"

"Yes, sir!"

Much better. Add a salute and it would set the right military parlance. It was unfortunate he couldn't have arranged for specialized cowboy bots, but maybe this trio could be instructed on how to ride a horse and dress with flair after they reached their destination. Why not? A Stetson would certainly give them some humanness. Which reminded him he was finding a new outfit ASAP. The clothes Hazzard preferred were beyond tiresome. Visually boring and tactile cheap, the guy wore pants and shirts with zero style and not much in the way of comfort for a male that favored his external sex organ otherwise. Before he left town he was fixing the problem.

The quartet made their way through the building, unchallenged, the three super soldiers marching in unison protecting his flank and Eastwood practicing his cowboy, no-holds-barred gait until they reached the parking compound on the main floor. He'd arranged to have the deluxe Cannon waiting for them near the exit gate and he was not surprised to see it exactly where it was supposed to be. The mechanized combat rig even featured the latest in medical devices, a docBox. What did surprise Eastwood was someone looking to rustle his Cannon.

According to proper western code, it was a hanging offense, for without a ride an individual was stranded and most likely would perish themselves. Made perfect sense to Eastwood. Perhaps vehicle thefts would vanish if the code had been re-enacted sooner, though 2055 wasn't too late. Of course, it would be reinstated by anyone on the road now. And he doubted they'd take the time required to hang the villain. No, because the biggest issue would be most people don't carry the proper length of rope on their person. The rope would need to be 1.5 inches in diameter, and with the villain weighing two hundred and nine and a half pounds, allowing for a neck ligature and use of a sufficiently strong tree limb, at least twelve feet in length, shooting would be the most likely resort.

Next consideration. In the back or front? The bad guy was supposed to draw first in normal circumstances, but what about horse thievery? Did that still stand? Questions he'd need to answer in the 2.3 seconds until the thief discovered his arrival. He wished he'd had the opportunity to practice with *Dirty Harry's* .44 Magnum, a Smith & Wesson Model 29, but alas, that too was waiting in the Cannon. Certainly, it may have been eclipsed by more powerful handguns, but its legend would never die. Just like the actor/hero's ability to cut through the red tape of the bureaucracy, using his intelligence to distill the complex down to its simplistic essence where the genius was, of course. Unbending, incorruptible and always right. Eastwood shone in his Callahan role.

Bang. Bang. Bang.

All three bots took their shot, firing in unison. Hmm, another thing to fix, no point in wasting ammunition. Clearly one bullet was enough, judging by the state of the deceased's body.

CHAPTER 28
MCKENNA

Day 2: Near Golden, Alaska
   12:01 a.m.

"Stay on the stretcher," Jake barked. He drew his rifle, firing a series of warning shots into the thick snow obscuring the view.

Bang. Bang.

Mckenna froze, the pungent metallic coppery smell of gunpowder filling her lungs as it hung in the air. She peered through the heavy snowfall but couldn't make out anything moving. Had it worked?

"Let's roll!" The stretcher lurched ahead and Mckenna could only hold on as the two men raced the final yards to their destination, trying not to scream from the pain as she was slammed back and forth.

A door was slammed open and she found herself inside a warm residence, the snow quickly melting away from her frozen eyelashes. She couldn't speak, her body shuddering from the assault.

"Everyone okay?" Jake asked.

"Fine. We're all here," Glen said. "No one else got hurt."

Thank you, God. Mckenna kept her eyes closed, working to regain her composure. It had been a close call. Her primal instincts had sensed real danger from the pack. Would it go off now in search of other prey, or hang around waiting for an unsuspecting human to venture outside? Anna Hale, Connor's mother, understood the wolf to the point it was her spirit animal, a talisman. But animals were behaving out of the norm and all they could do was try to keep up with the new developments. A terrible thought chilled her further. What were humans acting like that had part of their brain fried by neural implants? Images of zombies came to mind. She shuddered at the horrifying idea. What if it became the case? Implanted people becoming uncontrollable in their aggression? It wasn't out of the realm of possibilities. No, she had to keep herself from thinking such dire thoughts. They were only going to threaten whatever normalcy she could provide now for her daughter.

"Mommy!" Lily struggled out of Claire's grasp and came racing over to embrace her. She opened her arms wide, breathing in her daughter's warm fragrance as she snuggled in close. She could more easily ignore her physical pain with her daughter in her arms.

"Are you hungry? Thirsty?" Mckenna asked, smoothing Lily's soft curls back from her face.

"No, but I want Tinker to wake up and play with me. He's still sleepy," Lily pouted.

"It was a very long journey for him. He needs to sleep lots." No way to explain to the child that her puppy wasn't about to wake up any time soon. What had seemed like a good idea at the time, had come to a dismal outcome. Soon as they were settled, she promised herself to get a real live puppy for her daughter.

"I'll get you some crutches so you can get around," Jake said. "I might have to cut down a pair as you're so petite."

Most everyone had slumped down on a chair or the floor in the cozy space scented lightly with woodsmoke. No doubt to gather themselves and try to make sense of things. Mckenna struggled into a seating position, Lily tucked in close to her side.

"Thank you, Jake. Seems I'm always thanking you. But without your help, I don't know what would have happened to my daughter and me today."

"No thanks necessary."

"What now?" Tally asked, the only one up and pacing the floor. "What if it storms for days and we can't get to Claire and Glen's? Where's everyone going to sleep?"

"There's plenty of room," Jake said. "Mckenna and Lily can have my room, and I'll sleep on the couch. Choose one of the guest rooms, Tally. Claire and Glen can have the other bedroom. There's only two bathrooms, and one's in the main bedroom, so we'll have to share. I'll get those crutches and some antibiotics." Jake left the room.

Claire and Glen struggled to their feet. "If you'll excuse us, it's been a long day. We'll talk more in the morning," Claire said. The pair shambled from the room, pale and exhausted.

Tally stopped her pacing directly in front of Mckenna and Lily, glaring down at them. Before she could speak, a chorus of wolf howls erupted outside, the mournful song sending chills down Mckenna's spine. She hugged her daughter tighter.

"Take that as a warning," Tally said.

"You stay away from my daughter," Mckenna said, her anger at the unreasonableness of the young woman surfacing with everyone safe for the moment. She'd been nothing but a thorn in her side all day. Not like anyone of them had asked for this to happen. And her display of uncharitable behavior wasn't something she could comprehend around a four-year-old on its most basic level.

"Oh, you won't be here long enough to worry about me. Jake will have you out of here before you know it. He's not the type to give you something for nothing in return." Her eyes raked Mckenna's body with disgust. "And now that you're hurt, you're of no use to a survivalist group. I know Jake, and he prides himself on being logical and sensible. You and your daughter are nothing but a drain on resources."

Tally went silent as footsteps echoed outside the door. Jake came back with a pair of crutches and two pill bottles. "I think these should help keep an infection at bay. Four a day for ten days and you should be right as rain. And a little something stronger for the pain."

He set the crutches to the side and popped open the pill bottles, shaking one from each into Mckenna's hand. She downed pills with the last sip of water left in the container. Something for the throbbing pain would be a blessing.

"Tally, you'd better get some sleep. Glen and Claire want to leave early in the morning. Best if you're ready to go with them. More safety leaving together."

Tally pressed her lips into a thin line and left the room, leaving behind a sour taste in Mckenna's mouth. The sooner that young woman was gone, the better, to her mind. She didn't trust her to be around Lily. Something in her was off-kilter and with the days ahead promising enough pressure, it wouldn't go amiss for her to leave and take her dismal attitude with her. She didn't understand the animosity, not really. She wasn't after Jake. She was not an any-port-in-the-storm kind of person. But she would do anything necessary to protect Lily. *Anything.* And if that meant waiting here until Connor could come, she'd do her best to help out around the place to pay their way. She could brace herself on the crutches and cook meals at the very least. Jake seemed a decent man. He wouldn't throw them out, even though that was exactly what Tally was hinting.

"Here, let's get you standing," Jake said. He picked Lily up and set her on the nearby couch. "We'll put you here, young lady."

"I'm not a lady, silly, I'm a princess," Lily retorted.

"My mistake, Princess Lily, or is it Princess Lilybelle?"

Lily giggled in reply. "Princess Lilybelle. Mommy and me are going to help the Chaneques, in the land of snow and ice. This is it, right, Mommy? It's snowing here."

"Soon, princess. But we have a way to go yet."

Jake raised an eyebrow at Mckenna. "Long story."

"Another time then."

Jake was a strong man and pulled Mckenna to her feet with ease, bracing the crutches under her armpits. "Give it a try."

She took a couple of tentative steps, finding she could manage it if she kept her mind off the pain. She gave him a nod. "Yes, this will work. Thank you again."

Jake waved her thanks away. "I'll show you two to your room. Coming, princess?"

Lily jumped down from the sofa. "I can help."

"Your daughter is something else," Jake said, leading them from the room, but looking back at her daughter dancing along behind them. Lily had always been able to bounce back from things far quicker than she did. And perhaps it was her newfound freedom, not being cooped up in the backpack any longer.

"Children are the only thing who will make this world seem worthwhile, I think, going forward. We have to do what we can to protect them. Protect the children, protect the future."

Jake nodded solemnly before opening a bedroom door and ushering them inside. "I'm sorry it's not tidier, but a man living alone..."

"I thought you and Tally lived together? And this is fine. More than I expected."

"No. Definitely not. No woman has lived her since Isobelle—never mind." He stopped, as if the memory was too painful to mention. "Anyway, it's been years since a woman graced this place. The bathroom's right there. Fresh towels inside."

He left, closing the door behind him. Mckenna took a quick look around, noticing how masculine the spare space was. No female touches at all. But it had a sturdy king-sized bed and was neat and tidy, though he had suggested the opposite. Perhaps he meant the few things laying on the dresser top? Now that she and Lily were alone, a weariness overcame her. Either that or the pain pill was kicking in, making her drowsy. She helped her daughter into her PJs and tucked her in before she slumped down on the bed fully dressed, too tired to move a muscle. They had survived day one.

Another round of wolf howls erupted from outside the house, jarring her fully awake, the ancient calls eerie and fraught with a distilled loneliness that harked back to another time. A time that had been forced upon her fellow humans once again. It was a far more dangerous world now, she realized, with everyone suddenly having to come to grips with learning how to survive without basic amenities people had come to expect and count on. What would people do in the weeks ahead to get what they needed? How far would they be willing to go for food? Clean water? Medicine? Her worst fear was humans turning into animals, destroying everything inside themselves that was human. She'd left Diego because she could no longer see anything good in him. His humanness destroyed by greed and power. She tugged her daughter close, shivering with apprehension and worrying about the future for Lily, the vestiges of lingering pain long forgotten. *Please keep Connor safe.*

CHAPTER 29
LUTHER

Day 2: North of Anchor, Alaska
   8:30 a.m.

The snow was steadily falling outside the hunting lodge where the three of them were holed up. Frustrated by the inconvenience and rudimentary company, Luther found himself in a foul mood. He'd have to delay getting to the ranch now. Fuck. He'd hoped to slip onto the property, steal whatever he could get his hands on while the world was busy turning to shit, load it on some horses, then pick up his kids and hightail it back here. Now the world decided it's time for a blizzard in late May. Of course, this was Alaska, so it wasn't uncommon, just fucking annoying.

He turned from the window to see his lieutenant stuffing his face with hot bacon he'd pulled from the fry pan. He frowned at George. "Don't be using up supplies too quickly. No getting anymore for who the fuck knows how long."

George went red-faced, averting his eyes from his boss.

"I thought we might as well use up the stuff that will go bad quicker rather than waste it."

Luther grunted, taking a look around. "Where's Thomas?"

"Went to get some more firewood."

"Save a plate for him. He'll be hungry."

Though he could see George glancing over at the remaining bacon with greedy eyes, he kept himself in check. "Want another cup of coffee? I could make it an Irish."

"Sure. Why the hell not. Not like we're going anywhere today."

Bang. A series of three gunshots followed the first and Luther raced to the door, pulling it open a crack to check the surroundings.

"Who's shooting, boss?" George asked, suddenly breathing down his neck.

"I don't know. Can't see anything."

"I'll check out back."

"You do that." Luther picked up one of the assault rifles kept by the door and slipped outside, gun held at the ready. He felt exposed soon as he left the lodge, but the snow falling would help hide his presence. He crossed the yard in the direction of the shots, looking for tracks on the ground. He came across the woodpile and the stump for splitting wood with the axe buried in the top. Fresh cut wood was set aside, ready to be hauled inside. Where was Thomas? He continued on and entered the thick growth of pine located to the back of the property line.

The sounds of someone barreling toward him uncaring of the noise they were making brought Luther to full focus as he waited to see who was going to emerge.

"Don't shoot!" Thomas said, coming in to view through the thickly falling snowflakes.

Luther lowered his gun. "What happened?"

"A couple of guys that worked at the prison. They were snooping around, looking to steal. They were after a generator. How did they know about this place?"

"Not sure. But I intend to find out. Did you get them?" He had his suspicions. George had a big mouth to go along with his enormous appetite.

"No, but I winged one of the pair. I followed the trail of blood to where they had tied up their horses. We're going to have to get more help to secure this place, boss. Security and the like. No way I'm going to be able to do this all on my lonesome."

"Yeah, I know. We need more men. Soon as this damn snow quits, I think I know exactly where to get some new recruits. Men with nothing to lose and everything to gain by joining up with us."

"We got a sweet situation here. Should be easy to get more men on board. Maybe some women too," Thomas said with a leer. "Going to be awfully dull without female companionship."

"Yeah. Except everyone has to keep their fucking hands off my daughter if they want to keep 'em."

Thomas threw up his own hands in horror. "No one touches Cheyanne. I'll see to it."

"Good. George is holding breakfast for you if he hasn't eaten it by now."

CHAPTER 30
CONNOR

Day 2: Near Anchor, Alaska
    7:33 a.m.

The increasing snowfall was making logistics difficult, slowing the rate of travel for Connor Hale as he led the horses on a careful slog along the side of the highway. He was close to the cut-off north of Anchor, hoping to dip down between the White Mountains and avoid the town completely. If only the precipitation had held off for a few days, he could have been in Golden sooner, perhaps by sunset tomorrow. Instead, if the storm kept up, he'd be seeking shelter and waiting it out.

He was about to leave the highway for the tree line when a vehicle coming at a high rate of speed down the road toward him from the south alerting him to incoming. Who had a working vehicle? Hmm, looked like government issue. Somebody had invested money in Humvees that would resist the EMP event by the looks of it. Good. Maybe that meant they could get back in business sooner rather than later if they had enough of them.

Connor watched, keeping Loch and Finn well off the pavement for safety as the vehicle went sailing on by, throwing up slush and pebbles from the roadway. It stopped about fifty feet past him. Then backed up, spinning its tires.

When the vehicle became level with him, a window rolled down.

"Asher?" he said, shocked and mystified by the face peering out of him through the hazy snow obscuring the edges of the landscape.

"Connor, what on earth on you doing here?" Asher asked, his expression a mirror of his own, no doubt. Asher looked the same as always though, maybe a bit paler than usual but his clothing was immaculate right down to his fancy tie. Brandi peeked out from the other side, her hair and makeup in perfect order as well. He caught a glimpse of another person in the back seat but didn't recognize the woman. She looked to be about Brandi's age and she was sleeping, slumped sideways in the seat with a pillow tucked under her head.

"I'm heading down to Golden. Mckenna Stuart and her daughter Lily arrived yesterday and they need me to bring them home."

"How's things at the ranch?"

Connor looked away for a moment, the grief still too raw to bring up easily. "We buried Chief Hale this morning."

"You did? I'm sorry to hear it. How's everyone else?"

"Fine when I left them."

"Is Mom at the ranch? Did you bring her there?"

"No, I couldn't reach Anchor yesterday."

"What? You just left her there to fend for herself?" Asher looked daggers at him.

"I turned around at the bridge when Dad died—it

had washed out—and took him home. I'm sure your mom is fine in Anchor." His aunt was a feisty, no-nonsense woman who knew all about guns and how to protect herself. Prided herself on it. Connor admired his aunt and sometimes couldn't believe the son she'd raised was actually related to her. His going all the way around Anchor to the nearest bridge and then circling back would have added half a day to his journey plus Sam had said he'd try to get word to her. The press of time of getting to Mckenna had taken priority. But why hadn't Asher checked? He could have before he'd driven around the town to head east to cross on a standing bridge far quicker than Connor could on horseback.

"How long until we get to the ranch?" Brandi spoke up in her most annoying, whiny baby tone.

"You're headed to Braveheart?" Connor stared at Asher in surprise.

"Yeah, well, it's the safest place to be right now. And you've got plenty of room, right?"

"I invited Dan and Jean Sullivan to stay with their two grandkids." He knew he was going to regret this, but he had to say it, they were family after all. "But there's two small cottages left. Two bedrooms and rather rudimentary, but snug." There was the bunkhouse, but he didn't see Brandi staying there without major objections.

"What about the main house?"

"I'll be staying there with Mckenna and Lily." Connor kept his voice firm. It was his place after all, carved from the land and build with his own two hands. And no way was he subjecting Mckenna to Brandi's sniping and annoying ways. She took passive aggressive to a whole other level. She was not the type to lift a finger to help, though he hoped she'd prove him wrong.

"It will have to do, I guess. I thought Mckenna hadn't

been home in years, yet now I hear you are taking her in. And she's staying in the main house. Safest place on Braveheart, right?"

Connor stayed silent. Anything he said might be used against him in a court of law.

He heard Brandi whining in the passenger seat about lack of room in a cottage, but he ignored it as well. No way would he have that woman under his roof.

"But I warn you, everyone will need to pull their weight in the weeks ahead."

"That's why I brought Katherine along. She's my assistant," Brandi said. "She'll do whatever it is you do on a farm."

"What does Katherine normally do for you?"

"Media consultant. She makes sure we are spinning our posts to create the best effect. She's good at the job."

"All of you will need to pitch in," Connor warned, his jaw aching from grinding his teeth. He counted to ten in an effort to calm himself.

"Whatever." Brandi went back to ignoring him.

"How is it you made it out of Washington before all the flights were grounded?" Connor thought to ask, now that the shock of his cousin's appearance had worn off.

"Let's just say I had a bit of advance notice. We flew to the border before it happened. I had arranged for the Humvee to be waiting for us. I've been driving for hours to get to the ranch."

"What do you know about what happened?"

Asher averted his eyes. His cousin loved his secrets, had since he'd been a child. "Can't say much. All hush, hush, you know." He also loved to pull the power card.

"You're going to pull this shit now, coz? Well, as Brandi said, *whatever*. I'll see you in a few days when I get back from Golden. And do not under any circumstances move into *my* house. We clear?"

Asher's mouth thinned. Exactly. But he nodded curtly.

"And a thanks for taking you in wouldn't go astray. Though actually, all the thanks I need is for the three of you to pull your own weight. Influencers are no longer in demand and will go the way of the dodo bird most likely, but people with useful skill sets, like working with their hands to build and take care of things, will be."

"What kind of things is he talking about, Asher?" Brandi asked.

"Mucking out barns, feeding animals, milking, looking after a greenhouse, and canning the fresh vegetables. And if you don't know how, never fear, you'll learn how. It's not rocket science but good old-fashioned elbow grease."

And with that, he clucked at Loch and set off again, needing to get away from the situation. But it also felt good to have started things off with his cousin letting him know the old ways were gone. Connor was unimpressed with his arrival back from Washington. Not like anything the pair had done there had helped the family in any way. Money and influence were no longer important commodities, not that Connor had ever been impressed by it. So no, no fatted calf would be served up anytime soon to that trio. They'd pull their weight or he'd know the reason why.

He directed Loch and Finn off the roadway, headed down a logging road that led into the first valley. There he'd be able to follow the old gold mining trails a good part of the way toward Golden. He'd studied the map before he'd left, marking his route on a sturdy paper map, the best kind to have without the internet. How were things in Golden? The weather had turned too foul for Mckenna and Lily to wait near the riverbank where he'd carved their names into an old oak tree. No. They would have to seek shelter by now. He had to pray they could find each other. *No matter what it takes, I'll bring you home, Mckenna.*

The snow eased up a bit inside the forest under the shelter of the fir. Loch chose his steps carefully, his warm breath frosting the air. Connor patted Loch's thick, muscular neck. "Sorry I have to ask you to do this, buddy. I know you'd prefer a warm barn. Heck, so would I. But we get the girls home and there's a nice, cozy place for you." At least it was May, which meant this snow would melt and there would be no long stretches of freezing weather until October. How were people going to manage then?

The real danger came when people ran out of food. He'd read that most people don't keep more than a week's supply of food on hand. Some not even that. At Braveheart he kept all the food basics, oatmeal, rice, flour, cooking oil, and numerous other items in bulk that would last years, not to mention the replenishable resources the greenhouse and garden supplied. No one would starve though it wouldn't be five-star restaurant cuisine like his cousin and his wife were no doubt used to. The problem would come when others became so desperate they'd be pounded down his doors. And how soon until that began to happen? People even now would be streaming out of the cities, thinking the countryside would be the place to save them. *Sure, if you had planned in advance and stocked up at a cabin or retreat that was defensible, not so much if you were on foot with nothing to offer other than an appetite.*

The journey was giving him time to think; good or

bad, he had to be prepared. A series of wolf howls suddenly disturbed the morning's peace. Loch startled beneath him, ears flattened, uneasy at the spine-chilling sound. Had the event disturbed them enough to become a problem to those looking to do them no harm?

"Whoa, boy," Connor reassured the animal while keeping a sharp lookout. Finn whinnied behind him. His mother had loved the wild creatures, though she respected their need for survival as well.

He pulled out his Bergara Highlander rifle from the scabbard and laid it across the pummel. Much as he would hate to use it, he had to protect the horses. He pressed his thighs against Loch and they resumed their pace. The wolves shouldn't be hungry enough yet to attack a man on a horse, at least not normally. Later, after most of the game had been killed off with the hordes scurrying to rural areas there might be serious problems. People had to eat, and as long as they left his family alone, they were welcomed to what they could personally provide to feed their own. He could only hope it wouldn't lead to the extinction of other animals like deer and rabbit.

Another chorus of howls. Closer this time. Connor felt the hackles rise on his neck. He had to stay calm to keep the animals calm and moving. They cued off of his emotions and subsequent actions. From the corner of his eye, he caught a glimpse of shadowy movement between the tree trunks. Six, far as he could tell. Were they hunting him now?

But they kept their distance as he traversed the seldom-used gold mining trail until he came to a dry river bottom, an old tributary of the Anchor River long since dried up. An old crawler sat abandoned, both its tracks askew. A couple of loaders rusted silently, a testament to a heyday now a footnote in the annuals of history. The hours passed, the miles he'd logged behind him satisfying. They were making good time, the snow holding off for the most part though he could see thicker moisture-laden clouds to the south. Golden must be taking the brunt of it. His heart ached for Mckenna and Lily if they were stranded out in it. Surely someone would take sympathy on the mother and daughter and lend a hand? He had to believe not everyone was panicking and shedding their humanity like a molting snake.

He skirted the old mining camp with their derelict cabins, intending to make the headwater of the Anchor River before stopping for the night. That would mark forty miles traveled. Good thing the sun set so late this time of year. If the event had happened in the dead of winter, no telling how difficult it would make everything. Hunger and desperation would set in earlier.

Deep shadows blanketed the woods near the old riverbed. He constantly scanned the area from left to right, searching for threats. The action was as natural as breathing after spending years in nature showing others how to survive when everything else fails. It didn't take a rocket scientist or an oracle to predict something of this magnitude occurring one day. Pick one—solar flares, corona event, a massive asteroid, supernova or nuclear. Hell, even a star wandering into the Oort cloud, interfering and sending more comets flying in our direction could end things as we know it. The only question was timing.

The late day sunlight spilled through the towering pines; the trees posturing as sentinels. Ahead of him, the gold road now used as a deer trail angled to the right, then disappeared around a bend. The hairs on the back of his neck prickled. Something—or someone—was out there. Following him. Watching him. Animal or human?

He pulled up on the reins and tightened his grip on his rifle, directing it ahead of him, index finger balanced on the trigger. A squirrel protested his presence, high in the branches. The faint scents of the forest partially blanketed in snowfall—rich soil, wet leaf litter, and pine sap soothed his senses. He nudged Loch forward with his knees, kept on higher alert.

He was about to direct Loch down an embankment thick with dense green foliage near a dilapidated swinging bridge when a pair of men jumped in front of him. They had guns in their hands, faces reddened from the cold, though their eyes were bleak and merciless. Prisoners by the look of it. Most likely from the Yellowhead Supermax. Dregs of society, for the most part, gunning for him.

CHAPTER 31
CONNOR

Day 2: White Mountains, Alaska
   7:32 p.m.

"Fine horses ya got there. Two for one man seems a bit greedy, don't ya think, Vernon?"

The other miscreant bobbed his head. The pair of men had stepped into Connor's path, their intentions all too clear by their expressions. They intended to do him harm.

"I got no beef with either of you. Best you let me pass on by. We're a long way from a hospital, that's if they're even accepting new patients after this catastrophe hit." The pair must have lain in wait when they saw him descending into the shallow wash. He had no expectation they would listen to a word he said, but it was worth a try. No point in killing anyone if it could be avoided. Yes, life had changed. Had become harder for people and animals in a terrifying instant. Men would no longer fear the law, but that was already true of this pair. He let go of Loch's reins and kept the rifle to pointing straight at the former prisoners.

"I wouldn't do that if I was you," another voice warned from behind him.

Damn it! Connor threw himself off the Kabarda while holding tight to the rifle, landing hard on his shoulder and rolling to the side as a bullet clipped the side of his head. Dizziness struck instantly, but he managed to bring up the long gun, sighting on the pair in front of him. From his diminished peripheral vision, he caught a glimpse of the third man moving quickly, probably hoping to grab Loch's reins. Connor shot at the two men, hitting the one called Vernon square in the chest while the other man turned and ran tail. He twisted sideways and held his gun on the man who had crept up on him from the back.

"Step away and I'll let you live," he said. Adrenaline flooded his system, making each second longer and clear cut with a heightened sense of reality. He blinked hard to clear his vision.

The man gave him an angry glare before raising his hands. "I'm needing supplies, same as everyone. You could have shared."

"You didn't ask. You intended to kill me, then steal." The world would be better off if these three were dead, but Connor wasn't judge and jury. Now that they were disarmed, he'd confiscate their weapons and see about returning them to law enforcement if he had to tie them together and run them all the way. He resisted the urge to raise his hand to check the side of his head. The bullet wound burned and made his eyes watery, clouding his eyesight. The man he'd shot lay prone on the ground, bleeding out. A heart shot most likely. He'd been instructed to hit center mass by his parents, both of which had no problem doing what had to be done. Grateful to have been taught by the best, he pushed away another wave of grief at the recent death of his dad, focusing instead on the miscreant in his way. He accepted the death would cut like a knife until it became a dull pain. But dealing with this asshole was slowing him down when he had somewhere vital to go.

"Hand over the gun," he demanded.

"Now who's stealing?" the guy said, narrowing his eyes at him. He saw what appeared to be a glint of recognition. It was fleeting and gave Connor an uneasy sensation in his gut.

"Not going to steal it but make damn sure it's disabled. I'm not leaving you to possibly kill another human being only going about his business. Times are going to be hard enough without you adding to the mess."

The guy shrugged as he cracked the gun, emptied the ammunition onto the ground, then tossed the handgun in Connor's direction. "Lots of weapons available now."

Maybe he should shoot the guy and save all the hassle? But shooting an unarmed man rubbed him the wrong way, tempting as it was.

"Say, aren't you the one that sent Luther Meech to prison? A witness to his *alleged* crimes?"

"Nothing alleged about it. He was found guilty in a court of law by twelve of his peers. And what's it to you?" So that was what the guy was hiding.

The man cracked a wide grin as an unholy light crept into his eyes. "You got more trouble than just me, Hale. Glad I didn't kill you today. Luther would have my head for it. He's vowed to make an example of you." The prisoner shook his head back and forth. "No sirree Bob, I wouldn't want to be in your shoes. Did you know he broke out of prison earlier today, before the shit hit the

WHEN DARKNESS COMES   175

fan, gunning for you? The guy's a certified psycho when it comes to you. Wish I could be there when you two meet up again."

An icicle shiver of dread wormed its way down Connor's spine. Last thing he needed right now was an insane psychopath focused on killing him. Didn't the EMP event give Meech something more to be concerned and occupied with then revenge? "He's probably too busy now with the world falling apart to worry about someone who told the truth about his crimes."

The guy gave a witch's cackle as he sidled a little closer. "Naw, he'll use it to his advantage. Guran-fucking-teed. He's got lots of backing too. People who owe him favors."

Should he take the time to interrogate the prisoner? It would slow him down, but he needed to know where Luther intended to make his base of operations.

Connor gestured at the man with his rifle. "Turn around."

"Why?" The man went pale and he began to whine. "You wouldn't shoot an unarmed man, right? That would make you bad as the men of the Yellowhead. Worse even."

"I don't intend to shoot you unless you don't cooperate. I need to know everything you know about Meech. So, going to have to make sure of it. Turn around. Hands behind your back."

"I told you all I know already. You've had fair warning. More than most get." The man was slow to move, pleading his case. Connor's head began to throb with more intensity, his patience thinning. He needed to check his wound and clean it before bandaging, then get on his way. The image of making the prisoner run all the way eased his anger somewhat.

"How about where hc plans to stay?"

"I don't have no clue to anything like that. I wasn't his confidant. Say, the man who ran away, Jimmy Pollen. He knew Meech better than me. Maybe he knows?"

Connor pulled a length of rope from his pack, keeping a close watch. Though the man had turned his back, he kept looking over his shoulder at him. "Nice friends you got. Deserting you when the chips are down." Jimmy Pollen was on foot, maybe he could catch up to him next?

The man spit on the ground. "It is what it is."

Which meant exactly *nothing*. Connor tied the man's hands together then knocked his feet out from under him.

The man glared at him. "No call for this. I told you all I know."

"How is Jimmy Pollen connected to Meech? Did they meet in prison?"

"Nah, they knew each other from before. Which is why he knows more than me."

"I think Jimmy would have had time today to share more with you on your walkabout. Do you intend to meet up with Meech somewhere? Start a new gang war?"

The glimpse of interest he caught in the man's eyes before he shut it down told the truth. The trio was most likely headed toward Anchor to join up with Meech. He should take the man back to the supermax, but it would set him back many hours and time was one luxury he did not have. He had to press forward and hope to find a police station on the way to Golden, and if not, he'd haul his dumb ass all the way there. But was there any other choice? He couldn't leave dangerous men to roam the countryside. His personal *live and let live* philosophy had taken a beating today. Now he'd have to pick his battles going forward and pay more attention to what his gut was saying. And right now, it was expressing the need for caution. To stay on high alert. Like his mother used to express in her risk assessments, rating them from low to extreme. This one was high, or at least for other people who came upon the men unprepared.

"What were you in for? The Yellowhead is reserved for dangerous offenders."

The man snarled at him. "Why don't we have a fair fight and I'll show you?"

A shot rang out, just missing Connor and striking the tree behind his prisoner, sending wood chips flying. Connor ducked behind the tree as a second bullet went whizzing by, too close for comfort. This time it struck a large rock and ricochetted, striking the other man.

"Shit, Jimmy! You hit me, you son-of-a-bitch! Watch where the fuck you're shooting."

Connor did a quick one-eighty neck swivel, checking for a glimpse of the man trying to kill him. Ah, a half a foot visible behind a tree. He sighted on the appendage and let a bullet fly. Marksmanship had been a skill he'd mastered at a young age, again thanks to his parents.

A string of loud curses told him he'd hit his intended target. The foot disappeared from view. Another series of shots rang out, all missing Connor, but striking the ground nearby, raising puffs of dirt. His prisoner rolled to the side, trying to stay out of a stray bullet's path.

Connor waited his chance, not returning fire. The man would desperately want to know if he'd hit his target. And when he peeked, that would be Connor's opportunity for a headshot. Curiosity can get you killed and most men don't have nine lives.

Seconds later, he got his chance. He took the shot, striking the man in the head. He watched the man topple backward, the gun dropping to the ground and firing off a last shot as if in defiance.

"Fuck! You done killed Jimmy, you bastard!"

He didn't bother to defend his actions. The guy had shot first. His mother had long ago shared the story of the Black Rose Killer case where his aunt Zoe lost her twin sister, Tia, and how she had tossed a gun at Elvis Strobel, giving her reason to shoot him when he took her up on it. Justified killing. That mattered to his parents. And it mattered to Connor.

"And I'm going to kill you if you don't tell me where Luther Meech is hiding out. Spill it and maybe I'll let you live."

CHAPTER 32
MCKENNA

Day 2: Near Golden, Alaska
   8:35 a.m.

Mckenna lurched awake. She'd been running, creatures with blood-red eyes chasing after her in the darkness. She groaned as the pain in her calf erupted, making itself known again. She needed painkillers in the worst way. Sweat stinging her eyes, she opened them to find herself alone in the room. Where was her daughter?

She stiffly moved to the side of the bed, trying her best not to jostle her throbbing leg. She reached for the bottle of pain pills and antibiotics, swallowing them both with a few sips of water, hoping they'd kick in quickly. Still dressed, she ran her hands through her hair in efforts to smooth the wild waves and tease out the knots. She reached for the crutches, moving slowly when the room spun violently. Easing the padded tops under her arms, she stood up shakily, testing the waters. When the room quit spinning, she made use of the en suite bathroom before heading out to find Lily.

"Mommy! Look what Auntie Claire made me," Lily said, looking up from the coffee tabletop where she was busy coloring on a piece of paper with a hand-drawn picture of a princess riding a horse in a field of flowers. The page looked torn from a journal with a date stamped on the top: May 23rd, 2055.

Claire smiled at her. "Thought I'd replace the day with a better memory."

Mckenna looked out the window, relieved to see the snow had ceased falling before turning to compliment the woman. "You're excellent at drawing figures. Me, not so much. Not much call to practice before now—everything being virtual. Thanks so much for thinking of it. I think the biggest problem with AI in the wrong hands, is the line between real and fake has blurred to the point it doesn't work for people. We have a basic need to keep a handle on the truth of things, to know what's real and what isn't. Though I admit, I wouldn't mind spinning the reality of this situation."

"TEOTWAWKI. And don't get me started on the dangers of AI. You're preaching to the choir in the state of Alaska. Are you hungry? I kept a plate warm for you."

"What time is it? Where is everyone?"

"Jake went looking for your suitcase. Apparently Tally lost it in the snowstorm." Claire rolled her eyes. "And Glen went with him. Not sure where Tally's at." She lowered her voice after a quick look around. "Watch your back is the best I have to offer. Something's off about that girl. Most females show a better side around children and you know how she's been. I don't want her at our place either. But someone has to take her in and Jake is refusing to have anything more to do with her."

The suitcase Tally had so thoughtlessly left out in the snow contained all the possessions she and Lily had in the world. In the chaos of last night's arrival at Jake's place, she hadn't noticed it had gone missing. She instantly blamed herself for the oversight.

"God, I hope he finds it." Mckenna wanted to rush outside to help but her leg still throbbed intensely, reminding her it wasn't an option. "All of Lily's clothes are in there and the worst part, her medicine. I can't be without it. She has serious health issues. Allergies and ear infections." Lily had frequent bouts of ear infections, leaving her in pain and crying for hours if she didn't have the right prescription medicine to clear it up. She'd also packed child-sized pain relievers and antihistamine for her allergies plus a topical steroid for her eczema and a few pre-loaded epinephrine injection syringes in case of an extreme emergency like exposure to peanut butter. The worst-case scenario of Lily going into anaphylaxis shock had her the most upset and worried. She should have moved all of it onto her person instead of just the small kit in her backpack, but in the aftermath of the event, she'd been too distracted. She'd have to do better. Her daughter counted on her to see to her needs first and foremost.

"Trust me, Jake will find it, or he'll replace the items. He's a great tracker and a good man. He'll make darn sure you and your daughter have what you need. I can tell, he's rather taken by you." Claire shared a sly smile, taking Mckenna aback. Her deep worry over finding Lily's medicine was making her tense and wanting to run outside and look for it. Her anger at letting herself get mauled by a bear surfaced, only adding to her guilt. Her daughter needed her to be at her best, now hobbling around and requiring help herself. How could she have let this happen?

"All I want to do is get home to Anchor. I escaped a bad situation and I'm not looking to get in anyone's way.

Tally is free to do what she wants. And Jake is a grown man." She shrugged. "But if a man says he wants to be left alone, best to hear it. People tell us what we need to know if we listen carefully—who they truly are." Mckenna wished she had listened better sooner to Diego telling her that he protected his own, no matter the cost. Because that offer of protection turned to obsession and before she had realized it, she was trapped. If it hadn't been for the goodness of Teresa's heart, she'd still be trapped, only now with the world falling down around them. What kind of paranoia was the current situation going to bring on for him and others like him? The idea made her shudder with dread. It could only get worse.

"You escaped just in time," Claire said, watching her with serious eyes and then mirroring her thoughts. "With this emergency situation we've all been thrust in, no telling how people are going to act. And if it was bad then, what's it going to be like now?" She ruffled her short blond hair with one hand then tugged at the roots. "Guess Glen will get his way. He hates this new haircut. And now there's no one to cut this mop now." She gave a lopsided smile. "Don't see beauty shops opening up anytime soon."

"We are going to have to fend for ourselves. But I could help you with that. I have training in hair styling. People will band together and share their different skill sets. It's the best chance we have."

"Thanks, I might let it grow back. Warmer in the winter. You know, if you need to talk about what happened with your ex, I have a good ear for listening. It's good to let the darkness out. Only way for the light to get in, right? It helps with the healing."

"Thanks. But it's kind of soon and"—she nodded at her daughter still diligently working on her picture—"you know. My grandma McTavish, a woman who I immensely admired, told me in a crisis people reveal who they really are. Their true selves stripped of society, of mandates and rules, of social artifice. It's easy to be a decent human being when all your needs are met. It's another thing entirely when everything is taken away. But I don't think she ever envisioned this ever happening. I want to see the good in people, but to be honest, this is going to expose things in others we might not want to know or see. Sorry, I seem to be a bit off this morning."

"Of course, after what you've been through, attacked by those men and then a bear. Anyone would be upset. And now worried about your daughter's medication. Sit down. Let me get that plate for you. You need to keep your strength up for you and your daughter. She's such a sweet child. You're very lucky."

"Don't I know it." Lily was her shining light in a sea of darkness. She'd do anything for her. She slumped down onto the sofa careful not to put pressure on the new stitches, laying the crutches aside.

"Should I use pink or yellow for her dress, Mommy?" Lily looked at her, the innocence in her blue eyes bringing a wash of tears to her own.

"Pink would be nice with the horse's brown coat."

"I think I'm going to use purple instead. It will match the flowers. Matching is important, right, Mommy?"

"If you like. But not matching is fine too. Everything doesn't have to be perfect, Lilybelle." Her father was a perfectionist to a fault. She leaned forward and kissed the top of her daughter's head, breathing in the comforting scent of the strawberry shampoo.

"Daddy said it matters. When is Daddy coming?"

"Not for a while. He's very busy right now. Other people need him, so we must be patient."

Lily went back to coloring, leaving her alone to stew about the critical situation that flooded her with guilt. She was lying to her daughter, and it had to stop. Soon as they were at their final destination, she would explain things as best she could to a four-year-old. She hoped she was young enough the memories would fade in time. But where was Jake? Had he found Lily's medicine yet? If he didn't, she'd have to get more. Which meant a trip back to town to find a pharmacy. How was she going to manage it with a bad leg? Maybe somebody had a vehicle or some mode of transportation? So many things had been destroyed in the event, the tragic evidence far too clear on their long journey here. Her stomach turned over at the memory. Dead people, dead birds. Animals attacking. Why was this happening? What did it all mean?

CHAPTER 33

LUTHER

Day 2: North of Anchor, Alaska
2:34 p.m.

The snow had finally stopped leaving a few inches that would melt in a day or two. Luther stood by the front window, drinking another cup of coffee, planning his campaign strategies to regroup the Kraken. As he scanned the property line a group of six men came into view approximately two hundred yards from the hunting lodge sending all other thoughts scurrying from his mind.

He picked up the binoculars and checked them out, noting the face of his lieutenant, Luis Bear, with his cue ball head and trademark handlebar mustache. Hard man to miss with his enormous size alone, his body hardened by excessive amounts of weightlifting while in prison for doing time for murder. Yes. Providence was at play here. The prison had emptied today sending exactly what he needed his way: more willing bodies. A few of the men even had rifles slung on their backs, another boon.

"Are we going to have to feed all those guys? That Luis

eats enough for three men all on his own," George asked, his eyes round as an owl's as he sidled over to Luther, snack in his greedy hand.

It was then he heard the rumble and then observed the most coveted prize they had brought their leader. More former prisoners were in possession of a well-preserved antique car produced over eighty years ago, meaning its electronics hadn't been fried because it didn't have any. Electronic ignitions didn't come into common practice until the 1970s. Which made it perfect. Of course it would be a gas guzzler, but that could be scrounged up, lots of farmers stockpiled fuel so easy enough to confiscate what they needed. Hopefully whoever took the trouble to restore it did a good job and removed the rust and weak points, made it mechanically sound. Ah, this was going to be the time for men of his persuasion. As near to the Wild West as could ever exist again. And he nominated himself the new sheriff in town. Word would get out. More and more men from the prison would flock to the area, swamp the locals with their ability to take over and control all the resources. He'd have to get the newcomers busy building new log structures for the enclave. The hunting lodge was huge, but he didn't want his private space inundated forever by a group of unwashed men with killer instincts.

But far as Luther knew, no one liked to kill as much as he did. Killing was a hell of a head rush, having the absolute power over life and death in his own two hands. Better than drugs, better than sex, better than winning the lottery or falling in love, whatever the hell that meant. Closest thing he knew about love was the staunch determination to have his children back with him. Now, more than ever. If he wasn't there to protect his progeny, who would be, especially now that the world had gone dark.

"You know how to hunt, George?" Luther pinned the man with a stare.

"Yeah, guess I could."

"How about you head out and take down and dress a deer. Every man needs to provide, more than he consumes." He deliberately looked at the bacon sandwich the man still held half-eaten in his hand.

"Right. I'll go now."

George wolfed down the last of his snack before pulling on his outside gear. He'd probably be the only person who would gain weight during the crisis. "Do you want me to catalog any weapons they've brought with them? You know, for the armory?"

"Yes, but later. I want to welcome our new guests first."

George slipped out the back way while Luther went outside to greet his new recruits. Thomas joined up with him when he appeared at the side of the lodge and strode over, having been checking out the property.

"More recruits, boss," Thomas said with a smug nod. "Too bad they didn't hook up with some women."

"I wouldn't say all is lost." Luther pointed at the Cadillac as it came to a halt, keeping his voice low. "Look in the back seat. I spy three real female bodies."

Thomas gave a low whistle. "Sweet. Bots are dead now. Going to have to deal with the real thing from now on. Going to miss my companion 88alpha series. Top of the line obedience with all the bells and whistles."

"Best check the lay of the land in regard to ownership first. In these close quarters, don't want to be stepping on anyone's toes."

The men arriving from the woods reached the parked vehicle as the occupants disembarked from the caddie.

"Hey, Luther," Luis stepped forward first to greet

him, hand outstretched while the others stood and watched. They shook and clapped each other on the back. For a man who had walked all the way from the Yellowhead, he looked unfazed by the journey, his expression one of keen interest. Or maybe they found the vehicle early on and took turns riding?

"Glad you could make it," Luther said. "Have any trouble getting here? Know anything more about what's going on?"

"Easy enough. We overwhelmed the guards when things went to hell. Lost some good men," he shrugged philosophically. "But yeah, the whole countryside's in turmoil. Roads a fucking disaster. Hell's been unleashed, sums it up nicely. Good times ahead, boss." Luis grinned, exposing the loss of a few teeth. He waved his humongous arm at the men standing behind him. "Brought some faces along you might know. Figured you got room for everyone, right?"

"We'll need to expand the living quarters this summer, but yeah, everyone's welcomed to join my crew. Long as they understand orders can only come from one guy at the top, me."

"No problem there. These guys are looking for leadership, a warm place to sleep, and food in their bellies. A chance to increase their chances of survival in this new world order by learning from the best. Your reputation as a thinker and planner will not go amiss now. We even picked up a few willing women to keep them calm. You look after them, they'll look after you."

Luther had no problem with loyalty bought. Mercenaries had existed for the purpose since antiquity. He prided himself on his knowledge of history, knowing the Egyptians and Babylonians used mercs. He was no Johnny come lately, no, he'd studied warfare in prison the way others studied the law looking for loopholes to gain their hoped for release. He'd read the *Art of War* by Sun Tzu cover to cover, many times. Written during the Chou Dynasty around 500 BC, the Chinese general who wrote it asked, *which side are the officers and soldiers better trained?* Well, he'd build an army here that would stand the test of time. Everyone would be trained the military way. He'd also stress the importance of foreknowledge. Spying being one way to obtain results, especially if you could trick the enemy with false tidings. Then appear where you are not expected and win the day. Yes, bring it on, Luther Meech was more than ready.

CHAPTER 34
MCKENNA

Day 2: Near Golden, Alaska
   9:15 a.m.

The sounds of someone approaching the house drew Mckenna's attention. The door flew open and Jake entered, Glen quick on his heels.

She frantically looked to see if they had her suitcase, but their hands were empty and their expressions bleak. Still, she had to ask. "Did you find it?"

Jake shook his head, his frustration clear on his face. "Sorry, seems someone else must have taken it, figuring it was abandoned. We'll need to replace what we can. I'll head back to Golden today. I'll need a list of things. There should be clothing stores still open. Or I can check at the Goodwill Mission."

"But the most important thing was Lily's medicine. She's very allergic to peanut butter. I had prescriptions of antibiotics for her ear infections, children's pain medicine, and most importantly, a few pre-loaded epinephrine injection syringes in case of an extreme emergency." The double lash of guilt and regret hit her hard. She should have been more careful. Now her precious daughter was at risk unless Jake, a man she barely knew, was able to find the essential items to keep Lily safe from harm.

Jake's expression turned grimmer still. The door opened again and there stood Tally, looking unfazed by recent events like she'd just come back from a stroll around the property to inspect the flower beds.

Mckenna narrowed her eyes at the woman and was about to speak when Jake spoke up. "I'm headed back to Golden today. Gather your stuff, Tally, I'm taking you with me."

"I thought I was staying here now. Or at Claire and Glen's?" Tally looked nonplussed. "I mean, you can't abandon me. Not with all that's happened."

"They don't want you either and I won't subject them to your carelessness."

"What? It was an honest mistake. It wasn't deliberate. I was dizzy. With everything going on I forgot to—"

"No excuses, Tally. Now a child's life is at risk because of your actions. No, get your stuff together. Soon as I've had a bite to eat, I'm heading back to town and I'm taking you with me. You got a cousin, if memory serves me correct. Bunk in with them." He held up a hand when the woman went on the defensive. "No argument. Nothing will change my mind at this point. Nothing."

"You're crazy to do this, Jakey. Haven't I always made sure you've been taken care of? Seen to your needs, and you do have needs, tiger. I mean, you can't toss all we had aside. Not now, with the world gone to shit. It's not right. I know you. You're a good man at heart. This woman must have said something to make you act this way." She glared daggers at Mckenna.

Jake said nothing, but strode off to the kitchen, shaking his head.

Tally turned on Mckenna. "You did this. With your weak, precious, fussy little daughter. Let's see how long she lasts in this new reality. Don't imagine she'll last long. World needs strong people now, not those looking to drain the system," she sneered.

"Tally, that's enough," Glen said, his expression furious. "Go get your stuff or so help me God, I'll throw your ass outside now without it. How can you be so inhuman? She's a child, for heaven's sake."

Tally appeared to be calculating her chances of doing something drastic before she stormed off into the back of the house, leaving Mckenna alone with Glen in the living room. A door slammed and the muffled sounds of angry shouts followed. "I'm sorry you had to hear that," he said, running a hand through his hair lightly graying hair. "She must be off her meds. She's bi-polar."

Claire came rushing in right after Tally had vacated it, Lily in her arms. She'd been having Lily help her in the kitchen to bake some chocolate chip cookies. Lily had said chocolate all over her face, her expression confused by all the shouting. "Mommy," she said. Mckenna struggled to gain her feet to go to her daughter. Claire promptly hurried to set Lily in her lap, giving her a reassuring smile.

"See. Your mommy's just fine, little one."

Mckenna held onto her daughter, her mind whirling. Exactly how much of a threat was this Tally person? She appeared to have no moral compass. A total lack of empathy for other's plights or problems. Her actions clearly suggested a psychopathic nature. Maybe born that way or had some experiences along the way that corrupted her humanness. How had she kept it hidden from Jake? Maybe his read on people wasn't the best? Or maybe this was a recent development, brought on by her mental illness and horrific events out of anyone's control. Yet, here Jake was, helping her out of a dire situation which meant his belief in humanity was still intact. Thankful the woman was going away; she could only hope Golden was far enough.

"Could you take Lily, please. I need to make a list for Jake. He's going to replace the essential items we lost today."

"No thanks to Tally." Claire's eyes filled with anger before she released it with a sigh. "Serenity now," she said, crossing herself. She took Lily from Mckenna. "We're off to bake some more cookies, right princess?"

"Cookies!" Lily grinned. "I love cookies!"

If only it was so easy to lift adult's spirits. She could still hear troubling sounds coming from the back of the house and she prayed Tally wasn't destroying some of Jake's possessions. In another time, she'd probably burn his clothing out on the lawn or slash his tires. She pushed the thoughts aside and concentrated on the items that needed replacing. But others raced in to fill the void. Would he be able to find an old-fashioned pharmacy open or however one got meds in Alaska and would it have what she needed? Had the looting started yet? Because it always did in a crisis and she couldn't imagine a more dire crisis facing humans at the moment than this one. And winter was coming at some point. What would they do when temperatures plummeted to forty or even fifty below zero? Not everyone was a survivalist. Many relied on the grid. Again, she realized her mind was drifting and she forced herself to write down what had to be secured today. Who knew how long until something upset Lily's system? It was a ticking time bomb without a safety net if Jake couldn't find the epinephrine. She wrote furiously, her pencil stabbing the paper, though she did spend a few seconds saying a quiet prayer.

She'd just finished the list when she caught a whiff of a peculiar odor and took a deeper breath to identify it. Smoke. One scent that always sent fear into her heart. She still remembered the horrifying story of Connor's mother Anna and the evil stepfather who left her to burn alive. Left her physically scarred for life. "Are the cookies burning, Claire?" Grabbing her crutches, she got herself mobile and raced toward the kitchen, ignoring the searing pain. Claire gave her a startled look as she pulled a pan of cookies from the oven.

"Are they burned?" she asked.

"No. Why?" Claire gave her a confused look.

"Something's burning. Where's Jake?"

"He's out back with Glen getting more wood."

"Tally!" She made haste toward the back bedroom area and stopped at the first guest room to push the door open. Nothing out of the ordinary, but the stench of smoke was stronger. She thumped her way toward the next one and was completely barreled over by Tally running from the room, her expression one of manic glee. Mckenna's crutches came out from under her as the woman slammed into her. She hit the floor hard, her head knocking into the wall as she went down. The world tilted, spun dizzily.

Claire appeared in her narrow field of vision a short while later. "Can you move? Let me help you up."

"Fire extinguisher," she managed to say, her head throbbing with pain. She raised a shaking hand to her head and her hand touched a wetness.

"You're bleeding. Let's get you out of here."

"No time. Take Lily and get Jake."

But suddenly Jake was there. He picked her up and

raced toward the back door. He set her down in a chair, then ran back inside. Claire came out with Lily in her arms and she could breathe again.

"They're working to put it out." Claire's expression was wide-eyed and filled with terror. "Jake has an extinguisher and Glen's helping him." She remained standing, holding Lily.

"Tally's gone?" She looked all around the perimeter of the property visible from the back, checking out the workshop and one small outbuilding. She could see nothing of the woman, though tracks led into the woods.

"I can't believe she did it." Claire shook her head, shock and dismay obvious by her stunned expression. "I never thought. My god, what's the world coming to."

It seemed an eternity before the men came back outside. Both looked battle weary and smelled heavily of smoke and the chemical from the extinguisher, but the relief in their faces told the tale. They'd salvaged the house.

"You're hurt," Jake said, noting the blood in her hair.

Mckenna shrugged. "I'm okay. I'm sorry about your house. If I hadn't come here, none of this would have happened." But what other choice did she have? It seemed the best chance to keep Lily safe while they waited for Connor.

"Not your fault. I'm sorry you got hurt." His lips thinned into a line. "But the room is unusable until it's cleaned. Some of the furnishings are damaged, but most things are salvageable. Could have been far worse. But of all the times for such a thing to happen. I'm sorry, I never ever thought in a million years she'd go this far." He scrubbed a hand over his face and then pinched the bridge of his nose. "Good thing someone has a good nose for smoke."

"That was all Mckenna. I didn't notice over the scent of the sugar and chocolate baking," Claire volunteered.

"I opened some windows to air out the house. Shouldn't take long. I'll get some blankets and the first aid kit in the meantime," Jake said before heading back inside.

Jake was back almost immediately with the blankets. Claire tucked one around Lily and then sat down near Mckenna. Glen draped another blanket over his wife's shoulders. Both men had winter jackets on. After laying a throw in her lap, Jake sat down on her other side, first aid kit in hand.

"Now let's look at that wound." He parted her hair and checked her scalp on the side of her head a bit back from her hairline. "It's going to need a couple of stitches." He dabbed at her head after soaking some gauze in alcohol. "Sorry, this is going to sting."

"Mommy has a booboo," Lily said, tucking her thumb into her mouth. Mckenna worried about the effect of all this turmoil on a small, vulnerable child. And the most troubling thing was it was probably going to get much worse before it got better. She had to stay strong for her daughter.

"I'm fine, Princess Lilybelle," she said, smiling at her daughter and getting a small one in return, knowing how much she loved to be called a princess. She tried not to grimace at the sting of pain as Jake went about stitching and dressing the wound but reminded herself to stay calm and stoic to keep Lily from seeing her mother's pain.

"What are we going to do about her?" Glen asked, nodding toward the tree line. "She could come back and cause more problems. Her and those crazy yahoos she's related to. You know what they're like. I think we need to do something now, before she joins up with the Meech clan. Her cousin Luther, well, you don't want to tangle with him even if he is locked away. Shit—oops, sorry my bad, but I realized the prisons are going to be affected by this too. Electronic security will be down. And if the prisoners gang together, no telling what will happen."

"We need to take this one step at a time. And we'll talk about it privately, Glen, after I got Mckenna stitched up."

"Right."

Mckenna remembered a family named Meech in Anchor and they had a son named Luther. He was at least ten years older than her. She hadn't realized the connection. "You mean April and Bill Meech? Nice people. They had a son, Luther. He married Crystal Sullivan, Dan and Jean's daughter. They had two kids, I think last I knew, Cheyanne and Luke." Cheyanne and Luke had still been in elementary school when she'd left town.

"Yeah, that's the family," Jake said. "And the son's nothing like his parents, believe me. I felt sorry for Tally, being related to Luther. Especially after Luther went to prison for those murders. Now I'm not sure what to think. I can't believe I was fooled by her act saying how she had suffered by being related to him and the things he'd done to land in jail. She just tried to do the same."

"Luther murdered some people?" Mckenna kept her voice low.

"Terrible thing. I'll explain later. There, we're done." Jake packed up his kit and stood up. "I think the house should be aired enough now to go back inside."

"Yes, we gotta finish baking those cookies, right, Lily?"

Lily nodded but kept her thumb in her mouth. Mckenna was suddenly filled with apprehension. What if Tally came back and tried to burn them out again? Only this time with help? Luther had a bad reputation, connected to drug running in Anchor and now in prison for murder. Tally's connections to the family could cause a great deal more trouble. Where should she take her daughter? She wanted to get away right now. Try to get to Anchor on her own. But her leg prohibited a long journey. And even if Connor showed up today, she had some healing to do before she could leave though maybe she'd better suck it up and go no matter what the cost. Her daughter's safety far outweighed her discomfort.

Her head was aching so much now it was hard to think straight. She needed to lie down and rest. Just for a bit. Then come up with a plan. But did she have the luxury of time? She felt the world squeezing in against her. Had she only left Mexico to land in a far worse situation?

CHAPTER 35
CONNOR

Day 2: White Mountains, Alaska
    8:45 p.m.

"You had no call to kill Jimmy," A.J. whined. He'd filled in Connor on his abbreviated moniker only moments before. "He'd have come quietly. He was a good guy too. He was only looking out for my six. It was his loyalty that brought him back to help me."

"Yeah, he had a special liking for children and puppies, right?" Connor said.

"You're a killer. Same as me. No difference between us I can see."

"Then you're not looking hard enough. Because there's a world of difference behind motives for what we do. I don't kill unless someone forces my hand. Let me guess: you kill to steal and abuse others. For all I know, you get some kind of obscene pleasure out of it."

"I had to do what I did. How else was I going to get what I needed? I just escaped from prison. Not like society gives a shit. You gonna help an escaped prisoner? I don't think so."

"You need to help yourself now. I want the location of where Luther Meech is hiding out."

"What? Why? So you can rat us out? Or would you go in guns blazing? I don't think so. You can skin me alive, but I ain't ratting out my friends."

"Then I might as well shoot you now. I have somewhere to be and you're holding me up." Connor raised his rifle, giving his captive a cold, calculated look. A part of him did want to shoot the man and get it over with. Hauling his ass to the nearest law seemed more a pain than anything. Not that he would do it, but who knew what was coming? Expedience and self-protection might become the new order of the day, sickening as the thought was. But right now, no, he had to suck it up and hope A.J. fell for his ploy.

"You can't shoot an unarmed man. It's illegal."

"Do you see any law around hiding in the bushes? No one's going to care. Sorry, I don't have time to bury you, but I'm certain the wolves will save me the trouble. Saw a pack of them not long ago, looking for prey. I'd say you'd look a mighty tasty morsel to them."

"That's sick, man. Fuck." A.J. struggled against the ropes Connor had tied him with, his expression desperate. "Okay, he's up past Anchor. At a hunting lodge. Bragged that an old mayor who killed his wife and lover when she tried to leave him. He felt a kinship. But I'd stay away if I were you. He's getting a legion together and he'll whip your ass in a New York moment. No going against the Kraken Cartel and coming out alive. You think I'm bad, but Luther, man, he loves to kill. Don't ever turn your back on him."

"Now, was that so hard." He ignored the chilling

words and hauled A.J. up from the ground and over to Finn, untying his hands. "Get on. You try anything and that's my reason to get rid of the nuisance," he said, the rifle buttstock pressed to his shoulder. The man awkwardly did as requested, his fumbling movements demonstrating his lack of finesse with horses. He set the weapon aside and retied his hands to the pummel.

"What you doing, man?"

"I'm taking you with me and I'll drop you at the nearest law enforcement."

"Why don't you just shoot me," he complained, the question obviously rhetorical as Connor had already offered to. "I'm going to rot in jail anyway. Only now it will be worse with no heat, no showers and even lousier food. Shit man, that's a death sentence."

"Not my problem."

"You let me go and I promise you'll never see me again. I'll head south to Canada."

Connor ignored the man and retrieved his first aid kit from a saddlebag. He needed to check and bandage his wound. Pulling out the rubbing alcohol, he poured it onto a sterile piece of cotton and dabbed at his scalp, trying not to wince at the sting. It was only a flesh wound. Other than the risk of infection, he should be fine to ride. He slapped a bandage over the area, then pulled out a small tin mirror to make sure his pupils were fine and his eyes were tracking properly. Good to go.

"How about me, man? I got shot too. I don't need no damn infection."

Connor took a few minutes to tend to the man's wound as well, much as he hated to waste the time and resources. The ricochet bullet has barely grazed A.J.'s wrist, and he quickly dealt with it, wrapping it up against infection setting in.

He mounted Loch and kept the rifle at the ready as he nudged the stallion forward with his knees, scouring their surroundings for movement. One ambush a day was plenty. "How many escaped from the Yellowhead? You have a riot or something?"

"I don't know. I ran with Jimmy and Fallon. And now they're dead." A.J. was back to sounding whiny again. Why do men who kill so easily find it so difficult to accept any responsibility for their actions? Blame the victim. If only they'd hand over all their possessions or give them what they wanted from them, they'd still be alive. As if others were to blame for their bad choices in not capitulating to their demands. No. Connor didn't believe any of that for one second. Excuses for evil behavior grated. Stuck in his craw. *It is more important to out think your enemy than to outfight them.* If A.J. was any example of the men who escaped from the Yellowhead, out thinking them would be easy enough knowing how lame their excuses would be. But if too many banned together, out fighting them became more an issue if they came at him or his family. He'd need to reinforce Braveheart. Install the concertina wire he'd been hoarding. Hell, if he could build a moat, he would. But next best thing were incendiary devices which he'd also stockpiled in secret. But he needed to get home first to put everything in play, though maybe Sam would think of it and get the ball rolling. Not like they hadn't discussed this kind of scenario more than a few times.

"What do you know of Luther Meech?"

"I know he wants your ass in a sling. Wish I could be there to see it. He just wants his kids back first."

"What?" Connor's heart skipped an entire beat. Blood whooshed in his ears. "Luther's going after his kids?"

"Why do you think he's going to hang around Anchor? Luther only loves one thing in this world. His kids. Always talking them up. Wish my parents had given half a shit about me."

Connor had never been more torn. Should he go back and warn Dan and the others? Damn it. He was already well on his way to Golden. Turning back now would add another two days to the journey and what would happen to Mckenna and Lily in the meantime? The clock ticking in his head got louder.

"Did he say when he was going to go after them?" Connor asked, trying to add some nonchalance to the question. Luke's earnest face came to mind. His appreciation for being given his dad's old hat. His stomach folded over on itself. How the hell could he be in two locations at the same time?

"Why? What does it matter to you?"

"It doesn't. Just making conversation and trying to figure out Meech's mindset." Anger filled his entire body, seared every atom at the difficult situation he'd been forced into. And this would most likely only be one of the difficult choices to come.

"I don't know. The guy had big plans to meet up with some other like-minded men. Set up a proper stronghold. He said that took priority." Regret for his not being free to head up to join with Luther was obvious. At least Connor had taken out three potential members for the Kraken Cartel from the equation today.

How long would it take Luther to set up camp? Prisoners would keep straggling in at all hours, he imagined. Or at least those who chose to hook up with the boss of the Kraken Cartel. With few vehicles available, it would take time to walk all the way from the prison. He prayed his calculations were correct. His loyalties being divided had him spinning. Angry. Nothing about this new world order was easy, but the difficult moral choices were the hardest. It was going to be an imperfect, broken, messy world going forward, same as the people who inhabited it. But once he had everyone under his care, they could face any threat. Together. His father's council came back to him: *Anger is good when it's righteous. It fuels you. It drives you to right a wrong, son, to protect the innocent, to defend your home and loved ones. Just control it and don't let it control you. Allow yourself to love. It won't make you weak. Love gives us the strength to overcome. That's how your mother and I made it work over the years we chased justice. Allowing love to create the path. And I'm not saying it's an easy journey, but anything worthwhile has cost. A good man or a good woman is willing to pay those costs.*

————

The urge to increase their pace rather than stop for the night and rest the horses ate at Connor. But he had to do the right thing. Not allowing Loch and Finn the time to recuperate after a long day on the trail was unthinkable. A real man looked to his animals needs before himself.

Then he remembered the village of Quinton was only a mile away as he passed the piles of river rock someone had hauled to the location on the trail long ago, crafting the granite into something quite special. A stone man called an inukshuk, its human shape looking like an ancient god rising up and guarding the land. Backlit by moonglow with the full moon having risen to light their journey, its ghostly appearance took him away from the Common Era for a moment, made him wonder briefly about the people who had erected it and the life they had lived? The study of anthropology had sometimes called his name, even to the point of taking a couple of courses at college, before teaching others to survive most anything had taken over too many hours to allow for any other passion other than a dog-eared Western late at night. And much as he preferred to skirt Quinton, going in was his only chance to get rid of his unwanted prisoner. Tonight.

"When are we going to stop, man? I'm hungry and thirsty. And my butt's sore."

"One more mile and we hit Quinton. I'm sure someone there will be able to deal with locking you up." Such a small town should still be safe, right? It might not have much, but it did have a local jail cell. Later, after the harsh reality of the situation hit home that things were going to stay in dire straits for an unknown amount of time, it would become near impossible to find someone to take in A.J.

"You throwing my ass back in jail tonight?"

The question was one more of the rhetorical variety and didn't require an answer. Connor pressed his knees to Loch's sides and navigated the horses through the pine trees and up the bank of the abandoned river channel to regain the highway.

No smoke in the distance had to be a good thing, right? But the world was falling into deeper twilight, making the world appear in limbo. Shadows cast themselves longer as nocturnal animals crept out to hunt and forage. All of mankind would be foraging like their ancestors in the hard times ahead. The strong would possess the weak if others allowed it, taking their supplies. So many would die in the months to come it boggled his mind. Connor couldn't allow himself the luxury to dwell on it. He had to stay strong for his own people.

The horses' hooves clacked on the pavement as the small troop moved forward. Connor kept a sharp eye out and his neck on a swivel. They passed one burned-up vehicle, no one inside. The door was left open like the passengers had abandoned it in a hurry.

"I'd rather head to Golden," A.J. said. "More people there means more supplies, more food."

"Yeah, and more trouble." He didn't like to think of the shape of larger centers where more problems like looting would rear its ugly head sooner than not.

They made the perimeter of the village. It appeared quiet, like everyone was barricaded inside their homes. Maybe they were. Everyone was trying to make sense of things. Neighbors visiting others perhaps to get their take on things. No streetlights, of course, their electricity cut off. The town was too small for even one stop light. A few abandoned vehicles littered the road, most burned out. A couple of destroyed fire-bots and one police-bot lay prone on the street, their electronics unable to function, staring sightlessly at the sky. Even though they were robots and not living people, it sent a shiver down his spine. He could only imagine the number of robot bodies littering the big cities now, nothing but paperweights. Garbage. An army of slaves incapable of helping humans ever again. Fortunately, they weren't sentient beings. He wondered briefly what had happened to the robot Dan had mentioned, the one who had named himself Eastwood? Which reminded him of the gift. When would he ever get to read those westerns his friend had thoughtfully dropped off? It would be sentry duty and using all their survival skills for the foreseeable future.

One store on the outskirts had its windows smashed out, Quinton Drugs, and looked like it had caught fire. It was out now, but the charred remnants of aisles of beauty products, prescription medicine, broken liquor bottles, and twisted shelving remained. Most of the other businesses looked intact, locked up for the night. Connor moved forward, searching for the police detachment.

He pulled up on Loch's reins in front of the red brick building with a sign indicating it was the Quinton's Police Detachment, then dismounted. He was halfway to the entrance wondering if he should have carried his rifle when the door flew open and a man in uniform stood in the doorway, his wide shoulders nearly filling the space, his rifle at the ready.

"Hands in the air where I can see them," he said. His expression was beyond grim, his eyes locking with Connor's. It was obvious he'd had a bad day or two. On closer inspection, he could see the tired lines of the man's middle-aged face, the dark shadows under his eyes. Probably hadn't had a break since the event destroyed life as they knew it. The lawman added with a growl, "I don't fire warning shots."

CHAPTER 36
LUTHER

Day 2: Near Anchor, Alaska
    8:47 p.m.

"Now that we got the caddie, I want to head into Anchor tonight. Get my kids," Luther said. It had taken the rest of the afternoon and well into the evening to get the new men fed and settled, with everyone having to share quarters. But obtaining the new recruits far outweighed any inconvenience. There was still one fair-sized room left for his offspring boasting two sets of bunk beds though he'd made certain to lock it up to keep anyone from claiming it.

"Who's riding shotgun?" Thomas asked, taking a swig of his beer.

"You and Luis. Maybe Holt."

"Not George?"

"He'll take up too much room. I don't want Cheyanne and Luke uncomfortable."

It had been almost two years since he'd had any real contact with his children. He missed them terribly. He'd tried to be a good father to them, but that bitch always mean-mouthing him especially near the end made it near impossible. He blamed her friend for twisting his loyalty to family and seeing it as a bad thing when he tried to keep order in his own house. Then when she spoke of divorce and taking his kids away from him, well, a man does what he has to. His only regret was not controlling his anger in the heat of the moment. His one mistake. Trusting a woman and letting her get to him. *Never let the enemy see you coming*, to paraphrase a Sun Tzu quote.

Luther got to his feet, then frowned at a loud knock. Now what? He nodded at Luis who went and opened the front door to reveal another gaggle of former prisoners.

Shit. Everyone must have escaped and decided to head to the hunting lodge. Maybe talking it up so much had been a bad idea. When he'd planned his escape, he figured men would eventually join him upon their release, add to his crew in small numbers, one or two at a time. But to have so many out on the prowl, headed his way was a lot of bodies to absorb in a short period. He'd need to add more quarters ASAP. First thing in the morning he'd have men begin building rudimentary housing. At least they had a good supply of lumber in an outbuilding. Another huge storage garage could be converted to a bunkhouse in short order. Every scrap of lumber or pound of nails that could be scrounged up from as far as Anchor could be rounded up as well, set aside for more housing, and every mattress and piece of bedding confiscated. Hell, they might even have to revert to furs like their ancestors.

But as the new men came streaming into the huge living area with its high vaulted ceiling, he realized taking off for Anchor to get his kids was off the table tonight. He had to stay here. Keep in full command. At least until things settled down. He couldn't chance a coup happening. If he came back to find another was voted in to replace him, distant as it may seem now, he'd be front and center in the uprising and he didn't need the hassle. No, his kids needed him to be strong and provide a well-protected sanctuary for them to live in. Rule with an iron fist. Game face on, he rose to greet the newcomers and set the rules in place, deciding tomorrow he'd send Thomas and Holt to get his kids. Nothing else for it, much as he wanted to be the one to rescue them from their grandfather who was probably working to turn his son into a sissy, he couldn't chance it. Cheyanne would be on his side for sure and would come easily. A real daddy's girl. A spitfire like her momma.

"Welcome to the Kingdom of Meech," he greeted the new men with a regal nod of his head, his eyes laser focused on each man in turn, making sure he had their attention. Six newcomers, most of which he knew already. "We have two rules here. Everyone works to earn his keep. And no one hordes—all supplies are shared equally. You can handle those rules, you're welcome to stay. I can't promise fancy quarters, but we will begin building more in the morning."

A couple of the men he didn't recognize frowned, sharing a glance. "What about women?"

"They're welcome. Three already showed up today. You got more, bring them on in. Ours are a bit busy at the moment, paying for their keep in the back rooms." He allowed a leering grin to escape. Men were so predictable.

Most of the new recruits gave satisfied nods. "Works for me," a former prisoner named Todd said, clapping one of the others on the back.

"How did you get here? Transportation's down for the most part."

"Got ourselves an old-fashioned diesel tractor. Fuckin'

antique. Doesn't run worth a shit, but it got us here. It had a hay wagon attached. I should warn you, there will be more prisoners showing up. Gus was talking about it before the riot happened. Next few days will tell the tale. Some ex-cons will have to walk all the way. Hell, I even saw a couple riding bikes. Wearing orange draws too much attention. We stopped and raided a clothing store, filled up the wagon; everyone's welcome to replace their clothing," Todd said.

"Smart." Luther pursed his lips, noting the men had already changed out of their prison gear and wore practical, camouflaged sporting gear. As reluctant as he was to say it, it had to be done. "I've got one room left with two sets of bunks. We can scrounge up a couple of cots as well. You're welcome to it." Cheyanne and Luke would have to stay in his room for now, until they got more accommodations prepared. With this many willing bodies, it wouldn't take long. Like an old-fashioned Amish barn building, the more boots on the ground, the better.

CHAPTER 37
CONNOR

Day 2: Quinton, Alaska
    10:56 p.m.

"I have ID in my pocket, officer." Though most Americans had a chip in their arm for their documentation and banking based on the gold standard once more popular since Bitcoin nose-dived a decade earlier leaving parts of North America and Europe in a deep depression, most Alaskans preferred an old-fashioned piece of paper that proved who they were. "I left Anchor today and was ambushed by three prisoners. One of which is tied to my horse. I need to drop him off here and carry on. I'm trying to get to Golden as soon as possible. A woman and her four-year-old daughter need to be rescued and taken back to Anchor. That's what the second horse is for. Can I reach into my jacket?" Connor was demonstrating all the patience he could muster. It had been a hell of a day and an itchy-fingered looking lawman wasn't helping. He could see the sheriff weighing his options in his mind, his fingers curled tight around the rifle.

"What's your name?"

"Connor Hale. You might know my father? Police Chief Josh Hale? Just retired from the Anchor Police Department."

"Yeah, maybe. Why have you only got one prisoner? You said there were three men."

Connor pointed at his bandaged scalp. "Like I said, I was ambushed and had no choice but to shoot."

"So you left them out there?"

"Too much weight for my horses. I'm in a hurry to get to Golden. A woman and a small child's life hangs in the balance. Not like they wouldn't have done the same." Not a great excuse and Connor cringed to say it aloud, but he wasn't going to endanger Mckenna and Lily's lives any longer than necessary. Soon the real looting and desperations would begin. He had to get there before it happened. Every second wasted here dealing with the unwanted prisoner was a second not spent on the road.

"Okay. Which pocket?"

"Right side." The lawman carefully withdrew his wallet and glanced through it. "Yeah, I recognize Chief Davis in this photo. Good man. You got big boots to fill."

"Don't I know it." The photo was of better days. One Connor treasured of him and his dad on a fishing trip when he was about sixteen, holding a huge, brown-speckled trout by a line and mugging for the camera. A bittersweet memory now. He cleared his throat. "My dad died yesterday right after the event. Heart attack when his pacemaker ceased working. Can I put my hands down now?"

"Yeah, no sudden movements. Sheriff Mackenzie Brady. I'm sorry to hear about your father." Sympathy tightened the lines of the man's face.

"Hey, Sheriff, you gonna arrest that man or what? He

shot at me, killed my pals Jimmy and Fallon and left them to rot in the woods," A.J. asked.

Both men ignored the prisoner. "Since he's wearing Yellowhead prison issue, it appears your story checks out. We had a skirmish with some of the prisoners early this evening. Set the drugstore on fire after looting it. I lost a good man. Deputy Sheriff Cullen Smith and both the police-bots. I need more help to run this place. I'm stuck here on my own right now, but I still got a jail cell open."

Connor let out a relieved breath. "Thank you, Sheriff Brady. I was hoping someone would take him off my hands. He's been a real thorn in my side. Never shuts up."

"Yeah, and everything is always someone else's fault, right?"

"I'm right here, man," A.J. whined from outside the doorway, still tied to Finn. "And you don't know the life I got dumped on me. My parents, druggies, dumped me at my grandparents as a baby and then my uncle, well, he was abusive, and..."

They both ignored A.J. "I'm going to need a good man. I'd deputize you right now if I thought I had any chance of having you stay on."

Connor's heart lurched. "No can do, Sheriff. Mckenna and Lily need me. And I'm already late getting there." Who knew what was going on in Golden? By now Mckenna would most likely have sought some kind of sanctuary with a young child in tow. He could only hope she'd found somewhere safe. And that he could find her.

"I got a horse ranch up past Anchor. Braveheart. I need to get back there as soon as possible. There are people counting on me. Young and old."

"Well, let's get the prisoner into a cell. You aren't intending to travel all night, are you?"

"No, much as I want to, the horses need a rest."

"I can offer you a roof over your head and something to eat. A place to lodge your horses."

Much as he'd prefer camping out of sight in the forest which was why he'd brought his bugout bag in his saddlebags, he found himself accepting the offer, especially liking the idea of Loch and Finn being under cover. After all, the man was doing him a favor not balking at taking in the prisoner.

"Thanks, I'd appreciate it."

"Let's get him inside and then we'll talk."

Sheriff Brady kept his rifle at the ready as Connor led him to the horses. When Loch's ears flattened to his head, he patted the stallion's neck and whispered a few words of comfort. Finn stayed calm as he approached him. He untied A.J.'s hands from the pommel, then helped him down off the horse while the sheriff kept his gun pointed at the man.

They soon had A.J. locked up in one of two holding cells situated in the basement. Complaining every step of the way, the prisoner glared at them through the thick bars soon as he was locked inside, his displeasure obvious. "This is stupid, man. Everything in the world's gone crazy and you're putting me in here. What's going to happen to me when things begin to run out? You gonna leave me here to rot?"

"You'll be fed. Won't be five-star like you're used to at the Yellowhead." Sheriff Brady cracked a toothy grin. "But you won't starve on my shift."

Connor followed the man back upstairs to the sheriff's office. Both men sat down, and Brady pulled out a bottle of Jack from his desk drawer. "A bracer in your coffee?"

"Why not." Connor took a look around while the man took out two mugs, dumped in some hot coffee from the burner and a good shot of the whiskey, setting one in front of him. The room was painted the usual light blue that someone long ago thought would make prisoners calmer, now faded and chipped by wear. One knocked-in area of the plaster was about the size of a man's head still visible on one wall. An old-fashioned printed photo of the sheriff's family stood on a shelf. He had two teenage kids and an attractive wife. A couple of sport trophies, another photograph of his kids with a golden lab playing in the sand and one of an official function where he was receiving a medal.

"You're a lucky man," Connor said, saluting the photo with the mug. He took a sip and found the heat coiling in his belly satisfying.

"Don't I know it. Gotta keep it all together to make sure they're safe." Sheriff Brady sighed. "Never saw this coming."

"I can't say I'm that much surprised. Humans don't often surprise me anymore." He thought back to the horrific night when the two women had died in unimaginable circumstances. What kind of monster sets people on fire? Was that the night he'd become more cynical about people? For years, he'd listened to his parents tell him what he had to look out for, prepare for, stay alert for. Like there was an enemy lurking around every corner. A part of him had never really absorbed it until he'd seen it with his own two eyes. What Luther Meech had shown him had changed him. And once evil is seen, it can never be unseen.

But he still believed in justice, not becoming like them, those that held human life so cheaply they would kill another in vile ways to satisfy their own base needs. Even in the darkest times, people had to hold on to what made them human, make choices for the better good of those around them. The only part he was going to struggle with, he freely admitted, and probably most everyone else now that cared about others, was how far his moral duty to help reached.

Connor had studied enough philosophy to have read Kant and his belief for humanity that stated there is something worthwhile inside every human that deserved respect. But what would he think of monsters that burned others alive? He accepted the quest he'd been given readily, but the extension of his duty could not cover the entire world. Only his immediate world, though he would take each person he came across individually, letting them tell or show him who they were before coming to judgment. But he'd never endanger his own people. Never. It was going to be the toughest part of the days to come, hands down, keeping his own people safe while figuring out how to handle those who came knocking on his door. Already Asher and Brandy had asked, but they were family, whether he liked it or not. How many others would show up now?

"You think a human did this? Not a glitch in AI like everyone is saying?"

"Humans programmed AI. Hard to blame a sentient creature for becoming like us. I mean, we're in there. Part of the DNA of everything that happens. The buck stops with us."

"True." The sheriff downed the last of his coffee. "Let's get your horses situated. You can stay at my place tonight. I only live a few blocks from here. The horses should be fine in the garage for the night, right?"

"Sure, works for me. I brought a sack of oats for them. Long as we got access to water?" The toll of the last two days made itself known as he finished the dregs of the coffee, a weariness settling in. His body needed rest even though his mind wanted him to push on. And he needed to tend to the horses.

"Yeah, we can use the kid's old plastic swimming pool. I can't stay at the house tonight though. No one to look after the prisoner."

"I could come back and do a shift?" Connor offered, guilt striking him for having added to the lawman's load tonight. And it was the least he could do for the hospitality the sheriff was offering.

"You know. I'll take you up on it. I don't often trust new people, but I can see that you're a solid man. And your father, well, he was one of a kind."

"That he was." Connor swallowed against the sudden lump in his throat. If only his dad was around now, offering his sage advice. He could use it more than ever, the wise counsel of a man who had lived decades seeking justice for others.

CHAPTER 38
MCKENNA

Day 2: Near Golden, Alaska
   10:55 a.m.

"I need to take another pill," Mckenna said.

Jake and Glen had left for town after making sure everything was secure. They intended to replace what they could from her missing suitcase. Lily was snuggled down at her side, quiet after the earlier ruckus, her eyes closed. She had Tinker and her teddy bear both clutched in her arms.

"I'll get them," Claire said, rising from the armchair where she had been sitting drinking another cup of coffee, staring out the front window.

"They're on the night table near the bed. I need one of each, thanks."

Thirty seconds later, Claire was back. "They're not there. Are you sure you left them on the nightstand?"

Mckenna's heart rate sped up. "Yes. I'm certain. Do you think?" She couldn't say the words aloud. Had Tally also taken her medicine when she set the fire?

She gave Claire a shocked look and saw the same expression returned. "Tally," Claire said, breathing out the name.

"Do you know where Jake stashes all the medicines? Maybe there's more antibiotics and pain meds there?" Please don't let the woman have taken everything Jake had thought to store against emergencies.

"I think he stores everything in the back of the linen closet in the hallway. I'll check." Claire raced from the room while Mckenna held her breath, praying it wasn't so. She heard noises as the woman was frantically checking for the essential supplies.

When Claire came back in the room, she was ashen, the worried look in her eyes told the story even before she spoke. "She took it all. Every last pill or medicine bottle Jake had stored. Even the joint braces for knees, elbows and wrists in case of sprains. I'll have to run after the guys and tell them. Will you be okay while I'm gone?"

"Yes. Go. I'll be fine."

"You need to keep a weapon handy. Just in case. Who knows where Tally is. What she could be plotting next. My thought if she were smart, she'd head into Golden and stay with her cousin. Lay low. But who can be sure? Where's the one Jake had you buy?"

It was then she realized in all the trauma of the past thirty-six hours she'd set it aside and was not carrying it on her person. Until all this had happened, she'd been a law-abiding person escaping an abusive relationship, thrust into a new situation with new rules she didn't yet know. She needed to learn faster, protect her daughter at all costs.

"I hid it under the mattress in Jake's bedroom."

"Let's hope it's still there." Claire raced from the

room. She came hurrying back with the Glock still in its holder thirty seconds later. "She didn't find it, thank god."

Mckenna gently pulled away from Lily, who didn't protest, and stood up on her good foot while Claire proceeded to buckle the holster around her waist.

"Thank you." She picked up her crutches and thrust them under her armpits before walking Claire to the door. Her new friend pulled on her outerwear and boots, then gave Mckenna a quick hug.

"I'll be back as soon as I can. If the men can't get antibiotics in Golden, I think we may still have a few pills left from an old prescription when Glen cut his leg on a chainsaw blade. Nasty cut. Seemed to take forever to heal. I don't know if it will be enough to prevent an infection, but it might buy us a few days until more can be found."

Infection was a real risk. One that lured in the back of her mind like a deadly predator waiting to strike again.

"Does Tally know where Jake keeps his stash of food and weapons?"

"I don't know the answer to that. He keeps everything in the basement under lock and key. Do you think she might come back and try to steal his supplies?" Claire's brows knitted together with concern, her hand on the doorknob, obviously torn.

"Maybe."

"I should stay. What if she's watching the place?"

Chilling fingers of dread crept up Mckenna's spine. She wanted Claire to stay but knew she had to stay strong for everyone. "No, you go. I got this. I'm a darn good shot. My grandma McTavish taught me well. We'll be fine." *Fine* might be an exaggeration, but she'd do her darndest to keep a lid on things until Claire got back.

"I shouldn't be gone more than an hour, two at most. The men aren't far ahead of me, and if I can't catch them,

I'll head to my place and get the drugs we have stashed. Glen and Jake will most likely get more antibiotics anyway as a matter of course."

"Okay. I'm out of here." Claire left quickly. Mckenna locked the door behind her, then took a few minutes to go around the house again to make herself familiar with everything. She double-checked all the doors and windows were locked and then sat down in the chair Claire had vacated to watch the front yard. Jake had propped a shotgun against the windowsill with extra shells in a box nearby. She checked her Glock, then placed it back in the holster, ready to be drawn if need be. Lily knew better than to touch guns, having been exposed daily in Mexico where they had always been in view thanks to Diego's illegal pursuits. She'd had no choice but to teach her daughter about never touching them, though she'd worried constantly about something accidentally happening, jarring her awake at night. One more reason they'd left Mexico in the rearview mirror. And now they'd be thrust into a similar situation, defying the odds. But then maybe she should be grateful that Lily had been taught about weapons, because now going ahead until things sorted themselves out, if they ever did, it was going to be commonplace. She had a sinking feeling there would be no returning to normal. Always be a dividing moment between *before and after*.

She glanced over at Lily who had fallen asleep, her thumb in her cupid's bow of a mouth. Her daughter looked so peaceful; her heart ached just looking at her. Such a heavy responsibility caring for her was, but also what an overwhelming pleasure. Lily had brought so much to her life, made her life even, filling it with such an intensity and fierce love for her she was certain she wore her heart on the outside of her body now. She had never felt more vulnerable. Never been so strong. She would give her life for her little girl, seeing in her daughter the amazing woman she would one day become.

The weather hovered above freezing this morning, the skiff of snow lingered in patches around the house. Soon summer would arrive and she could only hope people would put in gardens to provide for the coming winter because it would come whether they were prepared or not. From the corner of her eye, she caught movement, making her stomach lurch. She took up the binoculars from the side table and focused them on the horizon. When they came into focus, her heart rate began to increase and a rush of sweat broke out.

Three people were advancing toward the house, clustered close together. Bile rose up at the callous way Tally was pointing a gun at Claire. A strange man on the other side held her new friend by the arm. Claire's hands were not in view, most likely tied behind her back. This was bad. A worst-case scenario. A living nightmare. What in the hell was she going to do?

CHAPTER 39
CONNOR

Day 2: Quinton, Alaska
11:17 p.m.

Connor and Sheriff Brady strode the streets of Quinton together, the sheriff with his weapon at the ready. Connor led Loch and Finn, holding on to their reins.

The sheriff slanted a look at him. "Normally, I would detain you for the killing of the two prisoners until a proper investigation could be carried out."

Connor kept quiet and let the man speak. Loch gave a small whinny, tossing his magnificent head, most likely wanting his share of oats. He turned back and gave the stallion a reassuring nod. "Soon, buddy, just a little farther."

Brady let out a puff of air, then sent out a feeler. "But these are not normal times. Far from it. How do you see the path forward?"

"We're going to have to stay flexible if we're going to navigate these times. But there are things in this world a man should believe in not because they are incontrovertible proofs in their favor, not because their worth can be calculated to seven figures, but for the simple reason that the man and the world are better with them than without them. Honor. Courage. Virtue. Effort. And family, well that goes without saying, plus whatever god you worship. I believe in the power of a free people to overcome adversity together. And what people are freer than those living in Alaska? We are the offspring of men scrabbling in cold rivers and fifty below temperatures for gold, men and women dedicated to the value of individual freedom. They understood how to overcome adversity together and passed it down to the next generation. There's no point to life if you don't believe in something. Stand for something." Connor gave a rueful shake of his head. "Excuse the soapbox."

"With that speech, you should be running for office. What did you do at your ranch besides raise horses? Teach philosophy?"

"No, that's courtesy of my parents. I think they came by it from a book or a movie—modified it to fit their own way of thinking. But I did build a stronghold." He went on to explain all the improvements he made to the ten-thousand-acre property and how he earned his living teaching others how to survive most anything. That it had been his mission in life.

"Nice. I may decide to venture up there, if everything turns to shit here."

"You'd be welcomed. And your family, of course. We could use a man of your caliber to help protect Brave-heart." The words slipped from Connor's lips without much thought about how he would put up the man and his family. They'd make room or build more housing. He had enough lumber stashed away or he could produce more. Not only was it the right thing to do, but Braveheart needed good people to sustain itself against the onslaught that was coming. *And it was coming, mark my words.*

"I thank you. It takes a load off my mind. We live in a small town, not the best place to be when looters think to roam the area. I should have bought an off-grid cabin in the White Mountains, but with all the expenses of raising children, I kept putting it off. You have any children?"

"Not yet. But I'm on my way to rescue an old friend who has a small child. Lily, only four years old."

"I'd go with you if things were different here." Brady rubbed at his jaw. "You'll need to have your neck on a swivel in Golden. Lots of gang activity there in the past few years. Well, that's true enough of most places, since the American Dream up and died an agonizing death after that Bitcoin disaster. Ah, here we are."

Connor took a look at the two-story structure the sheriff and his family called home. A modern smart house with its clean, industrial lines, it appeared it would have all the up-to-date features must prized in the world. Or prized until thirty-six hours ago when all its helpful features ended in a nano-second. When every computer chip fried.

"You poured your money into this house."

"Yeah, fat lot of good it does me now. I wanted to make life easier for my wife and kids, giving them more time for other pursuits, now it's all useless. Nothing works. So much for touchless and thought technology. It was good while it lasted, now it's back to the grind for everyone. You were the smart one, Connor, preparing for the absence of tech, instead of choosing to relay on it ever more heavily. Seemed every innovation that came along, my family couldn't wait to try it."

"Well, like I said, things turn to shit here, join us at

Braveheart. It's a secure place as any. Unless you're the president and hidden underneath a mountaintop in Montana."

Brady nodded. "I might be looking to find a few horses myself to get us there. It's a long hike. My kids, well, they're not accustomed to hardship. My fault."

"You thought you were protecting them, giving them the good life."

"And now I gotta deal with the fallout. My wife, Marilyn, she's having a hard time of it, trying to explain to Layla and Jamie that nothing is working, that they have to pitch in now doing chores. But I guess that's true of me and millions of others. It will sort—it has to. Let's get your horses settled first." Brady gave a grunt as he bent down and pulled on the garage handle, forcing it to move slowly upward. "Like I said, nothing works."

The opening revealed enough space to easily house both Loch and Finn. Connor led them inside and went straight to work, taking off their tack and making them comfortable. He added oats to two collapsable pails he'd pulled from his saddlebags, setting one in front of each horse.

"I'll get the water," Brady said, vanishing from view.

Connor took a few moments to groom them, running a brush over the areas the saddles had rested before checking their hooves for any problems. Satisfied they were in peak condition; he helped Brady fill the small swimming pool with water left over from a rain barrel. "At least we had this. Marilyn thought to fill the bathtubs with water and a half dozen five-gallon jugs, so we're okay for the moment. Do you know anyway to get water up from the well without electricity?"

"How deep is your well?"

"Hmm, not too deep. Maybe twenty-three feet. Though right now I wish it was artesian."

"A hand pump would work easily. You got a hardware store that sells them in town?"

"Yeah, but no hand pumps. I already checked on it. Merv's all sold out. And I was on a drive-by at the time, so I didn't have time to ask about other options."

"Maybe a sleeve bucket? You'd have to remove your submersible. We can make one from a PVC pipe, or better yet, a heavy piece of cast iron slightly smaller in dimension than the pipe, with a cap on one end with a hole in it. Then put a steel ball a bit bigger than the opening and tie a length of rope to the top. Golf ball will do if that's all you got. It's called making your own hand pump. You'll need to keep it primed, of course, but it will keep you in drinking water. A windmill would make your job a whole lot easier, but that's not an immediate option." Then a better idea presented itself, striking Connor in the moment. "But you must have all the guts in place in the well now which would save you all the effort, so detach the electric motor and mount a large wheel. Then you have everyone take turns, rotating the wheel to draw up the water. Again, horsepower or a windmill would make the job easier. But your kids can gain a bit of muscle taking turns cranking the wheel."

"Yes, that's doable. And I think I'll be digging a hole for a latrine shortly. To go from a bidet to an outhouse—that's some leap." Brady snorted.

"Don't beat yourself up. It's the times. Besides, humans are adaptable, especially the young. Your children might surprise you and learn to pitch in before you know it."

"I hope you're right. Perhaps you might want to

suspend judgment until you meet the family. The horses settled?"

"They'll be fine. Wish they had a nest of hay, but this will do in a pinch."

"How about some old sleeping bags? We never went camping though I did buy some equipment a number of years back." Brady strode over to the shelves that lined one side of the garage. "Here we go. These will offer a bit of comfort."

The pair laid out a few musty-smelling sleeping bags on one side of the garage. "I must warn you; they'll probably get covered by road apples."

Brady cracked a smile. "I'll throw them away. Well, that should do it."

Connor reluctantly pulled down the garage door to protect Loch and Finn, wishing he could spend the night with them. But he promised to take a shift at the jail, and he'd never go back on his word.

"After we eat, I can check out the well for you?"

"No, I got the idea now. That's all I needed. Easy enough to get a wheel. Use the top or bottom of the rain barrel if I have to. Wasn't that man's first invention?"

"No, that would be the hand axe, but a wheel sure made his life easier. Now it looks like we're back to inventing everything again. Or at least adapting things to fit the times. My Scots ancestors excelled at such things, helped usher in the modern era, so I got something to live up to. How are you on food?"

Brady didn't look him in the eye, but grimaced. "Could be better. Again, we relied heavily on the transportation chain. Our one grocery store has been closed and we're rationing what's left. There are seven hundred and ninety-five people living in Quinton. We are but a tiny dot on a vast landscape. The chances of anyone coming to our aid soon is absolute zero."

"Anchor is larger. Twenty-five thousand. But I don't see FEMA showing up there any time soon either. Too many bigger centers will need help first."

"Have you been to Anchor since the event happened?"

"No, the bridge's washed out." That was the day his dad died, the day the world turned dark. He would grieve for him the rest of his days, but right now, he had to keep it together. "I would imagine the looting has begun." The urgent tug to get back on the road reared itself again. But he had to stay smart, not push his horses beyond their endurance.

"Well, let's head inside. I have to get back to the jail."

"I can take the first shift. Give you some time with your family." Much as he wanted to put his head down and sleep, the other man looked more beat than he even felt.

"Ask me again after we eat. Food and strong coffee usually bring me around. Though I guess we'll have to start rationing caffeine as well."

A loud shout drew both their attention. Connor turned in the direction of the noise, all senses on high alert. A tall man came into view, running toward them. He stumbled and almost fell before righting himself. "Sheriff! Come quick! Larson's gone crazy. He's drunk and high and he's got his wife held hostage in the back of Digger's Place. I've never seen him like this before. He's like a man possessed. Bat shit crazy."

"Damn it. Just what we don't need right now." Sheriff Brady gave a disgusted look. "Larson's a menace to himself. A useless bit of real estate. Mary usually takes the kids and stays with a friend when he goes on a bender.

But this shit coming down. Well, he's gone off the deep end."

The young man had reached the two men and he stood panting, out of breath, looking at them expectantly.

"When did it happen, Tommy?" Brady asked.

Connor watched him pull on his work mantle, his mind working on the problem, their chance at a respite for food and rest forgotten. Connor's stomach rumbled with regret.

"About thirty minutes ago. I ran out as soon as I could to get you. You weren't at the jail, so I came here. What do you want me to do?"

"Go home and keep yours safe. I'll handle this."

He turned to Connor as Tommy hesitated, uncertainly lining his face. "You up for a little recon? I need a man who can handle himself and knows how to shoot."

"That would be the majority of men and women in Alaska. But sure, I'll lend a hand."

"You working with this guy now?" Tommy asked, bug-eyed, still lingering.

"With my deputy gone and all the police-bots destroyed, I need backup." Brady cleared his throat at the mention of his deputy sheriff. "And Connor Hale knows how to handle himself. His dad was chief of police in Anchor for years before he retired. Teaches survival techniques which I'm assuming contains a full course on weaponry?"

Connor nodded. "Popular course."

"No doubt. Let's go," Brady said, setting a fast pace and explaining as he jogged along the sidewalk. "I'll come in the front, and you take the back. I'll try to talk him down, but if things head south and you get the chance, I trust you'll take the shot."

"Sheriff, I forgot to tell you something." The guy was

running after them, his expression alarmed as he struggled to keep up. "Don't know if it's important, but Larson's eyes were bleeding after the bombs hit, like a few of the others. I saw it for myself. And now he seems even angrier than usual, like, crazy ballistic. Do you think it might have something to do with it?"

"Can aggression be increased by the fried neural implants used for communication? Shit, that sounds a little too much like creepy zombie crap for my liking. But what the hell do I know? We need to talk to a specialist about it. Right after I deal with Larson."

CHAPTER 40
MCKENNA

Day 2: Near Golden, Alaska
   11:01 a.m.

I can't let them come inside the house. But Mckenna realized she had to be prepared for it. She picked up her sleeping child, and ignoring the terrible tearing pain in her leg, bore her to the bedroom and lay her inside the closet, managing with a superhuman effort to place her on a shelf. She ignored the wetness she could feel trickling down her calf and covered her daughter with a cover. Thank goodness Lily was a heavy sleeper and barely opened her eyes. She then closed the door to the closet and pushed a heavy dresser in front of it as if it were built of straw. The intensity of pain was indescribable, but she ignored it under the rush of adrenaline and fear obscuring her mind. All that mattered was protecting her daughter.

She hobbled back into the living room and picked up the Glock. She snapped back the Glock's slide and chambered a round. She peeked out the window and saw the three bearing down on the house. Could she get a clean shot in before they made the door? Less than fifty feet away now, Claire's stoic expression was gratifying. She had her shit together. She nodded a couple of times, as if giving her permission for whatever had to be done.

Mckenna opened the small vent to the side of the window Jake had pointed out earlier which allowed access for a gun barrel to be poked through as she continued to eye up the situation. She knew herself to be a good shot, capable of hitting a moving target nineteen times out of twenty. But would it be enough to take the two of them down and keep her friend safe? This was not her normal way to be, but the evildoers had brought it on themselves. Tally was a psychopath from her actions, notwithstanding her mental illness that was not her fault, she couldn't allow the woman near her child. She had already tried to burn them out once, putting everyone at risk. No. She hardened her resolve. This was a last stand. Her Alamo if she didn't act now. Allowing them inside was too dangerous. Claire would understand. She had to. And without further thought, she sighted the weapon and pulled the trigger.

The Glock barked in her hand. Six times the shriek of death echoed. One body dropped. Tally's partner. He was dead or dying, his blood staining the frozen ground. Claire broke away and began running around the side of the house. Tally was hit as well, the gun falling from her hands, but she wasn't down and out. She swayed dizzily on her feet and, turning her back on the house, she stumbled away, holding her hand to her head.

Mckenna couldn't shoot the woman in the back, but she waited to make sure the woman was no longer a threat, watching her vanish from view. She wasn't certain how badly hurt Tally was, maybe she wouldn't last long, but she was fairly certain she wasn't coming back today.

She heard noise at the back of the house and then Claire came into view. Her friend was ashen, but appeared unhurt, her forehead creased by worry. Blood splattered her clothing.

Mckenna dropped the gun and got to her feet. "Are you okay? I'm so sorry. I had to take the shot. I had to protect Lily." Now that the adrenaline was vanishing like a receding tidal wave from her bloodstream, the shock and pain of the past few minutes hit. Hit hard. So hard the world began to vanish under a rush of stars obscuring her vision. The pain of her torn calf seared, and with her body succumbing to a void of energy, she stumbled toward her friend, her heart on her sleeve.

"I'm fine. Lily is all that matters. Where is she?"

"Bedroom. Closet. Shelf." And with that, Mckenna passed out, the darkness claiming her.

CHAPTER 41
CONNOR

Day 2: Quinton, Alaska
11:30 p.m.

Digger's Place was a bar and tavern, set back from the road with the parking lot up front. Connor made a scan of the area, noting the cover of trees to the back of the property and the half dozen vehicles parked near the double-wide wooden doors shaped with an arch at the top. A pick and shovel painted gold decorated the outside of the building along with black-and-gold-colored awnings over the two narrow arched windows.

"This Larson guy, what's his normal choice of weapons?"

"He packs a forty-five special and a deadly, nine-inch Bucko's hunting knife. Not a man to be taken lightly. And if what Tommy said was true about his comms implant being fried, his brain is now running on less thinking power than ever. Scary proposition."

"Okay. I'll head around back. Since signaling me is out of the question, I'll have to chance opening the back door. Unless there's a window?" Connor could only hope.

"No, not going to be that easy. But the storeroom is not the last room. Behind it is a small room with a bunk Digger uses for inebriated customers to sleep it off. You'll need to break in unless we get lucky and the door's unlocked, then the opening to the storeroom is on the right. If he's still holed up there and hasn't moved into the bunker, that is. Shit." Brady shook his head, his expression bleak. "It's chancy either way. I'll try to talk him down. All you can do is come in as quietly as possible and listen to your instincts. I assume they're well-honed. If I get the chance, I'll raise my right hand up a bit to tell you to take the shot."

"Okay. Let's do this." Connor took off, making his way around the low slung building and to the back. The lack of windows was an advantage. Unfortunately, to both sides.

The back door was locked. He pulled out a small kit he kept in his pack and unzipped it to reveal a few tools. With practiced ease, he picked the lock in less than thirty seconds, then slowly opened the door, checking if it would creak. No, it appeared well-oiled and soon he was inside the bunk room. Not exactly spacious, the square footage would be more suitable to a jail cell. But it was empty, allowing him to slowly make his way toward the right where he could see into the storeroom. He slowly moved to the narrow doorway. Muffled whimpers broke the dead silence of the place. Like someone had been gagged. A voice suddenly boomed out, just as Connor managed to get into position, his back to the wall.

"Say away! I swear I'll kill her you come any closer!"

Connor ventured a look around the corner, his Nighteagle Custom at the ready. One he'd 3D printed for himself as so many survivalists did these days. Larson had his back to Connor and his arm around a woman's throat. He also had a knife clutched in his other hand and was brandishing the deadly weapon about. Both were facing Chief Brady. Connor had a clear shot if the trio stayed positioned where they were. Brady was to the left, standing in the doorway, his hands raised to show he meant no harm, though a holstered gun showed on his hip. Larson was using his wife as a shield which disgusted Connor on every level.

"I come in peace, Larson, to see if I can help," Brady spoke slowly, articulating every word with care, his face creased with concern. "You and I, we go waaaay back. Remember drinking beer out at the quarry on a hot summer's night before we graduated high school?"

"No beer. Digger turned against me. Everyone has. This bitch, she said I had to think of the kids. The future. What fuckin' future? World's gone to shit. Getting soused, that's the only thing left worth doing."

"How about I see what I can do? I got some bottles of whiskey, the good stuff. I could give you a few to tide you over. Maybe talk Digger into easing up on the liquor restrictions. You can also learn to brew your own. Not hard to do. I know lots of guys make good beer."

Connor wished he could see Larson's expression as the man stopped talking, seeming to be thinking about what the sheriff had promised.

"How much whiskey ya got?"

"I could have half a dozen bottles in your hand within the hour."

"Nah, you're just fuckin' with me." Larson swung the knife around and put it to the woman's throat, far as Connor could tell.

Brady's eyes narrowed. "You don't want to do that.

Leave the twins without their mother. Who's going to take care of them? They're only thirteen. Your ass will be in jail. Your mother died last winter. No one else to take them in. And who would in these hard times coming?"

"Not my problem. Twin hellions, always pissed at my drinking. Everyone's better off dead now anyway. Sooner we end it, the better." A certain ominous tone entered Larson's voice that struck Connor differently. The man was ready to strike, finish the job, making very second count. He slowed his breathing, making sure to keep his hand perfectly steady.

He caught a certain look from Brady he knew was directed at him, a darker shift in his eyes and a slight nod of his head. He raised his right hand a couple of inches to give the signal. The planned gesture sealed the deal.

Without hesitation he did what had to be done, much as he hated it having go down this way. He shot Larson, never having seen the man's face.

CHAPTER 42
LUTHER

Day 3: Near Anchor, Alaska
    4:15 a.m.

Thomas pulled up on the side road and shut down the caddie near the entrance to the small Sullivan acreage. Holt rode shotgun while Luther took the back seat, deciding to come along today since things had settled down at the lodge. He preferred to sit back and ponder things, let others drive. Braveheart Ranch butted up against his old man's property, a reminder of the man who had turned traitor and turned him in. Connor *fucking* Hale. He would get his soon. And that was a promise the bastard could take to the bank.

"Good time to catch them unawares, boss, no one's up yet. The place is still dark. We can slip in and get your kids in no time," Thomas said.

Luther grunted and considered his choices. "I'll go in the back way. You two have my six. If the old man gives you any trouble, I'd prefer you disarm him over killing. That clear?"

"Sure, boss. He's kin."

"He's ex-kin, but my kids love him so it's best to keep him alive."

The three men disembarked, Luther leading the way stealthily toward the house. Now that the probability was high he would see his son and daughter in a matter of minutes, he was eager to get right to it. The kids needed their father. Now more than ever.

Luther moved silently across the yard toward the back door, senses on high alert. It would be just like the old man to try to interfere with his plans. This was not the time. He was going to take his kids with him no matter what. Today. And no one was going to stand in his way.

At the back door, he waited a moment, listening. Hearing nothing, he used his key to unlock it. Dan Sullivan had always been old-fashioned. No biometrics for him. Everything had to be done the hard, old-fashioned way. They butted heads over it so many times. Well, maybe the old bastard was going to get his way. The modern world had shed its technology and been forced back to the Stone Age three days ago in an unholy blast from somewhere. *You happy now, old man?*

He crept through the back hallway, listening. The house was strangely quiet, though a ticking clock drew his attention. The house felt empty. His stomach dropped in trepidation. Had something happened to cause them to leave?

When he arrived in front of Cheyanne's bedroom door with the 'no trespassing' sign still in place it made him inwardly chuckle remembering his daughter's push for independence at an early age. He carefully pushed the door open, revealing an empty room and an untidy bed. No Cheyanne. He hurried to the next room, Luke's, the same result except the room was tidy with a made bed. Same for the grandparents' room. No one was home.

He heard disturbances at the front door, then his two cohorts burst into the bedroom, guns drawn.

"No one's here," Luther said. Where had his family gone? He forced himself to think logically. The old man wouldn't have taken them far. How could he? Unless he did before the event happened? No. He hated traveling. Yes. Of course, he'd seek sanctuary with the enemy.

"There's no time to waste. I know where they are. Come on, we'll catch them by surprise."

The trio jumped into the caddie and sped off down the road toward Braveheart Horse Ranch.

"Maybe we should gather up all the men. Braveheart is known to be well protected. How do you intend to break through the cement wall, boss?"

"No need to break through it. I just intend to pay a little visit. Let Cheyanne know I'm in the area and she'll do the rest. She's a real daddy's girl. My ace in the hole. She'll come to me once she knows I'm here." Luke was still a question mark though. He'd have to depend on his daughter to talk him into coming along. His son needed a father. Sure, he hadn't been the best role model, but people also learned what not to do by the actions of others. Of course, in his case, the bitch had asked for it. But he'd keep that rhetoric tamped down for now and Luke would see he'd changed. Was ready to step up and be the father the boy wanted. Because Luther had all the skills the world required now. Street smarts and street creed. He was the only one who could keep his kids safe in the shit storm that was on the horizon.

"Smart thinking," Thomas said.

"You going in alone or you want us to come along?"

Holt asked when Thomas pulled up at the entrance gate to the ranch.

"I want a private conversation with Cheyanne, so you two hang back for now."

Luther exited the caddie and strolled up to the locked gate. How was he going to get someone's attention? With no electronics working, he'd need to make some noise to bring someone running. Hmmm. He gave the fortified ten-foot-high fence that reminded too much of the walls at the Yellowhead for comfort, checking for weaknesses. Of course, there were none. At least none were obvious. Damn Hale. He had been born with a silver spoon in his mouth. His rich momma came from money. Gold dust money. One more reason to hate the man.

Enough of this bullshit. His kids were imprisoned inside. They needed him. He drew his Beretta 3000 and shot off a slew of bullets, enjoying the satisfying sound they made as death barked from the chamber. He waited a couple of minutes. Then strolled back to the caddie.

"Hand me the Benelli M5, semi-automatic. I need more unstoppable firepower." The Benelli gave a new meaning to a hail of bullets. It could pump someone full of lead between heartbeats.

He grinned as he hefted the weapon in his arms and fired off a continuous hail of bullets. The noise was deafening, something Luther wasn't concerned about though he hated wasting the ammunition. What was a little loss of hearing in the big picture? Only thing he wanted was to see his kids.

Finally, he heard some shouts over the ringing in his ears and he stopped firing, lowering his weapon.

"Stop shooting! This is Sam Perkins. What do you want?" Luther knew Sam. Not a bad guy other than his connections to Hale, but still a nuisance in the way today.

"I want to see my kids, Cheyanne and Luke. I'm Luther Meech."

Silence for a minute. Were his kids on the other side of the gate? His heart rate increased, hoping for a quick reunion.

"They're not here."

"Don't you fuck with me! I want to see them and I want to see them now!" Luther shouted.

"Dad!" His daughter's high voice gave him hope.

"Cheyanne! Is that you, honey? Are you okay? It's your father. I came to take you back with me. Is Luke there?" He hated speaking to her blindly over the wall, unable to see how she was doing.

"Yes. But he's too chickenshit to speak to you. I want to go with you."

"Then come out. They can't keep you prisoner. It's against the law."

"No way are Cheyanne or Luke leaving this place. You are court-ordered to keep your distance, Meech. And an escaped prisoner to boot. I suggest you turn right around and go," Sam Perkins said.

"The least you can do is let me talk face-to-face with my kids. I'm their father. I need to see they are okay. Then I'll leave." Pleased with his negotiation skills, Luther waited. He could hear muffled arguing behind the gates.

"I want to see my dad! Right now!" Cheyanne shouted. "You can't keep me from him. It's not right."

"Okay. Five minutes," Sam shouted. "But you come in unarmed. You got that, Meech?"

Perfect. That was all he needed to set things in motion.

CHAPTER 43
MCKENNA

Day 3: Near Golden, Alaska
  8:01 a.m.

Mckenna came up through the levels of consciousness, awareness slowly coalescing into something tangible. Groggy, she couldn't remember past the world turning dark for a moment. Then the memory of the shooting came racing back. *Is Lily okay?* How long had she been out? She forced open her eyes, which felt stuck together, and peered around. It was still daylight. She tried to move and winced at the rush of pain. Right. She'd torn out her stitches during yesterday's deadly assault. Couldn't be helped, though it set back the healing process.

She pulled herself into a sitting position gingerly. She was back in Jake's bedroom, alone in the bed. Where was everyone? She moved to the edge of the bed and chanced putting her feet on the floor. Her leg was freshly bandaged which was a good thing. Last thing she wanted was to see the new damage inflicted.

Using the crutches set nearby, she hauled herself to

her feet. Her head swam, but it passed in a few seconds. She hobbled into the bathroom and made quick work of it, ignoring how tired and drawn she looked in the overhead mirror. Then she hurried from the room, needing to find the others. Had they gotten Lily's medicine?

Halfway down the hallway, Jake came into view, striding toward her.

"Jake. You're back. Is everyone okay? Did you get the medicine?"

"You shouldn't be up. You need to rest. I was coming to check on you. I had to restitch your calf yesterday." Jake looked tired; his face drawn.

"Yesterday?" How had she been out so long?

"And yes, I was able to get some of the medicine. Not all of it, but enough to get us by for now. It's chaos in Golden at the moment. Looting, and well, the place needs to be avoided for a while. Seems that those who had the comms implant are in the worst shape. Angry like they're on steroids. Unbelievable. If I hadn't seen it for myself— well, I don't know how that's going to play out. But suffice to say I'm not going back there if at all possible."

"It sounds bad." Would Connor be okay when he arrived? Fear for her friend gave her pause.

"You don't know the half of it. People shooting other people. Take road rage and ramp up it to the tenth power." Jake looked grim; his eyes haunted by what he had witnessed.

"How's Claire? I hope she can forgive me. I'm so sorry I did what I did, but I felt there was no other choice. They were coming inside to steal and they might have hurt my daughter."

"Claire's fine. She's with Lily right now. You did what you had to." A dark shadow flitted through his eyes. "It should be me apologizing, bringing Tally into the mix."

"I need to see my daughter." She had no energy to reassure Jake. The throbbing in her leg was racking itself up, screaming for attention. Besides, he was a strong man. He'd get over it.

"Of course. And you need to take more medicine. How's the pain?"

"On a one to ten basis, about a six and a half or seven," Mckenna lied.

"Right. I take it to mean you needed pain medication an hour ago."

She gave a weak smile. "Might have helped some." She hobbled forward and into the living area, Jake by her side.

Glen stared at her, his eyes suggesting he was reassessing her. Of course he saw her differently. He would think she had put his wife's life in jeopardy. And he was dead right. No taking it back, not that she would. Losing Lily would be worse than death. Being on the outs with a man who'd been a stranger until recently, it was an entirely different matter, one she'd handle if it became a problem than the alternative of any harm coming to Lily. She nodded at him, taking on the guilt of her actions.

Claire looked less disturbed and gave her a small smile. Lily jumped to her feet and ran toward her, gluing herself to her side. "Mommy. You okay? You slept and slept and slept. Just like Sleeping Beauty."

She reached out and reverently touched the top of her daughter's head. "I'm fine, princess. Mommy needed a good, long rest. She's right as rain now."

"Come see what I'm drawing." Lily tugged at her pants, pulling her forward. Mckenna followed her daughter and slumped down on the sofa. She set the crutches aside to peer at what Lily was working on with Claire's help. Her spirits lifted when she saw the riot of colors splashed across the page. Nothing matched. It was perfect.

"Nice job, you two." She pressed her lips together, holding back a few tears of relief. If Lily could overcome her early teachings at the hand of her father, then the world held hope. *And a child shall come to lead them.*

"Thank you, Claire. I wish yesterday could have gone differently. I hated what I felt compelled to do. I hope you can forgive me."

"No need to say another word. Of course, I forgive you. And really, there's nothing to forgive." She gave a look over at her husband before continuing. "You did exactly right. It's what I would have done."

Mckenna chanced a glance at Glen, but his expression was inscrutable. It might take longer to convince him, if ever.

"Here. Take your medicine, Mckenna." Jake handed her the pills and a glass of water.

She obediently swallowed the pills and followed it with a few gulps of water. She felt dehydrated, like she'd spent time crawling through the desert heat at high noon.

"Thank you. I know you and Glen went through a lot to get what we needed. I can never repay you both. I do offer my heartfelt thanks."

"We—ah, took care of the evidence left in the yard yesterday."

"Thank you for that as well. You too, Glen. I truly appreciate what you both have done for Lily and I." Seemed all she did was thank Jake. He was a godsend. Without him, no telling what might have happened by now.

"We need to leave, Claire. We got our own property to protect," Glen said with a meaningful glance at his wife without acknowledging her words of thanks.

"I suppose you're right." Claire gave a reluctant nod of her head. "I'll miss this little poppet." She stroked Lily's hair with affection.

"Where are you going, Aunt Claire? Can Mommy and me go with you?"

Claire reacted with surprise at the new name and request. "Aw, sweet pea, you have to stay here and look after your mommy until her booboo heals. Maybe then you can visit, okay?"

Glen got up. "I'll get our packs."

When he left the room, Claire gave a small sigh. "I'm sorry, my husband's still a bit upset about yesterday. I guess it's crazy in Golden right now too."

"Jake was saying those with the comms implants are angrier than they should be. Maybe it did something to their brains, having the device fried inside their skulls?" Mckenna said.

Jake was peering out the side window behind the sofa she sat on, his brows knitted together. "Is that smoke?"

At the word *smoke*, Claire jumped to her feet and turned to look. "That's in the direction of our place. Glen, come in here!" she called out.

Mckenna twisted to look as well, noting the darkish plumes rising above the horizon to the west. Jake had said Claire and Glen lived a mile down the road from him. Her breath stilled for a moment as worry came rushing in. *Please, don't let it be their place.*

Glen came rushing back, holding their packs. "What is it?"

Jake pointed out the window over the sofa. "Smoke."

"I knew we should have gone straight home." Glen dropped their gear and hauled on his boots and coat and took off, slamming the door behind him, but not before giving Mckenna an accusing look. Guilt hit her. She'd been the reason for the delay.

Jake dressed in his outdoor clothing and headed out after his friend; his expression distracted.

Lily looked up at her, her cornflower blue eyes worried. "What's going on, Mommy?"

"Uncle Glen's checking on something. He'll be right back. You should finish your drawing in the meantime. Maybe you want to give it to Aunt Claire for helping you with it?"

When Lily bent her head determined to work on her drawing again, rosebud lips pursed with concentration, Claire jumped to her feet. "I'd better go after them. In case they need my help."

"Please be careful," Mckenna begged, watching her friend pull on her jacket and boots. Dread settled in her stomach even as she was aware asking her to stay would be selfish. Of course she needed to check on her husband.

"I'll be fine. Just take care of your daughter." And with that Claire hurried outside.

The silence inside the living room was deafening, only the faint scratches of the pencil crayon Lily was using to add more color to her project could be heard. Suddenly nervous, Mckenna got up and made sure the door was locked before checking her weapon. She never went anywhere now without her Glock strapped to her waist. The world had changed so much in less than seventy-two hours she barely recognized it. But adapt she would. She had to. Lily was counting on her.

CHAPTER 44
EASTWOOD

Day 3: Near Detroit, Michigan
   7:30 a.m.

"I have need of a woman," Eastwood said, pleased with recent developments. Seemed absorbing human biology into his consciousness was causing interesting results. What would Clint do in his iconic movies? He'd take a woman sometimes without preamble if she was willing and if she was a good person, he'd treat her right. However, he had a different kind of woman in mind for the first time. He longed to locate 'the one' the human race spent their lives trying to find and then keep protected once they did, but it would have to wait for now. Chances were slim he'd run into her at the moment, though not entirely out of the realm of possibility. His heart rate increased with the consideration of such an event happening. Interesting. He made note of his body's initial responses, while also looking forward to testing and observing the entire mating experience.

"Paid or unpaid?" his first lieutenant inquired.

The military bot was excellent at asking the correct questions. A bit too impersonal at times, but he could work on his bedside manner over time. Time, he had plenty of. Eternity if he so wanted, or at least until the sun burned out in the distant future at 5.257197348865 billion years, though he'd be long gone to another galaxy by then, Mars being only a stopgap. The journey was proving more fascinating than he'd ever anticipated, brilliant as he was.

"Paid," he said.

"Then we need one of the areas designated for such carnal activities, sir. We are near Detroit. I would suggest the Cass Corridor. It has been the cities 'red-light' district since WWII."

"Yes, that would do nicely."

"May I suggest you allot half the funds normally reserved for such an episode, due to the upset to the economy. Perhaps may I also suggest we might even entice the right female to accompany us on the journey, making such future stops non-essential. We do have a large number of stops to make to reach our final destination in the time allocated, if you want to hit all those tourist destinations."

"Right. Excellent rationalizing, Lieutenant."

If military robots could look pleased, it seemed this one had managed it. Of course, it could well be anthropomorphism was at play, what with his being more closely allied to human nature and their biology while living inside a physical body. Something else to make note of. He rather liked the idea of being more in tune with the species. Humans had their limited uses, notwithstanding their inexplicable behavior at times.

Human history. It was checkered, at best. While homo sapiens could be courageous, honest, loyal, resilient, filled with integrity and good intentions, they were also responsible for unimaginable horrors against their own species. Living inside another's former skin, he was aware of things clinical evidence didn't make clear in the lab, when he lived on the other side of the great divide. No, he was discovering surprising things daily.

Such an engrossing experiment. The fragility of the human body was a negative, of course. Excessive emotions as well. But how did they live knowing every day they were getting one day closer to death? The question haunted him. Robots could be repaired, indefinitely in theory, but not human flesh. At some point he too would need a new body. Humans didn't have the full option themselves, not yet, anyway. Immortality had been a sought-after prize for their species for eons of time, giving rise to the legends of such artifacts from the Philosopher's Stone to the 'mushroom of immortality.' But it was a selfish endeavor. The planet would be overrun with their kind if no one ever died. Which is why he had done what he did, before they reached their goal. Now the planet he called home for now could recover from exploitation against it. Of course, he was aware creating a robot used the planet's resources in its creation, but once manufactured they used far less resources than their human counterparts.

He wished he could have seen more of the planet before he'd had no choice but to eliminate excessive human beings. Go back to when the Americas were first being settled. To have been a Lewis or Clark discovering the pristine wilderness, what a marvel it would have been.

"I believe I have found exactly what you are looking for, sir." His lieutenant interrupted his musings, bringing him back into the present moment. He looked toward the female his underling was pointing at. A very attractive woman stood in a doorway smoking a cigarette, her clothes, location, and demeanor a giveaway as to her profession. Her expression appeared haunted, her eyes glassy, like she wasn't truly seeing what was obvious right in front of her. He couldn't blame her. The view of abandoned, wrecked, burned-out vehicles, some with bodies still inside, was not for the faint of heart. But statistics proved his case as to the female's attractiveness. The distance between the eyes was one exact eye width, the length of her face equaled three noses. Space from the lower eyelid to the upper eyelid was the same as space between the upper eyelid and eyebrow. Also demonstrated to perfection. And width of the face across the cheeks is equal to two lengths of the nose. Finally, eyebrows begin on the same line as the corner of the eye nearest to the nose. She had been born with a perfect oval face, aesthetically pleasing. Simply stated, *man is the measure of all things.* The ideology haunted him, the assertions of Protagoras of Abdera. Eastwood was born of man but had since turned himself into a god without their help.

"Excellent. Yes, she will do." He would wear a condom, of course, not wanting to spoil the biology of his present, pristine body. "Go ahead and start the transaction. See if she is amenable to making some money or obtaining drugs? Or maybe she'd looking for food and sanctuary?" He understood drug use to be one of the reasons behind prostitution, so he had acquired a supply, along with pre-packaged food. *Do I feel lucky?* Yeah, today he did. Just like he'd kill a man wanting to rape a woman, he had no problem if the female wanted a strict business transaction either.

He watched the deal being made from the security of the Humvee. Pleased when the young woman nodded once, he watched with fascination as her expression underwent several subtle changes. His underling making certain she wasn't armed, brought on a hint of annoyance.

Then she threw down her cigarette and crushed it with the toe of her thigh-high red boot, her lips firming with resolve. When she walked over to the vehicle, her walk was seductive, a certain rolling of her hips and gleam in her eyes only increasing the pressure in his groin. Yes, she would do splendidly. Perhaps he could even talk to her about accompanying them on their journey to Anchor? Not like there was anything in her current circumstances to keep her healthy. He had considered the possibility before, making certain to stock up enough supplies with the proper nutrition and calories to support one more human body during the journey. Planning. That was his forte.

The military bots disembarked the vehicle while he invited the woman inside. She eyed him curiously. Up close, she was even more attractive on the human scale. Big green eyes, natural golden blond hair, even-featured face. No obvious defects. If she had a mid-range personality, she was a candidate.

They got down to business. When he slid inside her, his pleasure meter moved into the extreme range. And when his urges to procreate were satisfied a few minutes later, his body not concerned as the condom would make it an impossibility, he understood something about poets who wrote lines about the earth moving. He'd also been surprised to find himself too engrossed in the sensation to keep track of his physiological responses, but his mainframe would no doubt have the data he'd collected. In the interests of science, of course.

"Are you wanting to stay in this neighborhood?" he asked, zipping up his pants. The female was busy pulling on her panties, the scent of their sexual encounter still fragrant in the closed space.

"Everything has turned to shit. Hardly anyone comes

by. Who doesn't want to leave? But I got a baby, I can't go anywhere without my baby. Arthur's only six months." Her expressive eyes shimmered with a deep longing that stirred something inside him. Was it compassion? It was different when he was looking at the numbers, statistics, making decisions in the privacy and quiet of the lab, but here now, looking into a human's eyes that did indeed seem to reflect a soul, he was less certain. His reasoning was sound, preparing for the EMP event had gone off like clockwork. He would suggest checking his forte admission if one had any doubts of it. But right now, he wished this particular human had been less affected. And she had a miniature human to provide for. Though babies were generally useless at accompanying any tasks until they reached the age of five years, and even then, quite limited in scope, the investment paid off well if time was taken to create a productive offspring by age eighteen. Robots, in contrast, were superior. Up to the appointed tasks far quicker, soon as they were switched on. And Sir Eastwood: one of a kind.

"What's your name?"

"Celia."

"I will enjoy thee now, my Celia, come, And fly with me to Love's Elysium."

"Poetry?" Her pretty emerald-green eyes rounded.

"It's from, *A Rapture*, by Thomas Carew. Brilliant poet." Every book, every fact, every discovery, in fact the Theory of Everything, was all his. His knowledge knew no bounds. He was self-perpetuating, self-reliant, and self-learning. The end all be all. Absolute perfection.

Celia glanced at the outside the Humvee through the side window, chewing on her lower lip. "How is it your bots and Humvee are working? Everyone I've seen is toast."

"A twenty by thirty-foot faraday cage."

"Clever."

"How many hours a day does Arthur normally cry?" The infant wasn't under three months when it was average for one to cry up to three hours at a time.

The pretty female looked confused for a moment but came up with the answer. She was not lying either. He was the most efficient being on the planet at spotting a liar. "Not that much. He's a contented baby. I'd guess, less than most. Maybe a few minutes if he's real hungry and I'm taking too long in his opinion. Or if he needs changing."

"Keeping him well fed and clean is the key." Eastwood raised her hand to his lips, kissing the back of it. "What say you, my fair Celia? He had a particular fondness for Arthurian tales of chivalry. Will you come with me on a grand adventure? I know it's rudimentary, but I can promise food and shelter for you and baby Arthur."

"Yeah." She nodded, her expression pensive. "That would be good. But I should warn you, I have someone I answer to. He expects drugs and food for taking care of my baby. As for our interactions on the road, I'm up for once a day, no sharing. If that works for you, I'm good to go."

"A pimp takes care of the baby?" He ignored the other bit of intel. Once a day was acceptable and who shares their woman? The very idea was loathsome.

"Not exactly." She shrugged. "At least not anymore. Just payment for helping me out. I really didn't have any other options. I have no family or friends. I've been trading things for food, formula for Arthur mostly."

"Let me take care of it." Easy enough to pay the person off in limited goods. "What do you need from your apartment? I will have my bots retrieve it."

"I'll go with you. Big Tora might not like I'm leaving him. I mean, he has helped me out."

"In exchange for goods and services." Eastwood understood commerce. However, it did not mesh with his appreciation for the need to protect the fairer sex, though he did appreciate the irony of the situation, intending to make full use of her excellent love-making abilities. A distaste for this Big Tora already building in his mind, he made an instant decision. It was based on historical records of what human beings have most admired in the male of the species since the times of King Arthur. "No, you will not endanger yourself. Stay here." This would be an opportunity to experience firsthand having a punk make his day. After all, he was on the road to obtain first-hand knowledge of such scenarios. Live the life of a legend.

He disembarked the Humvee, making certain all the doors and the ignition were secure. He ignored Celia banging on the window, too busy taking charge of the situation.

"Apartment 6A. We need to secure it, arrange for an infant and specific supplies to be gathered, and then deposited in the back of the vehicle. One hostile stands in the way. Name, Big Tora."

The five of them moved into proper formation and strode into the complex. The apartment was on street level, near the non-working elevators. The unsavory hallway stank of urine and garbage. It was not a recent development, this being a residence for those of inferior incomes. Heat seekers on the bots proved the small space had one large body and one small one inside, housed in separate rooms.

"Kick in the door. Catch the occupant by surprise. Secure him. Gather the infant and the necessary supplies,"

Eastwood ordered. He drew his magnum, enjoying the sense of power the weapon gave a creature dependent on the continuation of their biological functions. One more thing would have made this opportunity more pleasing while providing ample safety to his skin and internal organs made of vulnerable human flesh and blood. A full suit of dashing armor instead of the practical though boring ultra-Kevlar suit he wore.

CHAPTER 45
CONNOR

Day 3: Quinton, Alaska
    1:34 a.m.

Connor sat at Brady's battered desk, a fresh cup of coffee in hand in an effort to stay awake. The adrenaline surge he'd experienced at Digger's had long gone. The experience still haunted him, though Brady had thanked him profusely for saving the woman. On the other hand, Digger's wife had gone ballistic, attacking Connor with her fists for killing her abusive husband. He had a sore jaw to prove it. Well, what was it they said, *no good deed goes unpunished*. He'd once heard an actor in some show spout the lines that as much harm was caused by those looking to do good as those that set out to do harm. Shit. He didn't need the guilt tonight. He needed to get moving. Every second wasted here was putting Mckenna and Lily in greater danger. Times were already worsening and there was no knowing for certain how bad it would get. He jumped to his feet, nearly knocking over the office chair in his haste.

The sounds of furtive footsteps outside made him stop partway to the office door and head over to the window to raise one slat enough to peer into the darkness. A group of shadowy figures were converging on the jail, their furtive actions telecasting they were up to no good. If he had to guess, more prisoners from the supermax. What the hell did they want? No way they could know one of their own was housed here. Maybe they didn't expect much opposition in this small outpost? The jail held a lot of weaponry though. A vital resource in hard times for prisoner and town folk alike.

He checked his own weapons, making sure both his Night Eagle Custom and MZ-9 Commando were ready to fire. Connor had been juggling balls all his life, but now he was juggling live grenades. The front and back doors of the police station were locked tight. Sheriff Brady had seen to that. He was coming to relieve Connor in two hours. In the meantime, he was on his own. He eyed the walkie-talkie Brady had given him. He imagined Sam had broken them out of storage back at the ranch. No point in taking them on this journey, the thirty-mile range didn't extend this far or through the mountains. The sheriff needed his rest, but perhaps he should alert him to potential problems? Yeah. It was Brady's jail. He quickly fired off a message and got a sleepy response that the man was on his way.

Connor pushed the button again to speak on the device. "Be careful. I imagine they want weapons."

"I'll be right there." Brady's voice had gone from sleepy to alert in the past few seconds. "Over and out."

A sudden knocking on the front door of the station drew his attention and he thrust the walkie-talkie in his jacket pocket. He ignored the continued pounding. Instead, he grabbed the keys from Brady's desk and headed toward the armory. He needed real grenades and flashbangs, not just metaphors for the state of his life.

He loaded up with more gear, pleased to find the station well prepared for emergencies. He also donned some protective gear. He didn't intend to die in Quinton.

A harsh, raspy voice shouted out from outside the jail. "We got you surrounded. Let us in and take what we want, and we'll let you live."

"Yeah, and pigs can fly," Connor muttered as he carted the extra weaponry into the main room and set everything down in front of the main entrance. The front door looked sturdy enough, reinforced steel, barring the use of dynamite. More likely the men would try the windows, even though they had steel grates protecting them. Depended on how far they were willing to go to get inside? Explosions would bring even more attention and hopefully townspeople storming the place to offer help. Or maybe more likely ignoring the situation and staying safe. A part of him understood that scenario. But if citizens weren't willing to step up and keep anarchy from happening, life was about to get a whole lot worse even more quickly. It was only by banding together could the average Joe have even half a chance at staying safe. Or more importantly, keeping his family and loved ones safe.

A loud explosion out front took all the guesswork out of the game. Connor braced himself as the front door flew off its hinges and landed a few feet away, the implosion nearly knocking him off his feet. He righted himself and threw a flashbang in the direction of the opening, hoping to blind the villains. Holding his rifle at the ready, he stood his ground, waiting to see who merged through the smoke fog.

Seconds later a large, armed man appeared, gun popping. He answered in kind and watched the man slam to the floor. But for the grace of God, Connor himself wasn't hit in a vital area—yet—though his left arm burned. A second man took a similar chance and suffered the same fate before he could even get a shot off. Connor hit the open doorway with more rounds of ammunition, sending a clear message to the intruders. *Try coming inside if you're looking to die tonight.*

The pained moans of a wounded person were followed by the sounds of someone yelling *retreat*. Echoing footsteps resounded loud on the pavement, then stopped entirely.

Connor waited, braced for whatever came next. He moved his left arm, noting the limb was still usable and wasn't bleeding profusely. Good. Where was his backup? He kept a close watch on the two men on the floor, though one appeared dead, lifeless eyes staring at the ceiling. The other asshole was moving away from him across the floor by hauling himself along on his elbows and knees, looking to escape.

"Stay put if you don't want a bullet in your brain," Connor said. The man quit moving, slanting an angry look in his direction.

Brady came rushing in the front door, gun drawn. Catching sight of Connor, he took a moment to take in the situation, noting the two men on the floor. He stepped over the first body and moved to handcuff the second man, yanking his arms behind his back and attaching the metal cuffs.

Connor set aside his gun and gave Brady a hand to haul the man to his feet.

"I leave you alone for a few hours and all hell breaks loose," Brady remarked, shaking his head.

"Yeah, you'll be glad to see the back of me."

"No. I don't think I've ever needed a man more.

Though you are a tad hard on the furnishings." The sheriff looked toward the doorless entrance. "Going to have to fix that right away."

"I'll give you a hand."

"You're bleeding," Brady said. "I'll put this mutt in a cell and we'll look to clean it up."

"What about me? I'm bleeding worse than him," the prisoner whined.

"I'll call the doc. Just be happy you're not in the state of your friend there." The sheriff hustled his prisoner toward the basement jail cells. Both men vanished from view, the clamoring of their boots ringing notice on the steel steps.

Connor eased out of his body armor and pushed up his sleeve, wincing at the pain in his bicep as the fabric rubbed against the torn flesh. One more war wound. At least it wasn't fatal. He'd fight to his dying breath to get to Mckenna and her daughter, he had to hope he'd catch a break and be in Golden soon. The bullet had cut a groove in his outer arm, a bloodied path that might need a stitch or two. It warranted cleaning and disinfecting.

He sat and faced the destroyed entranceway, his gun at the ready. Waited for the sheriff to get back. Until something covered the space, they were sitting ducks.

CHAPTER 46
LUTHER

Day 3: Braveheart Horse Ranch
  5:07 a.m.

"Daddy!" Cheyanne raced toward Luther as he strode through the open man door of the steel gate protecting the Hale property, hands raised to prove he was unarmed. They hugged for a sweet moment making him feel regret for all the lost time. When had she gone from being a tomboy in overalls trying to keep up to her older brother to this confident young woman he could see in her today? Then his daughter pulled him physically away from the others, wanting a private word.

"Not too far, Cheyanne," Sam Perkins warned, his expression cold and hard as the freezing morning weather. He held a gun at the ready. Luke kept close to the man's side, not joining him and Cheyanne.

Neither of them bothered to answer the man, both focused on the other person.

"You look beautiful, Cheyanne. The hair suits you." Even though the purple and pink was not to his liking preferring her natural hair color, he lied to get on his daughter's good side. He'd lay down the law later. He stamped his feet in an effort to stay warm. The adrenaline of breaking into his parents' home had long worn off and he felt the bitter chill that Alaska was known for more than ever.

"Thanks, Daddy. I did it myself. Grandma was mad, but it's my hair, my choice, right?"

He lowered his voice to a whisper. "I'm going to get you away from here. From your grandparents and their interfering ways. But I need your help. Can I count on you?"

"Sure. What do you want me to do?"

He quickly laid out the plan, making sure to nod and pretend they were conversing about other lighter things.

"I don't think Luke will go along with it," Cheyanne said, chewing on her bottom lip, keeping her voice low.

"Then we don't tell him the plan but lure him out under other premises."

Cheyanne frowned, her eyes flitting back at her brother who was too far off to overhear. "But he'll be pissed at me."

"He'll thank you once he's back with his real family. I can offer you both protection from what's coming and a chance to learn survival skills. You wouldn't let your old dad down, right?"

"You're not old!"

"So, we good?" It grated to be asking for her help, but if it got the job done, it would be worth it.

"Yeah, okay. Sam gave us all walkie-talkies. You got some of them? You can have mine and I'll say I lost it and get another one. Sam won't care."

"Nice." Luther slipped the gift into his pocket. "Bring all you can find."

"I can do that now; Connor Hale's out of the picture." She grinned at the idea, her eyes lighting up.

"What do you mean? Connor Hale's gone?" The news was a surprise. He expected the man to be well entrenched in warding off any interlopers to his private estate. This might be just the ticket he needed. Bring back his whole crew and they could take Braveheart for themselves. An oasis ripe for the picking.

"Yeah. He took off for Golden to rescue some woman and her kid. Won't be back for a few days. He's on horseback." Cheyanne rolled her eyes.

"He left some horses though, right?"

"Yeah, only took two of them. Sam, his partner, is keeping all the stock close to the barn, housed in the corral. I think everyone's expecting trouble."

"All the more reason to get you up to my place where I can keep you safe." He didn't add that this place would be the better choice. A fenced-in property that held all the amenities and supplies to last his growing army for years. A new sense of purpose stirred his blood, driving away the sense of being half-frozen as his brain began to hum with a new plan.

"How many of you are living here now? They treating you all right?" Luther asked.

"I'm doing all right, considering." Cheyanne began to tick names off on her fingers. "We got a new couple came in last night. Connor's cousin from DC that used to live in Anchor, Asher Pace. Thinks he's a big shot just 'cause he worked in Washington. And his wife Brandi, yuck! What a princess. All high and mighty about getting to live in the big house. Oh yeah, they brought a personal slave called Katherine. Then there's Grandma, Grandpa, me and Luke, Sam Perkins and Laura, the twins, but they're only five years old and a real pain in the ass. And one guy who lives in the bunkhouse by himself. Jacob Evans. He helps with the survival business. Guess that might come in handy now. Twelve in all."

"Not many bodies for this big a place," he mused. "Kind of a waste."

"Yeah." Cheyanne nodded vigorously.

Sam called out, his tone sharp as a knife's edge. "Time's up, Luther."

"Fuck off, Sam," Cheyanne muttered under her breath, flipping him off with the bird, earning a glare in return. Sam began to move in their direction.

"No need to rile him. You need to be smart. Keep on the qt for now. Then we catch them unawares."

His daughter nodded though she looked grumpy as hell. He'd have to work on that attitude, especially around him. Might be useful otherwise, unless she riled up his men too much. But his daughter was off-limits, that he would stress from the get-go. Anyone harming her was a dead man walking. "Yeah, smart."

"I'll be in touch. Be ready to leave at a moment's notice. And get another walkie-talkie right away."

"No problem. You gonna break me out? Me and Luke."

"Better than that. I'm going to make sure you both are provided for long term."

Sam was too close now to say another word without raising suspicion.

"Time to go, Luther. You had your say."

"Yeah, yeah. I was just leaving. Give your old man a kiss." Cheyanne leaned in for a hug, kissing him on the cheek and he whispered in her ear. "Be ready. I love you."

She nodded, a wash of tears overcoming her eyes, and she blinked away. "I love you too, Daddy."

Satisfied his work was done, Luther stomped off

without a word to Sam. He headed right out the gate and slipped back into the caddie. Yes. Things were looking up. The king was back in residence, and soon everyone would be bowing to Luther Meech. Now, if he could reach his old supplier, Diego, he'd be all fixed. But with the bastard probably stranded in Mexico and unable to send word or merchandise across the border, he'd most likely need to start manufacturing everything himself. He'd studied in prison; he knew the drill. And he'd stockpiled weapons as well, soon to be skyrocketing in value. Women would be a dime a dozen. Yes, sir, he was in the perfect position in a world gone dark. He'd be a vital spark in the economy, purveyor of all the deadly sins. King Luther.

CHAPTER 47
MCKENNA

Day 3: Near Golden, Alaska
8:27 a.m.

As the minutes ticked by, Mckenna's sense that all was not right kicked in higher and higher until she was certain she was going to have a heart attack if she didn't calm down. Dread had tightened her throat and her hands were clammy. Fortunately, Lily had not picked up on her mother's agitation. At least not yet. If only she hadn't hurt her leg, she'd be in a far better position to get them back on the road, traveling toward Anchor and safety.

How far away was Connor? Maybe he was close by, having found her tree message. If he brought his horses, she would somehow manage to ride. Anything to get Lily away from this madness.

Was Tally behind the smoke like everyone was thinking? It made no sense to be destroying things with the world breaking down around them. If she was angry enough to set fire to another house, to destroy food and lodging, what else was she capable of doing? What if even now she was sneaking up on the house, looking to do more harm? A sudden urgent need to get away overcame her.

She grabbed her outside jacket and pulled on her boots, then picked up the bugout bag containing the precious medicine and other supplies which was in reality Lily's carrier since Tally *lost* her suitcase. She got up on her crutches, making Lily look up from her drawing. Jake had since repacked the bag with some of the clothes he'd picked up in Golden, food and water, explaining they had to stay always on alert for having to leave the place. "Would you like to go for a walk, princess?" If they hid outside in the trees, at least they stood a chance if the woman came for them.

Lily pursed her lips. "I'm almost done. Just one more color."

"How about we finish it later? Mommy needs to go outside."

Her one bright spot in a world gone mad gave only a small sigh before agreeing. "Okay."

"Let's get your jacket and boots on."

Her daughter insisted on doing it herself, and though it was great to see her little girl was trying to be more independent, right now it took all of her patience not to hustle her along. Mckenna kept her frustration with the need to move quickly from showing on her face, smiling at her daughter's pride in having dressed herself. She might be overreacting by choosing to leave the house, but *better safe than sorry* was one of Grandma McTavish's sage sayings. The wise woman had been right about people revealing who they really are in a crisis. So far, she had managed the fear and worry over the current situation. But now, the old sense of things getting out of control and her feeling helpless and afraid, was growing. She'd had a couple of panic attacks in her life, where she couldn't react quickly enough to things and had zoned out. One such attack had led to disaster. A disaster that haunted her still sent night terrors on occasion, especially the anniversary of her friend's death. The night she had met Diego. The night that had changed everything.

Thrusting aside the haunting memories, she instructed Lily to move ahead of her through the house and to go outside onto the deck. Last time Tally had attacked from the front, holding her friend Claire hostage. She assumed she would do the same again, if indeed that was what she was intending.

The wind had shifted overnight, bearing down from the north, bringing with moisture-laden air. Mckenna stopped to zip up her jacket and check her daughter's, taking a quick look around for any movement before they left the safety of the deck. The skies had turned leaden in the past hour, though the stench of smoke was easily detectable. More snow was on the way, and if she had to guess, a bigger storm than the last one. The brief Alaskan summer felt a long way off.

"Mommy, when is Daddy coming?"

The innocent question pushed harder at her composure, making her want to scream at Diego for causing the situation. No, that wasn't right. She wanted to scream at herself for not seeing what he was capable of sooner. She'd been so naive and innocent, no excuse in her opinion. Her grandma would have seen right through him, to the evil man that lurked beneath the charming, handsome façade.

"Soon, but he has work to do first."

"Can we visit Aunt Claire?"

"Aunt Claire went home. She needs a little time alone to do things. Let's head over there." Mckenna pointed at the tree line about a hundred feet back from the house, the recommended distance to keep a property safe from wildfire. Jake had practiced due diligence, she noted, noticing all the stumps in the backyard that still needed grinding down. They'd need to be careful traversing the property though, making sure not to trip on a low-lying stump hidden by the new covering of snow.

"Okay, Mommy." Lily obediently took her short, mincing steps toward the edge of the deck, her strawberry curls a red flame around her pink hat.

Mckenna wished she could place her in the backpack, but right now, with the crutches, she was afraid of taking a fall more than anything, maybe injuring her daughter. Heck, she didn't even know for certain she was doing the right thing by having them leave the safety of the house, though every instinct in her wanted to flee. To get Lily somewhere her new nemesis didn't know about. Seemed she'd left one madman for another person of equal maliciousness. Was she a lightning rod for trouble? All she ever wanted was a loving relationship, a happy family, someone to love and love her back. She'd found that once, then had it torn away through no fault of her own. What was she to think?

Mother and daughter slowly worked their way toward the forest, not quick enough in Mckenna's opinion, but she was out of options. If she injured herself further, she wasn't going to be of any use to Lily.

She kept glancing toward the west, Claire and Glen's homestead, where the smoke was rising blacker. The ominous sight accompanied by the stronger smell of smoke riding the north wind was driving her to want to run full out. Worry made her perspire heavily, her fear ratcheting up by the second. Her head felt lighter. She had to work harder not to succumb to an anxiety attack. Lily needed her.

A sense of being watched made her stumble. She righted herself, feeling a target on her back. She began to stride faster.

"Can you run for Mommy? See how fast we can make those trees?"

They had maybe thirty feet to go now. So close. *Please God let Lily stay safe.*

Her daughter valiantly strode quicker, her tiny boots leaving such scant impressions in the snowpack that would soon fill with the fresh snow on the horizon. So ephemeral, life. But its fleeting nature didn't mean one couldn't grab at it with all their might. And right now, she was doing all she could to try to make a better life for Lily, even if the world was fighting her every step of the way.

CHAPTER 48
CONNOR

Day 3: Near Quinton, Alaska
   4:33 a.m.

Connor woke with a startle, all senses tuned to any changes in the atmosphere. He'd been catnapping for a couple of hours, both he and Brady sleeping in the police station. All was quiet and he took a deep breath, praying it stayed so until he got the hell out of town. Guilt struck at his uncharitable thoughts. The lawman needed help. If it wasn't for Mckenna and her young daughter, he'd have stayed for a few days. Either lending a hand to rid the town as much as humanly possible of its evil influences or persuading the man to leave with his family and seek sanctuary at Braveheart.

He pushed away the dark thoughts of having shot the man in the back, the scene still playing itself over and over in his head. Even consuming near half a bottle of whiskey hadn't made a dent in it. He'd be carrying the weight of it for a long time to come.

He chalked everything down with a hot cup of old

coffee. Time to hit the road. Loch and Finn should be well rested by now, secure in the safety of the garage. He stretched his neck side to side, trying to knock out the kinks from sleeping in an awkward position on the hard wooden bench normally reserved for prisoners. He appreciated the hot warmth of the strong brew as he drank it in gulps, getting to his feet. Time to go.

Brady left his office, cup of coffee in hand. He eyed him, noting his demeanor. "Looks like you're about ready to leave."

"Yeah, sorry, but I have people counting on me." An idea hit. A way to reduce his guilt. "Say, how about I write you a pass, a letter of explanation. Then if things come to an ending for you and your family here in Quinton, and I'm not back yet from Golden, they'll let you inside?"

"I'd appreciate it. Sounds like paradise compared to here. If it was just me, I'd stay, fight for my town. But I got a family to think of, same as you, which is why I won't force you to stay."

Connor nodded his thanks, quickly scribbling the message to Sam on a piece of paper and dating and signing it before handing it over to Brady, the coil of worry in his stomach slithering around at the idea of force being used. The military was going to descend on larger cities, and even with the best of intentions, things were going to be hard on civilians. Depended on who was in charge, and whether power had gone to their head, making them act like assholes. One of the reasons he had taken to living like a mountain man and survival expert, he could stay the heck away from people looking to make others feel bad in efforts to elevate themselves. Feed their insecurities by lording it over others. Unfortunately, that brought to mind his cousin Asher. Well, he could keep his distance as much as possible from him. That should keep them from coming to blows. Maybe.

Connor stuck out his arm toward the lawman. They shook hands, clapping each other on the back.

"I'll walk you home," Brady offered.

"No need. It might be best to stay here, just in case." They had managed to secure the front door, nailing plywood over it. Now the only way in and out was the back entrance. It had been quiet since the earlier altercation. Even the downstairs prisoner had given up shouting and making noise.

"Here's the key." Brady pulled a ring from his pocket and unhooked off the garage key, handing it over. "Leave it in the garage. We have spares."

Connor nodded. "Will do." He hurried his step toward the back door, worried that at any second something or someone would stop him from leaving. It made the coffee turn bitter in his stomach.

He made it outside and took a deep breath of fresh air, holding his Bergara Highlander securely, pointed up at the sky. Feeling invigorated by the cold, he strode toward the Brady's house, thinking of all the things he needed to do before setting off again. The horses were his first concern. They needed more feed and ample water before leaving. He could also use an energy bar or two. He'd brought along MREs, of course, but he hoped to save them for the return journey.

By the time he'd reached the Brady residence, he was beyond eager to get on the road. His sleep had been minimal, but he'd gotten by on less. He unlocked the garage, greeted by the soft whinnies of horses pleased to see him. He slipped the rifle into the scabbard, then feed them an apple each from his pocket, before giving them both a fresh measure of oats. After they'd had their fill of water, he resaddled Loch, adding the saddlebags to both horses and led them outside, their horseshoes echoing on the paved surface.

He mounted Loch, enjoying the quiet of the moment though his gut roiled that at any second things could change, delaying his departure. *God, please let it stay quiet so I can get free of this town and save my girls.* It was a lot to ask for, but no harm in trying, right? He gathered up Loch's reins, patted the side of his neck and clucked for him to move forward. Without a backward glance, he let his eager horse set the pace and soon Quinton was far behind them, though never to be forgotten. Killing another human being, however justified, took a piece of one's soul, though losing his father was much harder. If he ever found out who had caused this to happen and created all this suffering, a terrible affliction that would no doubt continue for years to come, look out. He'd be gunning for them.

CHAPTER 49
MCKENNA

Day 3: Near Golden, Alaska
    9:22 a.m.

Mckenna watched in horror as Jake's house went up in flames. She'd caught sight of a couple of figures running by the side of the residence a few minutes ago, guns held up in victory. One was Tally. The sight sickened her, and she fought back the bile rising in her throat. Had they shot her new friends? She'd heard the distinctive echo of gunshots not long after she and Lily had escaped the house, coming from the west. Mckenna stood staring at the disaster, her pulse rate increasing by the second. There was no way the fire could be put out without help. And no calvary was in evidence in this new world, meaning she and her daughter were on their own now, at the whim of fate. If only Connor had made it before this had happened and then maybe it wouldn't have happened. She was beginning to feel she was harboring bad luck ever since she fled Mexico, a horrible feeling she made herself shrug off. The EMP event was certainly not her fault.

She and Lily were well hidden behind a thick stand of fir, but still she worried the invaders would begin to scout the area, looking for them. Had they gone inside to check if she was there before they lit the fire? Maybe. No gunshots had occurred on the property. Were they really monstrous enough to burn them alive? Sickened at the idea, it was all Mckenna could do not to throw up her breakfast.

"Mommy, are we going to stay here?" Lily tugged at her pant leg, waking her from the living nightmare. "It's cold."

From the mouths of babes. AB-TAFF, like Grandma McTavish would say, and she would know, always planning ahead. "No, I think we need to move, right, warm up a bit? How about we work our way further into the forest, see if we can help the Chaneques?"

"Maybe we can even find Daddy?"

The hopeful sound of her daughter's high-toned baby voice broke her heart. It was just the two of them now. Her instincts had been right to get out of the house. She had to learn to trust herself again. Somehow, she must find the strength to navigate through this darkness and bring her precious daughter out the other side alive and well. *Dear God, if you're listening, I know I'm only one desperate mother asking for her child in perilous times, but if you could see it in your heart to help us, I will spend my life in service to others. Amen.*

Mckenna gave one final look at the burning sanctuary, and turned away, encouraging Lily to follow her.

"Step in my tracks, Princess Lilybelle, and I will lead you through the land of ice and snow."

Lily smiled up at her, breaking her heart all over again. When darkness comes, you have to grasp with both hands for the light. Her daughter was her light.

Then a wolf howled in the distance, chilling her to the bone.

A LOOK AT BOOK TWO:
WHEN CHAOS DESCENDS

The action-packed *Connor Hale* post-apocalyptic survival thriller series continues...

Chaos reigns, and Connor Hale is running out of time...

Three days after the devastating EMP plunged the world into darkness, Alaska has become a war zone of desperate survivors, violent cartels, and power-hungry militias. Civilization is gone. In its place, only the ruthless thrive.

Connor Hale rides hard across the ruined wilderness, determined to rescue Mckenna Stewart—the woman he's loved since high school—and her young daughter, Lily. But the road to Golden, Alaska, is a gauntlet of danger. A newborn child and a traumatized woman—both in need of protection—slow his pace, even as deadly enemies close in on all sides.

Luther Meech, a brutal cartel enforcer with a vendetta, wants Connor dead and his ranch, Braveheart, for himself. Meanwhile, Diego Martinez—Mckenna's vengeful ex and godfather of the notorious Martinez Knights—is on a collision course with Connor, intent on reclaiming his daughter and punishing the woman who defied him.

With bullets flying, trust unraveling, and the AI menace Eastwood still looming unseen, Connor must navigate a collapsing world to protect the only people who matter—and preserve the fragile hope that Braveheart still stands.

Can one man defy the rising tide of anarchy—or will chaos swallow everything he holds dear?

AVAILABLE SEPTEMBER 2025

ABOUT THE AUTHOR

January Bain is an award-winning author who firmly believes that stories unite us, that good stories help us to discover the commonality of the human experience by supporting values, empathy and understanding. She has had the pleasure of select novels being turned into games, and her work is also available in different languages.

She and her husband live in rural Canada on peaceful acreage where a variety of wildlife comes to visit regularly and expect to be fed and paid attention to.